‖‖‖ ‖ ‖‖‖‖‖‖ ‖ ‖‖ ‖ ‖‖‖‖‖‖‖‖‖ ‖‖ ‖ ‖‖
◁ **W9-AMM-354**

ACCLAIM FOR MARK COGGINS'
VULTURE CAPITAL

"If you laid all the boring Silicon Valley authors end-to-end it would be a good thing. But they still wouldn't amount to half the insight Coggins lays down in his adventurous novel. Fast cars, nymphomaniac rich kids, billionaires with short attention spans and long money: a truer picture of Silicon Valley can't be found. In a world transformed through technology-driven change, we need new heroes, a new James Bond—Ted Valmont is it."
—CNBC

"Dry ice sarcasm…and plenty of nasty chuckles in route."
—*Wall Street Journal*

"*Vulture Capital* is a well executed, slightly twisted and weird, but completely believable story about the dark side of Silicon Valley's start-up community."
—*I Love a Mystery*

"Coggins has a talent for penning credible, often clever dialogue, and some of his more cynical remarks and observations about modern society might reduce a nun to gales of laughter."
—*January Magazine*

"*Vulture Capital* is another winner … Strong recommendation."
—*Deadly Pleasures*

ACCLAIM FOR MARK COGGINS' VULTURE CAPITAL

"A trip through the dark satanic mills of venture capital with Chandler or Hammett as tour guide."

"Coggins ...deftly using the tropes of classic private-eye fiction to give readers a cold, delightfully nasty look at the venture capitalists who rode to fame and glory on the tech boom. His eye is sharp and the details are crisp...From the boardrooms of Palo Alto to the wineries of Napa, *Vulture Capital* gives us Northern California in the 21st century, as noir as it ever was."

"Po Bronson, for all his talents, did not catch the Valley's entrepreneurial/venture capital lifeblood...as unerringly as Coggins does in *Vulture Capital.*"
—Salon.com

"Peppered with local landmarks and tech in-jokes, *Vulture Capital* exposes the seamy underside of venture capital, populated by back-stabbing partners, corrupt CEOs and nasty funding boards."
—*Silicon Valley Metro*

"Truly brings the California private eye novel into the 21st century"
—What Do I Read Next?, Gale Group

VULTURE CAPITAL

#2 in the August Riordan Series

VULTURE CAPITAL

Mark Coggins

BLEAK HOUSE BOOKS

MADISON | WISCONSIN

Published by Bleak House Books,
an imprint of Big Earth Publishing
923 Williamson St.
Madison, WI 53703

Copyright © 2002, 2007 by Mark Coggins

All rights reserved. No part of this publication may be reproduced or transmitted in any form or by any means, electronic or mechanical, including photocopy, recording, or any information storage and retrieval system, without permission in writing from the publisher.

This is a work of fiction. Any similarities to people or places, living or dead, is purely coincidental.

ISBN 13: 978-1-932557-57-2

FIRST BLEAK HOUSE BOOKS PAPERBACK PRINTING: August 2007
FIRST POLTROON PRESS HARDCOVER PRINTING: September 2002

11 10 09 08 07   1 2 3 4 5

Set in Adobe Garamond Pro

Cover and book design by Von Bliss Design, based on a concept by Peter Streicher
www.vonbliss.com

For the Pets.com Sock Puppet

"Even though the VCs have all the money in the world, he's the guy making it happen. They respect him because they know they can never be him—he's the fucking Marlboro Man, and they're on the sidelines."

—Anonymous, speaking of the Chief Executive Officer of a venture-funded start-up

AUTHOR AND PHOTOGRAPHER'S NOTE

THE AUTHOR WISHES TO THANK HIS FELLOW writers Donna Levin, Mike Padilla, and Judith Rascoe for helping him make *Vulture Capital* the best he can make it. Thanks are also due to Larry Berger, Steve Freedman and Ron Olson for their important contributions to the book.

All the characters in the novel are fictional, and while most of the places are real, they have been used in ways that are complete figments of the author's imagination.

Likewise, the majority of the photographs are true portrayals of the San Francisco Bay Area locales where the action takes place, but some have been included not because they are literal illustrations of a particular place, but because they suggest an atmosphere or a mood that is en rapport with the text.

Finally, both the author and photographer (although they are the same person) would like to give special thanks to his wife, Linda: the author for her incredible patience and support while he struggled mightily with the text, and the photographer for her willingness to help him lug heavy large-format camera equipment all over the Bay Area, many times correcting his lousy compositions for better pictures.

PROLOGUE

KTVC WAS THE STATION. AMELIA CRENSHAW WAS the reporter. Her producer, cameraman and the station van were arrayed along the narrow shoulder of Highway 280 while Amelia, microphone in hand, did a stand-up with the exit sign for Sand Hill Road looming behind her.

A top-of-the-line BMW SUV swept by them, barreling down the off-ramp. Strands of Amelia's luxuriant mane flew up, embedding themselves in the primordial ooze of her too-red lipstick. "This is Amelia Crenshaw for FUCK!" said Amelia as the hair came into her mouth. She turned from the camera and pointed the microphone at the producer like a gun. "I told you this was a stupid idea, Hal. Why can't we shoot this in front of one of the office buildings?"

Hal, a calm, slope-shouldered man with short hair and an earring, came up to her. He pulled the hair from her mouth and dabbed with a cotton ball at a place on her cheek where the red color had smeared. "And why can't you wear a muted lipstick with a lower petroleum content?"

Amelia responded by sticking her tongue out.

Hal touched up her foundation with a pad from a compact and stepped back behind the camera. "We can't shoot in front of the buildings because no one knows the names of the firms. Sand Hill

Road is what they know— the Hill. Home to the crème de la crème of venture capital. Now again from the top."

In a practiced gesture, Amelia smoothed the material of her wrap-around skirt and assumed a keen, eager-looking stance. She fixed the camera with a business-like stare.

"Despite the September 11th attacks and the shakeout in the dot-com market," she began, "*Venture Wire* reported today that pension funds, university endowments and wealthy individuals have committed a whopping $24.4 billion to venture capital funds that closed in the second quarter of this year. That's up sharply from $18.4 billion from the same period last year.

"And just where is all this new money going?" Amelia raised her eyebrows and inclined her head to signal a scoop. "Insiders say that wireless devices and biotechnology have replaced the Internet as the hot new investment area for the denizens of Sand Hill Road in Menlo Park, California—the location where many venture capitalists are based."

A quarter mile up the highway, a midnight blue Ferrari dropped from the fast lane all the way down to the exit lane. Oblivious, Amelia continued slyly, "But that doesn't mean that entrepreneurs seeking funding don't have their work cut out for them." The Ferrari put on its turn signal. "The cash may be there, but there are few things more feared in the Silicon Valley than facing a room full of 'Vulture Capitalists' to pitch your idea for a new company."

The blue sports car roared past, the turbulence from its wake flipping open Amelia's skirt to mid-thigh. With no further thought for the stand-up, she stamped her heel and turned to yell at the driver.

Red glow from his taillights and the name "Valmont" on his vanity plate were all that she saw.

FUNDING PITCH

"Doing a funding pitch is like defending your life at the pearly gates—except Saint Peter doesn't have a 15 slide limit."
—Co-founder, failed Internet start-up

THE GANGLY YOUNG MAN AT THE FRONT of the room swallowed hard and tugged at the knot of his tie. His dark suit appeared new and well made, but the material gave out too soon in the sleeves, exposing bony wrists and an inelegant amount of white cuff. In a nervous gesture, he pushed on the nosepiece of his thick plastic glasses. They failed to oblige him by riding any further up the bridge of his nose. "Could you...I mean, would you repeat the question?" he asked.

Ted Valmont looked up from the note pad he was doodling on and sat back in his chair. At 31, he was about the same age as the man at the front of the room, and nearly as tall. But unlike him, Ted Valmont's clothes fit him well: possibly too well. His black hair was combed straight back—with more than the proverbial dab of styling cream—and he had olive skin with regular features that were almost delicate. His eyes were a soft gray green, and in the diffuse light from the conference room skylight, they seemed to shine with amusement. He gave the man at the front of the room a sympathetic grin. "I'm sorry," he said. "I was just wondering—what is the advantage of using radar over infrared in this application?"

"Good. Yes. That is a good question," said the gangly young man. "I have a slide on that right here." Hunching anxiously over a laptop computer, he repeatedly depressed a key to advance the slides in his presentation. He stopped when one with the title, "Radar vs. Infrared in Automatic Flush Valves" was projected on the screen behind him.

"As you can see," he said as he straightened up, "there are two clear-cut advantages of radar over infrared. First, infrared works only on a line-of-sight basis. That means the sensor must be placed in plain view near the washbasin or urinal that it's meant to control. In a public rest room, where vandalism is often a problem, this has distinct disadvantages. On the other hand, a radar sensor can be installed anywhere—even behind porcelain fixtures, tile or masonry. A vandal would literally need a sledge hammer to disable one."

The young man fumbled a laser-pointing device out of his breast pocket and aimed it at the second bullet on his slide. "In addition," he said breathlessly, "radar is capable of detecting a more subtle range of motion than infrared. As you may know, the 'holy grail' in the automatic flush valve industry is providing an automatic flush capability for toilets. Infrared is simply not up for the job. It has been used widely for urinals because the decision of when to flush is binary: you are either standing in front of the urinal or you're not. But when a person uses a toilet, there is no longer a binary…I mean, there is a more complex—"

Tillman Cardinal, a genial-looking man whose curly, matted hair came to a blunt widow's peak like a spent Brillo pad, began to laugh. He reached over to Ted Valmont and poked him in the ribs. "What he means, Ted, is that when you lift up to wipe your ass you don't want the damn toilet flushing early. Be a waste of water."

Ted Valmont smiled and shook his head. Across the table, Mary Wong narrowed her eyes to glare at both men. She tapped a gold pencil on the table sharply and turned to face the presenter. "Go ahead, Roger," she said. "I think we've grasped your point."

The gangly man reddened and cleared his throat. "Yes. The key take-away, of course, is that with radar it's possible to determine the right time to flush. You can avoid flushing too early, or, ah, not at all."

"What about cost?" said Cardinal in more serious tone. "Have you estimated the manufacturing costs? Will they be comparable to infrared?"

Ted Valmont glanced down at the silver 1920s tank watch on his wrist. It was 12:35. As the presenter paged through his slide deck looking for manufacturing cost projections, Ted Valmont gathered up his note pad, cell phone and Palm computer. He stood and walked to the front of the room. "Roger, I'm afraid I need to leave for a board meeting at a portfolio company," he said, extending his hand. "Thanks for taking the time to come down here. I'll follow up with Tillman and Mary when I get back."

Roger shot his hand forward to grasp Ted Valmont's, dropping his laser pointer in the process. "Thank you very much," said Roger earnestly. "Basis Ventures is our first choice for venture funding. I really hope we can work something out."

Ted Valmont smiled, pumped Roger's hand and turned to go out the conference room door. As he pulled it closed behind him, his smile dropped and he chanted in a sardonic undertone, "Pleased to meet you, hope you guessed my name."

A sturdy, large-boned woman with wide shoulders and a tremendous bosom strode up to him from further down the corridor. "No sympathy for the devil, boss," she said matter-of-factly. "Leastwise, not around here."

Ted Valmont's smile reasserted itself. "You're right, Carrie. As Pogo says, 'We have met the enemy and he is us.' What's up?"

Carrie's voice dropped in volume and tone. "I don't know from Pogo, but your brother's on the line. He's been holding for a half an hour."

Ted Valmont stared down at Carrie's size 11 flats. "You told him that I'm booked solid this morning?" he said softly.

"Yes, boss, I did. But he's had some bad news. He said—well, he said that Christy's left him."

Ted Valmont brought a hand up to a spot below his breastbone and clenched it into a fist. He took a deep breath and stood motionless for an uncomfortable moment. "Put him on the line in the small conference room," he said at last, unclenching his fist. "I'll talk to him there."

Carrie acknowledged the request with a truncated nod and broke into a trot. "And I'll call NeuroStimix to tell them you'll be late," she said over her shoulder.

Ted Valmont stepped into a conference room next to the one he had exited and pulled the door shut. He went over to a gray, starfish-shaped phone and pressed the speaker button. "Tim," he said neutrally. "Are you there?"

"I'm never really all here, am I Ted?" said a voice like Ted Valmont's, but not like it: deeper, rougher and—just at this moment—much more slurred.

Ted Valmont took hold of the speakerphone by two of its feet. "Have you been drinking, Tim?"

"You bet. That's one thing I do better than ever."

Mashing a knuckle into the center of his stomach, Ted Valmont said, "Carrie told me Christy left. Did you two fight?"

A wounded, snarling sound issued from the speaker. "No, we didn't. She just packed her fucking bags and snuck out in the middle of the night. No mess, no fuss: lose the crip in one easy step." He laughed contemptuously. "But that's not why I called. I called to find out where the fuck that device is. You said that NeuroStimix would be ready for clinical trials three months ago."

Ted Valmont leaned into the speakerphone. "I said as early as May and as late as September. This is research and development, not cake baking. It can't be pinned down to a precise schedule."

"Oh, yeah? Well I can tell you precisely how long it takes me to empty my bowels: an hour and a half. Of course, that's only if Archie doesn't have to break out the heavy implements."

"Please, Tim—"

"Don't 'please Tim' me. Now what the hell is going on at that place? When am I going to get out of this fucking wheelchair?"

"I'm going to a board meeting today, so I should get an update. But you know there's no guarantee you'll be selected for the trials."

"Tell them they have to take me. You put money in the company."

"We've been over this already. I'll do my best, but there's only so far I can push it. It's a conflict of interest for board members—"

"You sanctimonious bastard! Nobody makes the millions you have without breaking a few rules. Now you won't even round the corners to help your own brother." The connection dropped with a brittle snap.

Ted Valmont reddened and propelled the speakerphone across the conference room table. "*Putain de merde!*" he barked, and launched out the door. He went down the bright hallway—passing several original Mark Citret prints—and into a spacious reception area paneled with cherry and ash woods and illuminated by dramatic columns of light beaming down from triangular skylights nearly thirty feet above.

A receptionist sat behind a U-shaped desk with a pair of crossed polo mallets tacked to the front. The telephone console in front of her flashed and buzzed at a furious pace. By the time Ted Valmont crossed the polished marble floor of the lobby, she had said, "Basis Ventures, would you hold please?" a half dozen times.

Ted Valmont pushed through tall, double glass doors, then paused to slip on a pair of minuscule oval sunglasses. He went down a sidewalk bounded by a carefully tended flower garden to a small parking area in front of the building. His car—a midnight blue Ferrari F355 Spider—was parked in a space with his name. He disabled the alarm and door locks remotely and levered himself into the low seat of the roadster. The car started with a throaty rumble, and Ted Valmont belted up and flipped the lever to retract the convertible roof.

He pulled onto Sand Hill Road and streaked up the quarter mile to Highway 280. Heading south on the freeway, he used the speech recognition technology in the car's hands-free cell phone to check his voice mail.

"New messages," he said to the microphone.

An anxious male voice came onto the line. "Ted, this is Dan Willhite from Infrisco Software. It's been three weeks since we sent you our business plan—"

"Delete."

A no nonsense female voice came next. "It's Sarah. Are you in this deal or not? I've got the green light from my partners. We'll put in six mil if you match it. That gets us each a board seat and 20 percent of the company. I—"

"Save."

Carrie's clipped speech filled the car. "Boss, Dr. Pettibone says he can't refill the prescription unless you come in for an appointment. I squeezed you in on Thursday—"

Ted Valmont wrung the steering wheel in frustration. "Reply," he said sharply, cutting off the message. "Carrie, you've got to get that prescription refilled for me. I can't see Dr. Pettibone on Thursday—or any other day for the next two weeks. If I wait that long, the damn ulcer will eat right through me. Please." He stabbed at a button to drop the connection.

On Shoreline Avenue in Mountain View, he fought lunch-hour traffic across Central Expressway and Highway 101 and continued until he came to Charleston Road. Futuristic buildings from a variety of high technology companies lined Charleston, including the imitation spaceport that comprised the corporate headquarters of Silicon Graphics. Passing the glitzier buildings, Ted Valmont pulled into the parking lot of a modest concrete tilt-up with a placard reading, "NeuroStimix Technologies." He glanced at his watch as he went up the walk to the lobby door. It was 1:10.

He greeted the pudgy black woman at the front desk as Betty, and after slipping off his sunglasses, inquired about her vegetable garden. Betty smiled uncomfortably and smoothed a nonexistent wrinkle out of her floral-patterned skirt. Her eyes crawled sideways to the corridor that opened on her left. "Fine," she said. "It's fine. We had some of the asparagus last night."

Ted Valmont ran his tongue speculatively over his lower lip and leaned down to scribble his name in the visitor log. "Keep me in mind if you have any surplus. Those tomatoes you gave me last summer were great." He looked up. "I'm running late again. Are they waiting for me? Usual room?"

Betty raised her eyebrows in a look of forced candor and nodded precipitously. "Everyone—" she stumbled over the word. "Everyone's there. The big conference room like usual."

Ted Valmont tugged on his earlobe with a thoughtful expression and walked down the corridor. No Mark Citret prints graced its walls, only framed enlargements of medical equipment from the NeuroStimix catalog. He passed the open door of an empty conference room and continued to a closed one further down. He knocked lightly, and without waiting for a response, pushed it open.

GEEK BE GONE

"Board meeting at a start-up? Think children's soccer match. Everyone swarms the ball without regard to their assigned positions— without regard, that is, for the long term."
—Co-founder, failed Internet start-up

INSIDE THE ROOM, THE SOUND OF A heated conversation choked off and the faces of five people—three men and two women— turned to look at the intruder. Ted Valmont met the discomfited gaze of the man at the head of the table. Middle-aged with a deep tan and a beak-like nose, his thinning hair had probably been both dyed and permed. He had a gold watch, a gold bracelet and a gold pinkie ring with a black onyx stone.

"Sorry I'm late," said Ted Valmont with the air of someone trying to smooth over an awkward moment. "I guess I just need a faster car."

The man at the head of the table snorted and stood up to shake hands. Ted Valmont gripped his hand firmly, kiddingly referred to him as, "Chuck DeMarco, CEO Extraordinaire" and moved around the room to greet the others. Coming at the end to a young man with soft pink skin and a protruding forehead, he said, "I'm afraid we haven't met."

"Alan Farr," said the man, proffering a hand with long, curiously jointed fingers. "I'm a senior engineer in product development."

"Very good," said Ted Valmont. "I'm eager to hear how work on the stimulator is going."

Farr looked over at DeMarco, and then back at Ted Valmont. "I've got a presentation and a short video to show you," he said finally.

"Then I won't hold us up any longer," said Ted Valmont, and settled himself into the chair next to bulkier of the two women.

"We thought we'd start with Alan's presentation," said DeMarco, "and then move to a discussion of the next round of funding."

"And here I thought you liked me for reasons other than money."

"Oh, we do, Ted, we do. But it's the whole Valmont package that we admire. It would be so hard to isolate one element from the others."

"Right," said Ted Valmont, leavening the word with irony. "What about Warren, then? Is he joining us?"

A flicker of annoyance crossed DeMarco's face. "No," he said. "I'm afraid Dr. Niebuhr couldn't be with us today. That's why we asked Alan to attend. He's prepared to give a full report on product development and answer any questions you might have."

Ted Valmont looked across the table to Farr, and watched as the engineer broke eye contact and stared down at his lap. "I see," said Ted Valmont. "Is there any particular reason why Warren couldn't make it? This does seem like an important meeting."

DeMarco's voice took on an edge as he replied. "Warren's off at another of his conferences. Not the best timing—I agree—but CEOs and Chief Scientists sometimes do not see the world in quite the same way. I guess this is one of those occasions. Now, shall we get started? We've got a lot of ground to cover."

"Sure," said Ted Valmont, lingering over the word. "Let's do it."

DeMarco motioned Farr to the other end of the table where a VCR with a multimedia projector stood ready. Farr bent down to fiddle with some switches and then stepped back and wiped his palms on the front of his shirt. He said:

"What you're going to see now is a demonstration of recent work with laboratory animals. The animal on the tape—a rabbit in this case—had its spinal cord severed at the 12th vertebrae, resulting in loss of motor function in the hind legs and tail. The latest version of the stimulator was then implanted, which in this configuration consists of a receiver placed under the skin with wires leading to electrodes that stimulate selected nerve roots just below the break in the spine. Power and control signals are fed to the stimulator using radio frequency induction.

"By replicating motor signals sent by the brain in normal rabbits, we were able to a recreate a considerable range of motion in the paralyzed animal." Farr gave a limp smile. "The tape shows this to good effect."

Farr lowered the lights in the conference room and then pressed the play button on the VCR. The image projected on the screen was starkly lit. It showed a gray rabbit lying on its side on a padded board. Held firmly in place by leather restraints, the fur on its back was shaved and a long scar was visible along the crest of its spine. Although the rabbit blinked and twitched its ears, its front legs were held motionless by the restraints and its hind legs appeared to have no life.

The room was suddenly very quiet. Ted Valmont leaned back in his chair and rubbed the pit of his stomach with a pained expression on his face.

Farr cleared his throat. "Now we'll see the results of a series of remote commands transmitted to the stimulator receiver from a master console. As the captions on the screen will indicate, the rabbit will be sent commands to perform the following movements in sequence: tail wag, left leg kick, right leg kick, and finally, simultaneous left and right leg kick."

Ted Valmont frowned in the dark. He watched as a caption flashed in a corner of the screen: "Tail Wag." The rabbit obliged by moving its tail to and fro with unnatural slowness—like the pendulum on a tired metronome. The caption for the left leg movement appeared, and the rabbit kicked the appointed leg in a spasmodic jerk. The movement of its right leg was similar and the "simultaneous" movement of both seemed anything but: one of the rabbit's legs jerked and retracted well before the other leg had moved at all. As a pair of hands appeared in the frame and began to unstrap the rabbit, Farr brought up the conference room lights and pushed the stop button on the VCR.

He looked down at the table, avoiding eye contact. "As you can see, the tape shows the tremendous progress we've made in replicating movements," he said dully. "But not so obvious are the other important advances that have been made with the technology. The size of the receiver, for example, has been considerably reduced, as well as the amount of power it draws."

Ted Valmont shifted in his chair. "Excuse me," he said. "I don't know about the receiver size and its power consumption—I'll take your word for that. But I do know about the rest of it. Warren Niebuhr had paralyzed animals standing on their own power with limited mobility nearly 18 months ago. This seems like definite a step backwards."

The pink color drained from Farr's face. The long fingers of one hand waved frantically like the legs of a crushed spider. "Yes," he stammered. "Well, we—we've had to make some trade-offs in order to get the size of the receiver down. We knew we'd never have a commercially viable product unless it could easily be implanted under the skin. And with Warren not here—"

"Please, Alan," put in Ted Valmont. "I'm sorry if it feels like I'm giving you the third degree. But Warren going off to a one week conference could not have had that significant an impact on the project."

Farr looked across the length of the table to Chuck DeMarco, who pursed his lips.

No one said anything for a long moment. The third man in the room—short, dumpy with gold wire-rimmed reading glasses—finally broke the silence. "For the love of Jesus," he said in too loud voice. "You're going to have to tell the man what's going on, Chuck. He's a God damned board member." He looked over to Ted Valmont. "The fact of the matter is Warren Niebuhr is missing."

Ted Valmont's face darkened with anger. "Missing?" he spat. "Exactly how much of this Kool-Aid were you going to let me drink, Chuck? Why wasn't I told immediately?"

The dumpy man began to respond, but Ted Valmont cut him off. "Thanks for falling on the hand grenade, Ernie, but this is something I need to hear from Chuck."

DeMarco cocked his head to one side and made a close study of his pinkie ring, twirling it around on his finger. "It's no big thing," he said languidly. "As I said, Niebuhr went to a biotech symposium in Napa. He was supposed to come back at the end of last week." DeMarco's eyes were cold but entreating as he shifted his gaze to Ted Valmont. "You know the man, Ted. You went to school with him. He's an irresponsible flake. This is not the first time he's gone off like this, and I'm sure it won't be the last. But that's almost beside the point. Quite frankly, Niebuhr hasn't been pulling his weight. All the progress that's been made in the last six months has been due to Alan and the other engineers. Bottom line: we don't need Warren—or as far as I'm concerned—want him any more."

Ernie grimaced as DeMarco said this last bit. The two women exchanged worried glances.

Ted Valmont drew in a deep breath. "You don't need the founder, principle stock holder and Chief Scientist," he said with low urgency. "You don't need the man that convinced me—against my initial judgment—to let you move from VP of Sales to President when Edwards had his heart attack. There's a lot you don't need, I guess."

DeMarco clamped his mouth shut. Bunches of muscles played along the side of his jaw.

Ernie held his hands up in a placating gesture. "Time out. Let's not let this get out of hand." He glanced at Farr and the two women. "Maybe it would be better if we talked this over in a closed session."

Ted Valmont rubbed his face, looked at DeMarco and Ernie. "Sure," he said in a cooler voice. "That's probably best." He turned to Farr. "Thanks for the update, Alan. I'll be interested to hear more about your work on the stimulator receiver at a later date."

Farr smiled weakly and hurried to pick up his things. The women followed his example and the three of them filed out in a silent procession, closing the door softly behind them.

DeMarco jabbed a manicured index finger in Ted Valmont's direction. "Don't you ever talk about me that way in front of my employees again."

"That's exactly what the Tsar said before the Bolsheviks shot him."

DeMarco drew back as if he had been slapped. He looked down at the floor and patted the back of his carefully coiffed hair.

"What else do we know about this?" said Ted Valmont. "Have we spoken with Laura? Contacted the police?"

"We called Laura on Monday when Warren didn't come into work," said Ernie. "She didn't want to go to the police and we didn't press her. We all thought having them involved would only prove embarrassing to Warren and the company when he returned."

"Not to mention spooking the investors."

Ernie took off his reading glasses and laid them on the table. He looked over at DeMarco, who had stopped patting his hair, apparently reengaged in the conversation. "Yes," he said, "we were worried about that too."

"You were right to worry. With Warren out of the equation, I'll never get approval from my partners for another round of funding." DeMarco opened his mouth to speak. "Don't even bother," said Ted Valmont quickly. "You do need Niebuhr and you need him working on the stimulator. That demo I just saw was pathetic. As far as I can tell, you're further from commercializing the technology today than you were when the company was founded. And that's after burning through $12 million in financing."

"You're painting way too bleak a picture," said DeMarco. "We've made good progress with the technology. We're on track. We just need you to follow through on your original commitment."

"Oh yeah? Let's ask our CFO here about last quarter. How did the final numbers shake out, Ernie? Close to the preliminary estimates you gave me?"

Ernie massaged the red spot on his nose where his eyeglasses rested. "Yes," he said reluctantly. "I'm afraid so. We had sales of $1.2 million on an expense base of 3.5."

"And that revenue number is down from last quarter—as well as being down from the same quarter last year. Correct?"

"Correct. We had a competitive advantage with most all of the products we spun off the stimulator research— like the specialized electrodes—but our competitors are catching up and that's put us under price pressure. We just can't hold the margins any longer."

"And how about cash?"

"We've got 600K in the bank, and I can probably borrow another 500 on the receivables line, but that will only take us part way through August."

DeMarco slapped his palm on the table. "All right, Valmont—you proved your point. You've got us by the short hairs. Now what would you like us to do? Pull Niebuhr out of a hat? Because if you haven't figured it out by now, we don't have a fucking clue where he is."

Ted Valmont looked at DeMarco and shook his head. "Was *Management for Dummies* too advanced for you? It's time to involve the police—well past time. Setting aside the impact on NeuroStimix, have you bothered to consider Warren's personal welfare? He could be sick, injured or worse."

"But Ted, we can't go to the police without Laura," Ernie said soberly, "and she's not having it. She's not crying wolf again."

Ted Valmont put his hand over his mouth and pressed his fingers into the skin of his face. When he took his hand away the imprint burned red on his cheeks. "All right, I'll try to talk some sense into her. And I can ask around at the winery—maybe he stopped in there." He turned to the dumpy CFO. "In the meantime, I want you to search Warren's office, go through his voice mail—whatever it takes to get a lead on him."

"Yes sir," Ernie said glumly.

DeMarco stirred in his chair. He spoke in a chastened voice. "But what about the financing, Ted? You heard what Ernie said about us running out of cash. We've got to get another round in or we won't make the August payroll."

Ted Valmont let out an exasperated growl. "No promises. Finding Warren is the main thing now."

He stood up abruptly and looked down at DeMarco. "I'm going. But there's one last thing: if you ever try to con me about the performance of this company again, I'll make sure that the only work you can get in Silicon Valley is herding shopping carts in the parking lot of Fry's Electronics. You got me?"

DeMarco blinked dumbly. He nodded his head yes.

Falling into the driver's side of the Ferrari a few minutes later, Ted Valmont lunged for the glove box. He pulled out a bottle of liquid antacid, flung off the cap and gulped down half the contents.

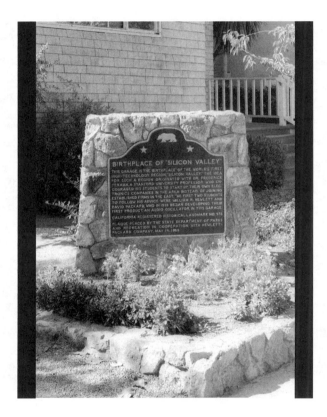

T 'N' T

"Bid For Surgery will be similar to a medical eBay."
—Kevin Moshayedi, CEO, Medicine Online, Inc

THE UNDERCARRIAGE OF TED VALMONT'S FERRARI SPIDER cleared the curb by the thinnest of margins as he wheeled the car into the driveway of a two-story, brown-shingled farmhouse near downtown Palo Alto. Parked in front of him was a Ford van with a wheelchair lift mechanism bolted to the rear door and a blue and white handicapped sticker on the license plate. The vanity plate number read, "HIDIVER".

Ted Valmont spilled out of the roadster and went swiftly up the driveway to the front porch. Here there were signs of remodeling. A smooth concrete ramp with painted metal rails came up to meet the older, fissured concrete of the porch, undoubtedly displacing a set of steps. Ted Valmont yanked open the screen door and twisted the old style ringer, producing a sound like an anemic bicycle bell.

The door was opened almost immediately by a ruddy, middle-aged man wearing a loose-knit black sweater and a pair of chinos. His sweater was pushed up to the elbows of both arms, revealing heavily muscled forearms, sparsely covered by fine blonde hair. The hair on his head was cut short, its original blonde color now mostly given over to a dirty, yellow-gray. He held himself calmly erect in the manner of an ex-military man and his eyes betrayed no hint of recognition as he took in Ted Valmont standing anxiously at the doorway.

"Hello Archie," said the younger man. "I came as soon as I could shake myself loose. How's he doing?"

Archie stepped to one side. "As well as can be expected," he said without enthusiasm, and waved Ted Valmont into the house. "He slept off most of the booze and now he's back in his office surfing the web."

"Checking out the cure sites again?"

Archie nodded curtly and fell into a leather sofa positioned against the sill of the front window. Ted Valmont came to rest on a Navajo rug in the middle of the hardwood floor. He said:

"Christy really left the way he described? Took off in the middle of the night without saying anything?"

Archie expelled air through his nose and let his chin sink to his chest. He looked upward under his brows at Ted Valmont. "Strictly speaking, yes. But the topic of her leaving was not a new one. And it's not as if she hadn't gone AWOL before."

Muscles in Ted Valmont's face tightened. "What do you mean?"

"I mean that she often spent the night elsewhere."

"The bitch."

"This is hard duty for a woman her age. I wouldn't presume to judge her."

Ted Valmont's eyes became cool and deliberate. "You're working for my brother, Archie, not her. You might want to keep that in mind. And why the hell didn't you clue me in?"

Archie shoved the material of his sweater further up one arm. "Because I don't work for you either, Ted. If Tim wants you to know he can damn well tell you himself."

Ted Valmont blinked and brought both hands to the place below his sternum. His shoulders sagged. "You're right, Archie. I just wish they hadn't gotten married so early. Christ, they were only juniors in college."

Archie said nothing for a moment, worrying at a loose thread in the fabric of his sweater with thick fingers. "Maybe it was better that way. At least he got one good year before the accident." He glanced up. "Ulcer bothering you again?"

Ted Valmont smiled tepidly. "Yeah. Big news there." He sighed, cleared his throat awkwardly. "Look—I apologize for what I said just then. It's all going to shit on me this week. No hard feelings?" He put his hand out and Archie stood to take it. "You know I appreciate everything you've done for Tim. Let me know if there's anything you need, won't you?"

Archie flashed a gold-toothed grin and threw aside Ted Valmont's hand. "You're welcome, Ted, and, no, I don't need any more money. I've told you that about a dozen times now."

Ted Valmont waved dismissively and went to the back of the house, going down a wide hallway thoroughly strafed by pictures, clippings, certificates and medals, all hung below eye level. He stopped when he came to a framed newspaper clipping lying on the floor next to a hammer and a box of nails, as if waiting to join the other items. He bent down to pick it up. Taken from the May 7, 1990 edition of the Stanford Daily, the headlines from the article blared:

T 'N' T EXPLODE AT UCLA MEET

Valmont Twins Take First Place in Diving and Swimming Events

Ted Valmont stared at the clipping without recognition, then produced a grunt of surprise and held it closer. Delight spread from his eyes to the rest of his face as he read.

A rasping voice broke his reverie. Issuing from a doorway just down the hall, it commanded, "Home. W-W-W-Dot-N-E-W-M-O-B-I-L-I-T-Y-Dot-C-O-M. Enter."

Ted Valmont returned the clipping to the floor and moved to peer through the doorway. Inside was a pale, gaunt, spindle-limbed version of himself, strapped into a heavy electric wheelchair. The gray-green eyes, though red-rimmed, shone with much of the same intensity, but the once handsome features were etched and wizened by hardship. And, in contrast with the sartorial obsessions of the original, this second Valmont wore a Stanford baseball cap, a Stanford sweatsuit and had leather splints buckled to both wrists. He sat in front of a desk with a personal computer, using a pointing stick to page through a web site. When he tired of this, he leaned down to a microphone and rasped, "Back." The web browser on the computer monitor flashed and reloaded a prior page.

Ted Valmont entered the sparsely furnished room. At one end was a sliding glass door, and at the other, the L-shaped computer desk. The floor was bare hardwood and the only other features of interest were a well-stocked trophy shelf and a tall metal stand with prescription drugs, tissues and a water bottle with a long straw.

"Hey, Tim," he said tentatively. "Good to see my speech recognition software getting a workout."

Tim swiveled his head around, then not so much grasped as hooked the joystick of his wheelchair with a claw-like hand. The electric motor made a whirring noise and the rubber tires backed smoothly away from the desk. Tim thrust his chin out in a brusque greeting to his brother. "The Microsoft version is a hell of a lot better than Valediction ever was," he said. "The only thing they haven't replicated is your packaging. Theirs is boring."

"Sure. That's the secret of my success. Form over function."

A horrible smile distorted Tim's features. "And I've got neither form nor function, do I?" He twitched the wheelchair closer. "Did you come to see how I was dealing with my latest disappointment?"

"Yes, Tim, I did."

"Well, Ted," he rasped caustically, "I hardly noticed it. It was like the tiniest prick of a pin on my big numb, lifeless toe. I can't let it bother me." He drew in a ragged breath. "I also can't clean my fingernails, can't floss my teeth, can't get the sleep out of my eyes, can't blow my nose, can't spit further than my shoulder, can't work a bank machine, can't fit under tables, can't drive, can't masturbate. Can't even tick this fucking list off on my fingers."

Tim glared stony-faced at Ted Valmont for a long moment and then his lower lip began to tremble. A sob caught in his throat and water squeezed from the corners of his red-rimmed eyes. "This can't go on, Ted," he sniffed fiercely. "You've got to help me."

A stricken look came over Ted Valmont's face. He hesitated, then moved self-consciously beside his brother and drew his arms around his shoulder and head. Tim thrust his head in Ted Valmont's stomach, darkening his shirt with tears and mucous.

When Tim spoke again it was with a hoarse, muffled voice that came from deep inside. "Has there been any progress at NeuroStimix? What happened at your meeting?"

Muscles knotted in Ted Valmont's shoulders. He closed his eyes and breathed shallowly through his mouth. "It's going well," he said in a self-possessed tone that lied even more than his words. "They've reduced the size of the receiver considerably."

"Then it won't be long now?"

Ted Valmont looked down at his brother and smoothed aside the hair on his forehead. He squeezed his shoulder. "No, Tim," he said gently. "It won't be long now."

THE POLO MOGUL

"There is, of course, a widespread impression in the entrepreneurial world that...all 3,000 venture capitalists in the industry are arrogant, know-it-all, heavy-handed, control-oriented jerks."
—Frederick J. Beste III, Venture Capitalist, Mid-Atlantic Venture Funds

TED VALMONT WENT DOWN A CORRIDOR AT Basis Ventures, stopping in front of an office door with "Larry Breen" marked on the nameplate. Although the door was shut tight, the sound of a bullying voice could be heard from within.

"I've told you this repeatedly, Samantha. All e-mails to me are to be formatted exactly 72 characters in width. This e-mail you sent me on the company picnic uses the full 80 columns. What are you? Brain-dead? Here—I'm deleting it now. If you expect me to respond, you'll resend it in the proper format. And another thing: there's a little something on your computer called a spelling checker. Use it!"

The door jerked open to reveal an urbane-looking woman with short black hair. She rolled her eyes at Ted Valmont and said with a practiced snideness, "I'm going to grind his face off with my emery board."

Ted Valmont smiled and nodded his agreement and then poked his head through the doorway to peer inside. Larry Breen sat behind a massive oak desk, hunting and pecking on a computer keyboard with two plump fingers. He was a heavy-set man with a florid complexion and a full, fleshy face covered partly by a Vandyke beard. His dull brown hair was thinning, and he wore it slicked back from a narrow point at the crown of his head. Beady, but fierce looking eyes glistened behind his large, aviator-style glasses.

Neither man acknowledged the other. Ted Valmont walked into the office and dropped into a chair in front of the desk. He formed a bridge with his hands and let his glance wander along the back wall. Grouped in a prominent spot in the center were three framed degrees: an AB and an MBA from Harvard, and a JD from Yale. As conspicuous as these appeared, they represented a mere island in the sea of polo paraphernalia surrounding them. There were framed, triple-matted lithographs of polo matches. There were yellowed pamphlets with the rules of polo written in old English. There were knee guards, breeches and gloves, and a polo shirt with the name Breen lettered on the back. There were blunt, half-inch spurs, a helmet, a whip, a bamboo polo mallet, and finally, a set of four horseshoes.

Breen continued typing for several minutes more, and then glanced up at Ted Valmont as if realizing for the first time that he was present. "Well, hello there, Ted," he said genially. "Have I shown you my latest toy?"

Ted Valmont tugged on his earlobe and grinned. "I'm not sure—it's a bit hard to keep track."

"Oh, I think you'd remember if you'd seen this. Take a gander." Breen pushed an oblong, Lucite prism forward on his desk. The prism sat on a walnut base and had a row of colored LED's embedded within it. It looked like a bad piece of modern art or a high tech paperweight. "It's a handsome piece, isn't it?" he asked.

Ted Valmont cocked his head to one side and looked down at the paperweight. "Sure," he said. "It looks nice."

The LED's in the paperweight glowed a vibrant red. Breen laughed and clapped his hands together. "You're lying. You think it's ugly."

Ted Valmont frowned. "Okay, I'll bite. How do you know that?"

"It's a lie detector. It detects modulations in the human voice that occur when a speaker is under stress, as when the speaker is lying his ass off. The LED's glow green if there's no stress, yellow if there's some and red if there's a lot. You definitely pegged it just then." Breen rubbed his hands together with mock glee. "Now the next time one of you comes into my office and tells me the fish are jumping out of the tank at a portfolio company, I'll know whether we really have a winner or you're just spouting off."

"Great. But since you just told me how it works, I can check up on you too."

Breen hunched his shoulders and held up his hands in a distinctly Gallic gesture. "Those who live by the sword," he said. "Besides, I think I'll keep it tucked out of sight over here." Breen moved the detector behind his computer and fell back in his chair in a contented heap. "Say, you want some popcorn? I know I do."

Breen pressed a button on his phone and leaned down to talk into the microphone. "Samantha, bring us some popcorn please. And don't leave any unpopped kernels at the bottom of the bowl this time. Come on now. Chop-chop." Breen released the button and smiled at Ted Valmont. "Was there something?"

"Yes, bad news over at NeuroStimix. It seems that Warren Niebuhr has gone missing."

"Gone missing as in left the company, or gone missing as in he really can't be found?"

"He went to a conference about a week ago and never came back. That lunkhead DeMarco didn't tell me about it until today."

Breen took off his glasses and began cleaning the lenses with the tip of his necktie. "I see. And what impact do you think this will have on the investment?"

"Frankly, I think it's just the olive atop the shit sandwich. The disappearance certainly hasn't helped the R&D effort, but it's apparent to me now that Niebuhr and DeMarco have been butting heads for some time—with the result that Warren has been disengaged for a lot longer than a week."

Breen put his glasses back on and looked at Ted Valmont with a sober expression. "I appreciate the clear-eyed view you're taking of this. Warren Niebuhr being a partner in your winery, and the, ah, situation with your brother must make it difficult."

Ted Valmont hesitated, evading Breen's eyes. "Yeah," was all he said.

Breen plunked an elbow down on the armrest of his chair. He ran his thumb along the tips of his fingers contemplatively while looking off in a corner. "Ted, in my role as Managing General Partner, I'm often called upon to be blunt. This is one of those occasions. You've got a good record with your picks for the Medical Fund II. Three out of five are on track for a profitable exit strategy and there's some reason to believe a fourth will make it too. With that kind of performance, you stand a quite reasonable chance of being promoted to General Partner in the third fund when we open it in the fall.

"That being said, NeuroStimix is not one of your successes. The technology, while alluring and possessing tremendous potential, has not matured at anywhere near the rate we hoped it would. In retrospect, it seems clear that more basic research at the university or government level is required before anyone could hope to make it the foundation for a successful commercial venture. Coupled with this are serious problems with the management team. The CEO and President, whom I just heard you refer to as a 'lunkhead,' has insufficient general management experience and is a poor people-manager to boot. And Warren Niebuhr, while brilliant, is moody, unfocused, and as this latest episode demonstrates, unstable and irresponsible.

"My point is this: your promotion—if and when it comes—will be based not only on the winners you pick, but the way you deal with the losers. It's time for you to realize that NeuroStimix is a loser and act accordingly."

Ted Valmont's thin smile was not amplified, or even confirmed, by his eyes. "Don't let anyone ever tell you that you don't know the meaning of the word blunt, Larry. I hear what you're saying, but I think it's still too early to pull the rip cord. If the NeuroStimix technology can be made to work, the rewards will be tremendous—both financially, and forgive me for being dewy-eyed and dreamy, in terms of the contribution we'll make to society. My brother is only one of millions of people in the world who live with SCI—"

"SCI?" put in Breen peevishly.

"Sorry. It stands for Spinal Cord Injury. I've gotten hip to all the jargon at the board meetings."

Breen nodded. "Better board meetings than People magazine articles about certain crippled movie stars. In any event, your reasoning is specious. We don't invest in companies simply because there's a tremendous upside. We invest in them because there's an upside and a reasonable chance of success."

"I know that. But there are things we can do to improve the percentages with NeuroStimix. We can shoot DeMarco and bring in a good athlete who's capable of managing a sophisticated R&D effort. And we can find Warren and get him back in harness. You said it yourself: he is a brilliant man. My read on the situation is that he is not as far from a commercially viable product as you think."

Breen locked his hands together behind his head. "How were the second quarter results then?"

Ted Valmont frowned. "Bad. They lost 2.3 million, and their revenues are down because of increased discount pressure. But the current offerings are just gravy. They are by-products of the stimulator research. The original business plan didn't call for revenue until next year."

"Yes, it's a tribute to your business acumen that NeuroStimix has a revenue line at all. I'll grant you that. However, expenses are much higher than originally projected, and that more than makes up for the dollars they have coming in. They must be close to the bottom on cash. Didn't I see them on Monday's Fincom agenda?"

"Yes, it looks like they'll run out of cash in August. I'll be proposing another funding round of eight mil on Monday."

"You have your work cut out for you, Ted. With the poor balance sheet and the Chief Scientist missing, I would be very surprised if the other partners didn't develop a case of short arms."

Samantha marched into the room with an enormous bowl of popcorn and set it on the desk in front of Breen.

"No, no," he grumbled. "On the side table, please."

She pounded the bowl down on a table beside the desk. Brushing Ted Valmont's shoulder not-so-accidentally with her hip, she continued past him through the office door.

Breen reached into the bowl and shoved a generous portion into his face. "I'm going to give you a little analogy from polo," he said, his mouth still brimming with masticated kernels.

"Swell," said Ted Valmont. "I wonder how that came to mind."

"It's a grand sport. I've told you that many times. And contrary to the adage about not changing horses in mid-stream, in polo its common practice to swap ponies in the middle of a chukker. Horses, like human players, can have a bad day and there's no point in riding around on a pony that isn't performing. But if you do elect to change, the game keeps going. No one stops the clock and no one waits around for you to return. Therefore, when you do decide to switch, you better do it early and do it quickly. That's the way it is in venture capital. We often pick the wrong pony to ride—it's the nature of high risk, speculative investments. But once we know we've got a bad investment, we need to get out promptly and put our money to work elsewhere. It does no one any good to keep flogging a loser."

Ted Valmont smiled weakly. "Let's just say that I'm not a polo player."

"What do you intend to do then?"

"Finding Warren is the key to all of this. I'm going to talk to his wife and nose around some in Napa."

"Do what you think best, Ted," said Breen, licking salt off the tip of his index finger. "But please don't ignore your other responsibilities. And be advised you will not have my vote at Monday's Fincom no matter what you do to locate Dr. Niebuhr. My mind is made up: it's time to switch ponies."

Ted Valmont brought a hand up to rub his stomach. "I understand," he said vaguely. "I guess I'll have to work that much harder to get the other General Partners' votes."

"Just so," said Breen, and reached for a remote control console. "Now, have I demonstrated my new stereo system for you yet? Wait until you hear—or should I say, experience—the cannon on Tchaikovsky's *1812 Overture*."

PALO ALTO PICKUP

"The odds are good, but the goods are odd."
—Female engineer, on the 6:1 single guy-to-girl ratio in Silicon Valley

TED VALMONT ANGLED HIS FERRARI SPIDER ACROSS two parking spaces in the garage beneath Palo Alto City Hall. He flung the car door shut and charged up the stairs two at a time to ground level, where he emerged on Ramona Street across from a bustling Silicon Valley watering hole. He bent to peck the cheek of a blonde with a pageboy cut who sat at a table near the patio entrance and hurried inside.

Young, casually dressed men and women mobbed dinner booths and pool tables on the ground floor. Off to Ted Valmont's right, above the general yammering, someone was shouting to make himself heard:

"Pets.com! Why not buy dirt online and have it shipped?"

Ted Valmont threaded his way to a wide stairway leading to the second floor. Cocktail waitresses whose dress had no common theme except the exposure of a bare midriff moved among a set of tables. A twenty-foot bar lined the back wall, and the sea of people that extended from it, around the tables and out to the stairway railing was packed even more tightly than the horde below.

Two women at a table in the other end of the room stood up and called together, "Yoo-hoo, Teddy!"

He picked his way to their table and embraced each in turn, greeting the first as Ginny and the second as Esme. Ginny was a petite Chinese with short hair, moussed bangs, broad cheekbones and a pouty, sensuous mouth. Esme was a tall, lithe brunette with green eyes and a strikingly handsome face that was almost feline. They asked him questions, introduced him to their companions and made a place for him at their table.

He sat down, and in reply to their questions, said he was there by himself and his was Pol Roger champagne.

The three of them talked about their time together at a failed Silicon Valley start-up that made pen-based computing devices, and Ginny's date—a tow-headed man named Tom—contributed anecdotes about his old firm, an Internet content syndicator that was in Chapter 11. Esme's companion was a woman. She had a lush figure, a dark complexion and black hair done in a long, single braid. She spoke with a French accent and said only that she was in her residency at Stanford hospital and that she did not like computers.

When the second bottle of champagne had been ordered and consumed, Tom suggested that they move on to the Empire Tap Room. On the short walk to the next bar, Esme's companion turned away from the group and disappeared down the dimly lit street. Ted Valmont shouted for her to come back, but Esme said in an undertone, "Let her go. She's just being French."

At the Empire Tap Room, the two couples sat in a booth near the back. The drinks, clientele and conversation were much like that of the prior establishment, but in a moment of drunken perception at a little past midnight, Tom squinted across the table at Esme and Ted Valmont and declared, "You two look a lot alike. You could be brother and sister."

Esme reached up to touch Ted Valmont's cheek. "I do see myself in him," she said slowly. "That must be the attraction."

This last remark saddled the party with a weight from which it could not recover, and a short while later, Ted Valmont pulled out a pocket-sized cellular phone to call for a limousine. They drove first to a condominium in Mountain View, where Tom and Ginny said good night. From there, the limo driver went up San Antonio Road to Highway 280 and then north to the exclusive town of Woodside.

In the driveway of his rambling, half-timbered Tudor style mansion, Ted Valmont paid the driver off and opened the rear door of the limo. He held out his hand for Esme, and grasping it, she slid across the seat and stood on shaky legs by the back tire. She pulled him close to her. "I want you to do me, Ted Valmont," she whispered in his ear. "Do me good."

He made no remark to this, but waved the limo driver off and guided Esme up the walk to the front door of his house. As he turned from her to put key to lock, she sighed and collapsed on the porch. Sparing only the briefest of glances behind him, he pushed open the door and strode purposefully inside to a buzzing keypad.

It took him several passes with fumbling fingers to enter the correct sequence of numbers, but finally the buzzing ceased. He hurried back to the porch and hefted the unconscious girl like a drooping bundle of rolled carpet, groaning as he straightened up. He lurched through the living room and down a long hallway to the master bedroom, where he flipped her onto the canopy bed. After yanking down the covers, he pulled off the girl's shoes, pants and shirt. Underneath she wore a man's white cotton tank top and a pair of white cotton panties. The tattoo of a Chinese character crested over the edge of her left shoulder.

Ted Valmont looked down at her and gnawed at his lower lip. Slowly, as if moving of their accord, outstretched fingers came to within an inch of her left breast—then snapped back to claw fiercely at the muscles in his neck.

"The perfect end," he pronounced thickly, "to the perfect week."

He shook himself and reached down again to maneuver her torso under the covers, placing her arms at her sides above the bedspread. He left the room, but returned a minute later with a pitcher of water, a glass and a bottle of aspirin. These he left on the nightstand.

In a guest room four doors down he collapsed onto the bed, not bothering even to kick off his shoes. He was asleep a moment later.

The distant sound of a ringing telephone awakened Ted Valmont at 9:46. He was on his back, in almost exactly the same position as he was when he fell asleep. His eyes flickered open and he brought the heels of his palms to his temples. He drew in a deep breath but it caught in his throat as he exhaled, precipitating a racking cough. The pressure from the cough made his face redden and his body went rigid as he gripped the top of his head like it was going to explode. With great effort, he choked off the cough, then rolled onto his side and levered himself upright.

He looked around the room with miserable eyes. The sun came full on through a large window behind the bed, causing him to squint painfully. He kicked off his shoes and stood up, his pants and shirt hanging off him like turkey wattle, crisscrossed with deep wrinkles. He padded out of the room, down the hall and into the master bedroom. Esme lay on her side, snoring lightly with one arm wrapped around her head.

Ted Valmont smiled at her, muttered, "solace through others' pain," and wondered out of the room to the kitchen where he downed two large glasses of ice water. He started a pot of coffee brewing and was just pouring out a bowl of cereal when his houseguest walked through the doorway. Still dressed in her underwear, she cradled her head with one arm and looked at him in an unfocused way through the eye that was not covered. "What did you do to me?" she asked in a depressed tone.

Ted Valmont stared at her for a long moment. "Nothing that came close to what you requested—unfortunately."

Pink color suffused through her cheeks. "I didn't mean that. I mean what happened to my head?"

"You passed out on the way into the house and knocked it on the porch or something." He frowned at her. "Come here. Let me take a look at it."

Esme went around the kitchen island and stood docilely in front of Ted Valmont. She took her hand from the back of her head and then winced as he parted her hair to probe the injury with gentle fingers. "You've got a bump the size of Mount McKinley, but at least the skin isn't broken. Did you take some of the aspirin I left you?"

"Yes. That was—that was thoughtful of you."

"I suppose. I'll go you one better and give you an ice pack for the bump. But that's about the limit of Dr. Valmont's medical knowledge."

He filled a plastic bag with ice from the freezer and pressed it to the back of her head. Moisture from the ice dripped out of the bag and ran down her neck. Ted Valmont watched as the drops rolled under her tee shirt and all the way down her back, settling at the base of her spine. Goose bumps appeared along the strip of flesh that was exposed between shirt and panties. She shivered and her nipples stood out beneath thin cotton.

Ted Valmont bit his lip and pushed her hand up to replace his own on the ice pack. "Go sit over there," he said peevishly, gesturing to the bar stools on the other side of the island. "You're making me jumpy."

A faint smile tugged at the corners of her lips, but she obliged him by sitting on one of the stools. She shifted in the seat, then crossed her free arm across her breasts—a maneuver that did not escape Ted Valmont's attention.

"What's with you, anyway?" he demanded. "I thought you gave up on men."

"So did Odile."

"Well?"

She bowed her head. "I don't know. I've got this weird thing for you, Ted. I was a total heel last night. Here I've been trying so hard to make it work with Odile, and the first time I see you again, I run her off and go home with you. She'll never forgive me."

"Do you live with her?"

Esme looked up from the counter. "What?" she said, surprised. "No, I don't. We were talking about getting a place, but we both wanted to be sure we were committed to the relationship. Some commitment, huh?"

Hair that was normally slicked down fell on Ted Valmont's forehead. He shoved it back. "If you don't live with her," he said mildly, "then she doesn't have to know you spent the night here. Just tell her that you got bombed and went home to sleep it off. Having boorish American friends who drink too much and only talk about computers is better than sleeping with a man—which you didn't, anyway."

"I guess," said Esme without enthusiasm.

"It is, believe me. Now go get dressed and I'll run you home."

Esme left the room and returned 15 minutes later dressed in clothes from the prior evening. She had combed out her hair and scrubbed her face, but there were heavy circles under her eyes and her skin had a greenish pallor. As ill as she appeared, she stood rigidly in the center of the kitchen with a new air of determination.

"You're right," she announced. "I've made a mistake, but it's not fatal. I'm going to walk up to Robert's Market and call a cab."

"It's no bother to take you."

"That's not the point. I don't want to chance Odile seeing you, and frankly, I don't want to see you myself. Ever. After I walk out of here, will you promise to stay away and never have anything to do with me?"

Ted Valmont let the spoon from the cereal he was eating clatter into the bowl. "If that's what you want."

"Fine," said Esme. "Good-bye."

Esme strode out of the kitchen and a short while later the front door opened and slammed closed. Ted Valmont shook his head, and after a moment's pause, pulled out the business section of the morning paper to check the closing price for Oracle.

WEDDED TO SCIENCE

"Into this void of potential mates comes a man you may not have considered before, a man of substance, quietude and stability, a cerebral creature with a culture all his own. In short, a geek."
—Mikki Halpin, author, *The Geek Handbook*

TED VALMONT'S OTHER CAR WAS A TOPAZ Jaguar XK8. He piloted it on a Byzantine course through residential streets of Los Altos, eventually pulling into the circle drive of a neglected ranch style house that was hunkered down at the end of a short block.

Toys and children's clothing of all sorts littered the yard, as well as newspapers, a variety of dead vegetation and an unusually high concentration of dog feces. Ted Valmont went up the chipped brick sidewalk to the front porch, where he found a phalanx of terra cotta pots populated with more dead plants and a blue plastic recycling bin filled with computer parts, wires and a tangled mass of half inch magnetic tape. There was a weathered note on the bin curtly informing the Niebuhrs that the city only accepted newspaper, glass and aluminum for recycling. The note was dated from the prior year.

Ted Valmont paused to examine an empty socket from the string of Christmas tree lights that still fringed the doorframe and pressed the bell. It made no sound. He balled his hand into a fist and pounded. A chorus of dogs began barking and the sound of toenails on hardwood could be heard as they scampered across the floor and assailed the interior door.

A child shrieked, "M-o-m-m-y! The door, mommy!"

With the sound of dogs panting to mark the time, Ted Valmont waited on the porch for nearly a minute. At last locks rattled open and the door was pulled back the width of its safety chain. Two brown snouts thrust themselves immediately into the gap, barking and licking furiously.

"Laura," said Ted Valmont, straining to be heard over the animals. "It's me—Ted."

"Stay back or you'll get trampled."

Ted Valmont stepped back as requested, but then watched help-lessly as two large dogs—each an uncertain mix of Irish Setter and Golden Retriever—launched from the doorway and jumped up to plant massive paws on his chest and stomach.

Laura Niebuhr appeared on the porch. Short and plump with milk pale skin, her unruly brown hair lay entirely flat on one side of her head, while jutting out in a series of stiff projections like curling roof tile on the other. She stamped her foot in frustration. "FORTRAN! COBOL!" she scolded.

The dogs paid no attention to her, vying now for the opportunity to acquaint themselves with Ted Valmont's crotch. She took a quick step forward and swatted each on the butt. They turned to look at her with solemn expressions and trotted back into the house.

Laura wiped her hand on the shiny blue material of her jogging suit. "I apologize for being so short on the phone," she said. "I know you think I should have reported Warren missing the first day after the conference, but you've never lived with the man. You just don't understand the dynamics."

Ted Valmont fought to suppress a smile. "I did live with him, remember? Freshman roommates."

"That's hardly the same thing, Ted. Come on—I made us some tea. I thought we could talk out on the patio."

They went into the house, through a dimly lit living room furnished in ersatz Colonial American to a sliding glass door that opened on the back patio. Outside was a set of rickety lawn furniture with frayed cushions that had been thoroughly chewed by the dogs. Laura poured iced tea from a plastic pitcher into a pair of Flintstones glasses and flopped into the closest chair. Ted Valmont pulled out one across from her, but after getting a good look at the seat, moved to another with more upholstery and less dog hair.

"What's all that?" he asked, eyeing a rusting pile of electronic instruments stacked against the side of the house.

"Overflow. The lab, the garage and the storage shed are already filled."

Ted Valmont nodded. "I remember he used to keep trays with half-dissected animals under our bunk bed in school. I could never get any girls to come over."

"I'm sure you made out just fine."

"I suppose so," he said, grinning a boy's grin. "Look, you're right—I don't understand why you haven't gone to the police. Aren't you worried about Warren?"

Laura Niebuhr dumped a package of sugar in her iced tea and stirred it with an index finger. She flicked tea from her finger to the ground. "I don't call the police anymore. It doesn't make me feel better and they don't do anything anyway."

"What do you mean?"

"I'll feel better when he stops running off. Calling the cops doesn't prevent that. As for what they'll do if I report him missing, with no evidence of a crime, they're not obliged to do a damn thing."

Ted Valmont frowned and brushed absently at dog hair on his trousers. "How many times has he done this?"

"Three or four, depending on how you count. The last time was a medical equipment trade show in Atlanta. He was supposed to be in the NeuroStimix booth demonstrating their products, but he came upon a defibrillator from a competitor that intrigued him. Guess the punch line?"

"No idea."

"He told the competitor he could improve the design and he spent the next two weeks in their lab working 16 hour days to make the damn thing better. For free."

"Did anyone know where he was?"

Laura barked a derisive laugh. "No one on this planet, anyway."

Ted Valmont blinked with surprise. "That's a little harsh, isn't it? He is your husband after all."

"From your lips to God's elbow."

"Ear."

"What?"

"You mean God's ear—not his elbow."

Laura ran her finger down the side of her glass, tracing a line through the beads of condensation. She looked up at Ted Valmont with a smirk. "Are you sure?"

He cleared his throat, embarrassed. "Have it your way. But if you don't mind, I'd still like to talk to the police."

"Knock yourself out. Detective Mark Whitten of the Los Altos police is the one I've given my business in the past. But if I were you, I wouldn't mention the name Niebuhr until you get in to see him. With any kind of warning, he'll hide under his desk and stay there until you leave."

Ted Valmont pulled a top-of-the-line Palm computer with wireless modem from the breast pocket of his sport coat. He slid out the stylus and tapped in a note with Whitten's name. He glanced up. "What about the conference. Can you tell me anything about it?"

"You sure want a lot of service with your tea."

"I didn't come to drink the damn tea, Laura. I came to get information to find Warren. Now how about it?"

Laura nudged the empty sugar packet with the bottom of her glass. "It was held at the Appellation Inn in Yountville," she said tartly. "Everyone was specially invited and most were executives from health care companies. BioTech Summit they called it."

Ted Valmont's stylus tapped in more notes. "You think Warren stopped in at the winery while he was up there?"

"Please. As far as I can tell, the only interest Warren has in the winery is cashing the checks."

Ted Valmont sighed and returned the Palm computer to his pocket. He reached for his glass and downed the tea in four gulps. Standing, he looked at Laura Niebuhr speculatively. "You will tell me if you hear from him?"

Laura smirked again. "You'll be the first to know."

Ted Valmont walked briskly down the front steps of the Los Altos Civic Center and headed back to his car. He did not look happy.

Sitting in the front seat of the Jaguar, he took out his Palm computer and tapped in more notes. As he moved the stylus over the writing area, the following appeared on the display:

```
MP report filed report 6/15 w/ LA
Police.

See Dep. Sheriff Norman Olken,
Napa.
```

An icon in the shape of an envelope flashed in the upper corner of the screen as Ted Valmont finished writing. He saved the memo and then tapped the icon with the tip of the stylus. The display cleared, "Receiving Message" flashed for a moment and the picture of a very attractive young woman in her early 20's painted in four segments. The words "Wine Auction?" showed below the picture, but there was no other text in the e-mail.

Ted Valmont tilted the display of the computer to the light and held it closer. He traced the stylus along the side of the girl's oval face in a near caress and then looked blankly out the front window of the car. After a moment, he shook his head, slid the stylus back in its holder and tossed the computer onto the passenger seat.

He started the Jaguar, put it into reverse and twisted around in his seat to back out of the parking stall, then abruptly returned the gearshift to park and snatched up the computer. He used the nail of his index finger to activate a button on the display marked "Reply", but the computer responded, "No return address." Ted Valmont threw it aside and drove out of the lot with a scowl.

He navigated the car over the San Mateo Bridge, through the rerouted Cypress interchange that had been destroyed in the 1989 earthquake, onto Interstate 80 and over the spindly Carquinez Bridge into the East Bay town of Vallejo. A few miles north of Vallejo, he left the interstate and after a jog on a smaller road, came onto Route 29, the main artery through the Napa Valley.

Gradually the countryside became patched with vineyards, their neat rows of vines—many of them newly planted—undulating over rolling hills. Wineries appeared by the roadside as well, buildings new and names unfamiliar at first, growing more venerable and well-known as Ted Valmont progressed through the valley.

Through the city limits of Napa proper, the road became clotted with the RVs, station wagons and mini-vans of weekend tourists. The temperature seemed to rise with the traffic, and inside the car Ted

Valmont switched on the air conditioning and carefully rolled up his shirtsleeves. At the crowded intersection with Trancas Street, he turned left, and coming through a short commercial district, veered off on Redwood Road to climb into the low Mayacamas Mountains, the range demarcating the western boundary of the valley.

The road zigged and zagged its way through a forest of scrub oak and stunted redwood and then abruptly the trees ended and terraced farmlands took their place. Acres and acres of old-growth Chardonnay and Cabernet Sauvignon clung somberly to hills obscured by the mist of a late-clearing valley fog. Ted Valmont gave the Jaguar its head, grunting with satisfaction as he threaded the curves of the road. At an intersection marked by a Val du Grue Vineyards sign, he turned off the main way onto a narrow track leading up the side of a steeply banked ridge. An imposing, turn-of-the-century stone building stood at the crest of the ridge. Its massive entry portal was marked by an arch of outsized sandstone blocks, and its irregular facade was checkered with narrow windows that looked like loopholes in a battlement. As an antidote for its dour countenance, brightly colored pennants with the image of a stylized crane streamed from the roofline to a point halfway down the building.

Ted Valmont parked his Jaguar in the ample visitor's lot and got out of the car to stretch. He walked around the side of the building to the courtyard beyond. In it stood a collection of idle equipment, including a winepress, a forklift and a pair of large stainless steel hoppers. Across the way was a modern-looking warehouse with a gaping entrance, and glittering beneath a bank of fluorescent lights, row upon row of tall stainless steel tanks. Workers in rubber boots and aprons maneuvered heavy hoses across the wet floor, and as Ted Valmont came up, the musty aroma of fermenting wine wafted out to him.

"Javier," he called out to one of the men. "*Està Bruce alrededor hoy?*"

A Hispanic man with a trim mustache and brilliant white teeth straightened up from his labor with the hose. He wiped his forehead with the back of his arm and smiled. "Hello Señor Ted. Yes, he's here. He's been messing with the Chardonnay blend for a week. Every time we think we are ready to mix the stuff from the oak with the stuff from the stainless steel, he comes running out to tell us he's not happy with the ratio. I think he's in his office rejiggering it again."

Ted Valmont shook his head. He said, "A true artist is never appreciated in his own time."

"And neither is Bruce Crane."

Ted Valmont laughed and reached up to slap Javier's hand, high five style. "So much for the Val du Grue winemaker. Please don't share your opinion of the absentee president."

"Well, we like the absentee part anyway."

"Great. I'll try to reestablish that condition." Ted Valmont saluted and turned to leave. "See you guys later," he called over his shoulder.

He went down a row of stainless steel tanks to the back of the warehouse, where he turned right and walked along windows that looked into the bottling room. A corridor opened on his left and he followed it to an open office door at the far end. Inside was a young man with red hair, a baby face, light skin dusted with freckles and an earnest, clean-cut air about him, like a Mormon on his mission. He was dressed in khakis and a starched white shirt and held a large wine glass with a half-inch of gold-colored wine. On the table in front of him were a rack of test tubes, graduated cylinders and a clipboard with notes written in a firm, square hand. Seeing Ted Valmont, he stood up from his chair and thrust forward the glass. "Try this," he said without preamble.

Ted Valmont took the stem of the glass, swirled the wine vigorously and then put his nose deep in the bell. He took a small sip of wine and rolled it around like a marble on his tongue. Bruce Crane watched the proceeding intently, and when Ted Valmont failed to say anything for several long seconds after he had swallowed the wine, Crane demanded, "Well?"

"Tastes like shit," pronounced Ted Valmont at last.

Crane grabbed the glass out of his hands and set it down on the table. "That's exactly what I'm afraid of."

"Relax, Bruce—I was kidding. Maybe it's still a bit closed-in, but I think you nailed it. What's the blend?"

Crane looked over his notes. "That particular batch is twenty percent three-year-old oak, with thirty percent two-year-old and the remaining from the stainless steel. Of course, the other variable is the vineyard. For the proportion that we aged in three-year-old barrels, I took sixty percent from Mount Veeder and forty percent from Stags Leap. For the—"

Ted Valmont waved his hands. "Enough already. I trust that you've taken all the factors into consideration. What is it exactly that you are worried about?"

"Well, you don't think it's gone tanky do you?"

Ted Valmont reached over to ruffle the other man's hair. "Christ, no. But if you think so that's probably a good sign. You said the same thing before the *Wine Spectator* gave us ninety-seven points for the 1999 Chardonnay."

"I suppose I did, didn't I?"

"Yes, in every one of the five years since we began this venture, you've made some dire prophecy about a selected varietal—not one of which has ever come true."

Crane sat down again and combed through his hair with his fingers. "It's different for you," he said. "This is just another venture to you. You've already made your fame and fortune playing the Silicon Valley whiz kid. For me, this is more than an avocation. It means something when I put my name on the bottle as winemaker."

"You're not going to start comparing me to all the retired dentists in the valley who have started wineries again, are you?"

Crane laughed. "No," he said, "this time I was going to compare you to the dental hygienists."

Ted Valmont ignored the gibe and pushed some of the equipment on the desk aside to rest his hip against the edge. "Speaking of dilettantes," he said, "you didn't happen to get a visit from our minority partner in the last couple of weeks, did you?"

"Warren? I'd have forgotten he had any involvement if it weren't for the bookkeeper bringing the checks by for me to sign every quarter."

"That's almost exactly what his wife said."

"Something wrong?"

"He came up for a conference at the Appellation Inn and never made it home."

Crane asked carefully, "Any reason to think it's serious?"

Ted Valmont stared down at the floor and rubbed the back of his neck. "I don't know. Laura certainly doesn't seem concerned, but you remember Warren's a co-founder at NeuroStimix."

"The company you said could help your brother."

"Yep. And if the stakes weren't high enough, my boss wants to pull the plug on their funding and he's made it pretty damn clear my promotion to partner is on the line—not that I really give a crap about that."

Crane nodded, his face a mask of polite concern. "Have you taken it to the police?"

Ted Valmont pressed three fingers into the spot below his sternum and grunted in the affirmative. "But they don't investigate adult missing persons cases unless there's evidence of foul play. Which reminds me—is there a wine auction anytime soon?"

"I can't even see your dust on that one."

Ted Valmont took out his Palm computer and powered it on. He set it on the desk and pushed it in Crane's direction. "Somebody sent this to me after I got done talking with the Los Altos police."

"Christ, Ted," said Crane, his eyes crinkling with amusement. "Now you got 'em hitting on you over wireless. I'm surprised she sent a picture with her clothes on."

"I don't think it's a come-on. Do you know who she is?"

"No idea—wait— isn't that Ms. January?"

"Fuck you," snapped Ted Valmont. "How about the auction?"

"There is an auction for the Migrant Farm Workers Housing Fund tonight. You'll be pleased to hear I took the liberty of donating a case of the '97 Pinot."

Ted Valmont straightened up from the desk. "When and where?"

"Maitland Winery." Crane smiled up at him. "I'll meet you there at 7. I wouldn't miss this for the world."

IN LIKE VALMONT

"The quality of deals is at an all-time high."
—Ann Winblad, Venture Capitalist, Hummer Winblad Venture
Partners, quoted in *The Wall Street Journal*, December 4, 2000

TED VALMONT CAME UP TO BRUCE CRANE. Crane was leaning against the mantel of a stone fireplace with a glass of white wine in one hand and a smoldering cigar in the other. Next to him was a hatchet-faced man of middle age with a crew cut and leathery, heavily lined skin. Milling around the trio was a larger crowd: mixed, affluent, casually dressed with a preference for western wear, yammering at a volume consistent with the consumption of at least one drink.

"Ted," said Bruce Crane with an enthusiasm that suggested he had crossed the one drink boundary. "I'd like you to meet Forrest Hawley. He's the winemaker here at Maitland Vineyards."

Ted Valmont shook hands with the hatchet-faced man. "Weren't you at Greystone before? Man, you guys made some great Merlot—especially the stuff from Selby Creek Vineyard."

Hawley smiled, revealing crooked, tobacco-stained teeth. "Thank you," he said in a flinty voice. "I actually liked the Napa Valley appellation better myself. I always thought the Selby Creek designation was something of a marketing gimmick."

Crane poked at Ted Valmont with his cigar. "That's just what I said about your Mount Veeder Reserve idea."

Ted Valmont held up his hands. "The only thing that proves is premium designations work. If I fell for it, there's no reason the average schmo won't either." He turned to Hawley. "Excuse the family squabbles. So what made you decide to jump ship to Maitland? Seems like you were on quite a roll at Greystone."

Hawley gave a twisted grin. "It was a tough call. It pretty much came down to two things. The first was I really wanted to try my hand at some other varietals, and that wasn't going to happen at Greystone. It's strictly Merlot and Cab there. The second was the opportunity to build up a winery from scratch—backed by somebody who was willing to invest to do it right."

"I gather Maitland didn't make his money cleaning teeth, then," said Crane.

"No—he's not one of the retired dentists, that's for sure. He's an industrialist of some sort. And he's willing to spend the dough. We've got an ultra-modern facility with capacity for more than triple this year's production. We've acquired four hundred acres of producing vineyards and planted about the same new. And we've even dug caves for barrel aging in the hills behind the winery."

Ted Valmont whistled. "I bet throwing around that kind of money has ruffled a few feathers. Lord knows Bruce and I weren't exactly greeted with open arms when we got started."

"You're right. A lot of folks think he's a rich latecomer with no appreciation for the business. Hence the auction. He wanted everyone to see he's a fundamentally a good egg who isn't treating winemaking as an expensive hobby."

Crane swirled the wine around in his glass. He sniffed at it. "It's opening up nicely, Forrest," he said. "How about your relationship with Maitland? You two see eye-to-eye on everything?"

"He can be something of a cold fish at times—no question. But I respect the man. He gives me a free hand, and as I said, he takes the business seriously. Both in terms of investment and in making an effort to learn what I've got to teach him."

A woman in a caterer's uniform came up to the group. "The auction is just about to begin, gentlemen," she said. "If you would take your assigned seats in the dining room."

The caterer gestured towards an archway at the rear of the room. Hawley moved to comply, but Crane took Ted Valmont by the elbow and pulled him close. "No sign of Miss January," he said in an undertone.

Annoyed, Ted Valmont jerked his elbow free and joined Hawley in a line of people going through the arch to a great hall with a stone floor and a high roof supported by untrimmed tree trunks. Narrow stained-glass windows projected rose-colored light at one end of the room, and at the other, a massive tapestry hung over a stone-mantled fireplace. A dais with tables on either side to display the wines being auctioned was set up in the middle.

The men found they had been seated together at one of a dozen or more trestle tables arrayed in front of the dais. The place card for the spot on Ted Valmont's left read, "Mr. Peter Mondavi," but his seat was empty. With no word of explanation, a young woman swooped in from behind and replaced the card for another, then disappeared in a blur of blue silk and strawberry hair.

"What in the heck was that?"

Forest Hawley cleared his throat. "That," he said, "was Maitland's niece. In theory, she's in the graduate viticulture and enology program at UC Davis, studying to be my assistant."

"Why in theory?" asked Crane.

"She's on summer break right now, but she only managed a single day at topping up the cabernet barrels before she abandoned all pretence and devoted herself entirely to the pool and tennis court.

She's the one thing Maitland and I actually butt heads over. I think he spoils her, but he won't hear a word against her."

"How old is she, then?" asked Ted Valmont.

Hawley frowned. "I don't know. How old are graduate students? Twenty-one or so?"

Crane chuckled and pointed at Ted Valmont with his thumb like he was hitching a ride. "That's what I like about Ted. Always careful to do the research up front. He's never once been charged with statutory rape."

Whatever response Ted Valmont might have made to Crane's remark was lost when the young woman returned to the table. He watched without comment as she pulled out the chair next to him and primly sat down. Undoubtedly the girl from the e-mail, she was paralyzingly beautiful in person. Her skin was ivory with peach undertones, her eyes a startling green. She wore a sleeveless blue dress that showed her sinewy and well-shaped limbs to good effect, matching espadrilles and an unadorned silver bracelet. When she parted her lips to run a delicate tongue across them, Bruce Crane let go of the breath he had been holding.

Ted Valmont smiled and reached over to pick up her place card. "Ms. Gabrielle Maitland, I presume."

Several hours later, Ted Valmont and Gabrielle Maitland walked together along a flagstone path on the grounds of the Maitland estate. It was pleasantly warm, and Ted Valmont had his jacket thrown over his shoulder. Gabrielle walked barefoot, having jettisoned her espadrilles under the dinner table. The path led around the back of the main house and up to the door of a small cottage. With a burst of girlish energy, Gabrielle leapt over the low stairs to the porch and landed on the wooden deck. She pulled open the front door. They passed together through the tiny sitting room and into a larger bedroom with an adjoining bath. A wrought iron bed dominated the room, and in front of that, a pair of freestanding wrought iron candlesticks rose to waist height. Gabrielle dialed the room lights up to a soft tone and then snatched a box of matches from the fireplace mantle. Ted Valmont watched as she fumbled with the matches—breaking two on the striking board before she got one lit—then bumped the candlestick with her elbow as she attempted to bring flame to wick.

He came up behind her and blew out the match. "Hey! Stop that," she said. "What's the matter? You have something against candlelight?" A slight British accent leavened her speech.

Ted Valmont put his arms around Gabrielle's waist. "I like it fine. But I didn't want to watch you burn the house down. Why don't you get us something to drink and I'll take care of the mood lighting."

She turned in his arms and, grabbing the back of his head, kissed him hard on the lips. "Right," she said as she pulled away. She pressed the box of matches into his palm.

Ted Valmont shook his head sharply as if to clear it from a blow and watched as she bounded out of the room. He lit the candles, returned the matches to the mantle and sat down on the edge of the bed. From somewhere in another part of the cottage came the sound of rattling crockery, then the pop of a sparkling wine cork, and finally the harsher sound of glass breaking on the floor. Several long minutes later, Gabrielle appeared with a tray. On it was a crystal flute filled to the brim with wine and a plain tumbler of ice water. Gabrielle put the tray on the cherry dresser beside her bed and handed Ted Valmont the flute. She took the tumbler for herself and sat down next to him.

"What's the matter?" he said, mimicking her. "You have something against champagne?"

She wagged her finger at him. "It's not champagne unless it comes from the Champagne region of France." She assumed a broad, Kentucky accent. "This here is good ol' American sparklin' wine."

"*Touché*, as they say in Champagne. But Daniel Boone you are not. How'd you come by the British accent?"

She looked down at his thigh and rubbed her hand along it. It was an odd gesture, somehow lacking in gentleness. "My mother moved us to England when I was twelve." She gave him a licentious grin. "I spent all of my formative teenage years there."

"I'm not going to touch that line."

"I read about you," she blurted, suddenly earnest. "In that book, *Valley Venture: The Story of Valediction*. When Uncle Douglas said you were coming to dinner, I was chuffed to bits."

"My being here can't have been that much of a surprise—seeing how you had more than a little to do with it."

"Whatever do you mean, Mr. Valmont?"

He scrutinized her features, then shook his head. "Go ahead—be coy. But don't believe a word you read in that book. The author made everything up."

"He didn't make up the fact that Valediction was the fastest growing software company ever."

"No."

"Or the fact that it was acquired by Microsoft for the largest sum they've ever paid for a private company."

"No."

"How about the bit where you seduced Bill Gates' wife to bias the deal in your favor."

"That he made up. I don't even know the woman. And seducing Bill Gates' wife hardly seems like the best way to curry favor."

"It depends on whose favor you're trying to curry, doesn't it? But whether or not the book is entirely accurate, what you accomplished was super. You must be proud."

Ted Valmont took a swallow of wine, nodding as he returned the glass to the tray. "Yes, I'm proud. But much of it was dumb luck. I was involved in two other start-ups before I founded Valediction, and both of those failed miserably. The difference with Valediction was that we developed a bulletproof speech recognition algorithm at just the time the market was ready to embrace it. Too much earlier and it would have been a novelty—a toy. Too much later and we would been beat by competitors. That's the way it goes in the Valley."

"So now you're at Basis Ventures, helping other entrepreneurs be successful."

Ted Valmont reached over and took hold of a lock of Gabrielle's hair. He tickled her cheek with it. "That's the hype on our web site. The real motivations are a lot less altruistic: greed and the desire to be known as king maker in the valley. At bottom, venture capital is a pretty ruthless industry."

"Attack of the vulture capitalists from Sand Hill Road."

"You got it. Sometimes I think we hurt entrepreneurs as much as help them."

Gabrielle leaned forward to put her glass on the tray, then pulled herself further back on the bed so her legs were stretched out in front of her. "How do you hurt them?"

"Oh, lots of ways. We take as much equity as we can get for the initial investment, we write ourselves favorable terms in the event of acquisition or bankruptcy, and we dilute the equity of the founders even further with additional rounds of financing—sometimes to the point where they actually have no remaining stake in the company.

"But the capper is that VC's just aren't very good at what they do. We're not very good at picking winners and, if the truth were known, a lot of people employed by venture capital firms would never make it in a real business. You know that old saying about teachers? 'Those who can, do. Those who can't, teach.' An apt corollary would be, 'Those who can't teach, VC.'"

She smiled. "I like Woody Allen's version better. He said, 'Those who can't teach, teach gym.'"

"I wonder if your average venture capitalist could even do that."

"What's left, then—Sex Ed?"

Without waiting for a response, Gabrielle took hold of Ted Valmont's shoulders and shoved him flat on the bed. She hitched up her skirt—revealing the pale blue material of her panties—and straddled him at the waist. Buttons flew like shrapnel as she yanked open his shirt.

Ted Valmont lifted his head awkwardly. "Hold on a second!" he yelped.

"Hush," said Gabrielle in a low tone. "Let's see how you do with your lesson." She bent down to kiss his chest and moved her hands along his sides and over the smooth muscles of his belly. When she came to his waistline, she took hold of his belt and jerked it open. The button and zipper of his fly were dispatched in a clumsy but expeditious manner, and soon Ted Valmont had his expensive wool trousers and silk boxers in a bunch around his ankles. His penis rose sharply, projecting a wavering shadow in the flickering light of the candles.

He let his head fall back and closed his eyes. "I'll do my best," he said vaguely.

Gabrielle scooted over to his side and tucked her knees beneath her. Placing a hand on his stomach and another on his thigh she brought her mouth down to his cock and kissed the tip of it. She teased her tongue around the purple head and gradually enveloped it with her lips. This produced an inarticulate moan from Ted Valmont.

Gabrielle brought her mouth softly down the shaft—almost to the base—and then made the return trip at an unhurried pace. She moved her hand from his thigh and cupped it around his balls.

Ted Valmont made more noises and Gabrielle continued the circuit up and down his cock, sometimes releasing him from her mouth to run her tongue broadly along the front of the shaft. As the pace of her caresses increased, Ted Valmont grabbed a fist full of bed cover and began to fidget urgently beneath her ministrations. He lifted his head to look at her. "Gabrielle," he said in a tight voice. "You're wonderful. But stop. Please stop. You'll use me up."

In a heavy, languid motion, he placed a hand on her back and ran it up to her neck, trying to dampen the bobbing motion of her head. Then, without warning, he inhaled sharply and bolted upright. He brought both hands around Gabrielle's face and pulled her to eye level. "What's on the back of your neck?" he asked in a worried voice. "There's some kind of wire under the skin."

Gabrielle brought her hands up to press his against her face. She leaned over to kiss him. "It's nothing, lover boy. It's just a memento from an accident I had when I was little."

"What sort of accident?"

Gabrielle smiled and pulled his hands from her face. She twisted round and sat with her back facing him. "Undo me and I'll tell you about it."

Ted Valmont chuckled. "I'd undo you even if you didn't tell me about it," he said in a looser tone. He undid the hook fastener at the back of her dress and pulled down the zipper. She shrugged out of her arms and the dress fell about round her waist. Her back was as toned and sinewy as her legs and arms.

"Now the bra," she said.

"I'm beginning to think this is just a way to avoid the question," said Ted Valmont, who nonetheless complied promptly with the request.

When the sheer silk bra had fallen away, Gabrielle stood on the bed and slipped completely out of her dress. Ted Valmont watched as she kicked it to the floor and returned to a place next to him, wearing only her blue panties. Her breasts—two perfect, creamy, vanilla scoops, each topped by a dainty pink nipple—swayed gently as she sidled closer to him, bringing their skin in to contact along the whole length of their hips and thighs. She brought her hand down to his still erect cock and closed her fingers about it. "Did you say something?" she whispered in his ear.

"Answer the question," he said, a pained expression on his face.

She released her grip but brought her hand back to stroke the front of his cock with two curled fingers. "Crikey, you are persistent. When I was 14, I was thrown from a horse and fractured my neck in the fall. I had to go in traction for several months, and the doctors decided to wire the fractured vertebrae in place to help them heal."

Ted Valmont's face convulsed. He grabbed Gabrielle's hand and pinned it to his leg. "My brother—" he began urgently.

Gabrielle giggled and pulled her hand loose. "Your brother what? Is a doctor? Relax, I've got several of my own. After I got out of traction, they told me there was no need to remove the wires—they provided extra support for the weakened bones—but over time they've worked loose and begun to protrude."

"Is—is there anything that can be done about it?"

Gabrielle returned to her caresses. "Do you mean is there anything that can be done to relieve the situation?"

"Yeah, yeah, that's what I mean," said Ted Valmont, shifting his rear end around on the bed.

"Yes, of course. I'm scheduled for a simple operation later this summer to have them out. The good news is my neck is stronger than ever and I don't need the extra support. Now, are you satisfied, Mr. Valmont?"

"Not exactly."

Gabrielle stopped what she was doing and slid off the bed to kneel on the floor in front of Ted Valmont. She unlaced his shoes and pulled them off, followed by his socks, pants and underwear. Ted Valmont yanked off his shirt and threw it over into the corner of the room.

Gabrielle stood in front of him. She brought her hands to her hips and rolled the fabric of her panties down, undulating her hips as she exposed more and more of her pelvis. When all that remained of her panties was a tight roll of fabric, she hooked her finger through them and slid them down her legs. She placed her hand over her closely cropped pubic hair and pressed on her abdomen. "Feel me," she said.

Ted Valmont reached across to touch her lips and brought away a finger shiny with moisture. He grabbed the firm cheeks of her butt and pulled her close to him. Falling back on the bed, he brought her down on top of him. He turned to roll into the superior position, but she blocked him with a surprising strength and pinned his arms above his head.

"Oh no you don't. There's more for you to learn."

Ted Valmont relaxed the tension in his arms, no longer straining against her grip. "Okay, teach," he said with a sigh. "What do you suggest?"

"A long, slow shag."

Releasing his arms, she planted a knee on either side of his hips and floated her pelvis just above his pulsing cock. She took hold of it and rubbed the head slowly along the moist lips of her pussy. She brought her hips down as if to impale herself, but by design or poor aim, his cock missed the mark and skittered up her belly. She rose once more to take him, but again he slid past her.

"Please Gabrielle," he said achingly "You're killing me."

She giggled, and took her hand from his cock. "You put it in me, Teddy. I'd like that." She arched her back to receive him.

Ted Valmont caressed her stomach and inner thighs with a trembling hand, then guided his cock to her pussy. He parted her lips with his fingers and pushed the head just inside her. Languidly, she rode down the shaft until she had taken his whole length. Ted Valmont groaned with pleasure, and Gabrielle leaned over to kiss him, her hair glimmering in the candlelight as it fell about his chest and shoulders.

Gabrielle moved on top of Ted Valmont with a quirky, athletic vigor for less than ten minutes before he exploded in a racking climax. Gabrielle did not join him. They cuddled spoonwise afterwards, but roused themselves twice more to make love, each time Gabrielle rebuffing any attempt on Ted Valmont's part to repay the pleasure she brought him.

At three-twenty, Ted Valmont fell into a heavy slumber. Gabrielle lay propped on her elbow, caressing his forehead as he breathed in a deep, regular cadence. At last, she got up to put out the guttering candles, then crawled back into bed to curl up beside him.

WALK OF SHAME

"[I]t was a company imagined by inexperienced bankers under thirty and…the bankers came from a leading and well respected firm. Ergo: A sure, certain 'win.'"

—Don Sussis, business columnist, explaining the investment analysis of Kosmo.com's venture capitalists

H ARD, FLAT LIGHT WAS STREAMING IN FROM two uncurtained windows when Ted Valmont sat up. At his side Gabrielle Maitland slept like a dead person, the position of her body unchanged from when she lay down. Ted Valmont slipped out of bed and walked quietly around the room, collecting socks, underwear, pants, shirt and shoes as he went. Behind the bathroom door, he splashed water on his face and tried to slick down his unruly hair. "Mr. Don Fucking Juan," he said to the disheveled image in the mirror.

Back in the bedroom, he picked up his jacket from where it hung on the bedpost and looked down at Gabrielle. A smile crept on to his face and he snaked a hand under the covers to pinch her butt. She did not stir. He brought the hand out and smoothed a strand of hair from her eyes. "Hey angel," he said softly. "I'm going."

Gabrielle's eyes fluttered half open and she smiled at him. She waved feebly with two fingers that peeped out from the covers and closed her eyes once more. Ted Valmont leaned down to kiss her. He opened his mouth to speak again, thought better of it, and went quietly out the door.

Outside he followed the flagstone path to the rear of the main house, then walked around the building to the winding drive in front. There were no cars anywhere along the length of it. Ted Valmont cursed the "frickin' valets," and shielding his eyes against the late morning sun, scanned the front half of the estate. His gaze came to rest on a barn at the far side of an acre or so of vineyards. Eschewing the dirt road that branched from the drive, he cut across the lawn and plunged into the vineyards, heading directly for the barn. He was part way up a row of trellised vines when a tall, white-haired man in coveralls straightened up from a rose bush at the other end. The man's nose was flat with prominent nostrils and a deep crease ran from either side of it to a thin-lipped, grim-looking mouth. He held pruning shears and several cut roses in gloved hands.

Ted Valmont checked his stride and stopped. The white-haired man looked at Ted Valmont without expression and turned his head calmly to spit into the bed of the rose bush.

"Lost?" he asked in a tight voice.

Ted Valmont forced a perfunctory smile. "It's not so much me as my car. I left it with the valets when I arrived for the auction. I'm not sure where they might have put it."

"They probably weren't thinking in terms of overnight parking."

Ted Valmont cleared his throat. "No," he said. "They probably weren't."

"You're Valmont, aren't you?"

"Yes, that's right. And you are—"

"Your host—Douglas Maitland."

"I see."

Maitland nodded as if Ted Valmont had made a comment about the weather. "I'm afraid I've been witness to too many of Gabrielle's flirtations to give them much weight. You'll find your car by the tractor barn. My foreman, Ramos, washed and polished it for you."

Ted Valmont looked down to mash a dirt clod with his shoe. "Thank you for your hospitality," he said slowly. "I hope you'll let me return the favor by accepting an invitation to Val du Grue sometime soon."

"Now you're making me out like some kind of pimp." Maitland grunted as he squatted down to wedge the maw of the shears around a sucker at the base of the rose bush. There was a dry snap and the sucker toppled to the dirt. "I think you'd better get on your horse and ride, Valmont."

Blood rushed to Ted Valmont's face and he pursed his lips in an angry fissure. He quick-stepped it around the older man and went down a track running between the rows of vines to the road that split from the driveway. He followed the road to the tractor barn, where, as Maitland had suggested, he found his car parked in the yard beneath an oak tree. A stocky Hispanic man wearing a backwards baseball cap was polishing the front bumper, whistling a tune under his breath. When he heard Ted Valmont's heels crunch on the gravel in the yard, he looked up. "Nice car, man. It really reminds you of the old Jaguar XKEs."

In spite of the exchange with Maitland, Ted Valmont grinned broadly. "Thanks," he said. "I just wish they made them with a manual transmission. All you can get is the automatic."

"So what? It's cooler to cruise down the road without rummaging around for the next gear all the time. And it leaves your hand free to stroke your *chica*." Ramos smiled. "Guess you got some major stroking done last night, eh?" He brought his arms to his sides and thrust his pelvis forward.

Ted Valmont's face became stiff and he reached for the car door and jerked it open. He flopped into the driver's seat and yanked the door closed. As he hunted vainly for the car keys, Ramos walked around to the car window. He leered down at Ted Valmont. "They're on the visor," he said through the glass. "What's the matter? Didn't get none last night? Forgot to refill your Viagra prescription?" He laughed rudely.

Ted Valmont pulled the car keys off the visor and shoved them into the ignition. He started the car and pulled quickly out of the yard, forcing Ramos to jump clear of the spinning wheels. As he pulled onto the main drive, the stocky Hispanic could be seen in the rear view mirror pumping his pelvis, laughing and waving his baseball cap.

After showering and changing clothes in his Yountville hotel, Ted Valmont drove to the Napa County Sheriff's Office. He marched through the door of the low-slung Mediterranean building to a dusty reception area with hard wooden chairs lined up along the wall and a vending machine for coffee with an "Out of Order" sign taped over the coin slot. A fresh-faced female clerk whose gun butt dug into the baby fat along her waist greeted him as he came up to the reception desk. "Can I help you, sir?"

Ted Valmont managed a warm smile that teased a matching one from the clerk's face. "I hope so," he said in a honeyed tone. "A good friend of mine disappeared after attending a conference in the valley. My friend lives in Los Altos, but the police there told me I should speak with a Deputy Norman Olken from this office."

The clerk's smile lost some of its warmth. "Who is the missing person?"

"His name is Warren Niebuhr."

"And your name is?"

Ted Valmont smiled again and put a hand on the desk counter. "My name is Ted Valmont. As I said, I'm a good friend of the missing man, and I'm also on the board of the company that employs him. The bottom line is I'm very concerned to find him for both business and personal reasons."

The clerk flexed the shaft of a Bic pen she was holding. "The department doesn't normally discuss open cases with anyone but family members."

"I understand that, but I have background information on Warren Niebuhr that might prove useful in locating him. And you're welcome to call his wife, Laura Niebuhr. I'm sure she would have no objections."

The clerk sighed and went to an open office behind the reception counter and picked up a phone. After a short conversation, during which she nodded several times, she returned to the desk. "Deputy Olken will see you. He'll be out shortly."

Olken was a dark-skinned man of medium build and medium height. He had a large, flat face with heavy bags under his eyes and several dark moles sprinkled over his nose and cheeks. His lower lip protruded slightly, his black hair was cut short and he smelled of Old Spice. He carried a clipboard and a Styrofoam cup.

Ted Valmont rose from one of the lobby chairs to greet him and the two men went to an interview room off to one side. "I'd offer you coffee," said Olken as they sat down, "but the machine in the lobby is busted and everyone in the office is too lazy to make it on Sunday."

"That's okay. I've got myself addicted to frou-frou stuff. Don't drink much of anything else these days."

"Then you wouldn't want any of our brewed battery acid." Olken leaned over to spit a stream of brown juice into his cup and then pulled a typed sheet from the clipboard. "You must be here about the car."

A faint look of disgust spread over Ted Valmont's features as it became apparent that Olken's cup did not hold coffee. "The car?" he said vaguely.

"Hmm, maybe not then. Toni said you're a family friend of the Niebuhrs."

Ted Valmont took out one of his cards and passed it over to Olken. "That's right," he said. "We went to school together. I also work at the venture capital firm that funded his company, NeuroStimix."

Olken took the card and looked at it briefly. He slipped it under the clip of his clipboard.

"You mentioned a car," said Ted Valmont. "Did you locate Warren Niebuhr's Citroën?"

Olken cleared his throat and shifted in his chair. It creaked loudly. "Yep, we did. I left a message about it with the wife early this morning, but she hasn't called back."

"I gather that Warren wasn't—that he wasn't found with the car."

"No, he wasn't. The car was abandoned on a back road near the town of Angwin."

"Angwin? There's nothing up there but cows and Seventh-day Adventists."

Olken smiled slightly, exposing teeth flecked with black tobacco. "The college is there too, but I guess you got the demographics about right. You don't think your friend would find a lot to appeal in Angwin, then?"

"Warren is not an outdoors person. I'd forgotten about the school, but he would only be interested in a big university with sophisticated labs or an extensive library. If you're asking me if I can think of any reason for him to be up there, the answer would have to be no."

Olken made some notes on his clipboard. He asked questions about Niebuhr's home life, his work and his habits in general, and Ted Valmont relayed the information he had collected in his conversations with the NeuroStimix board and Laura Niebuhr. Olken made more notes and then said, "That does it for me. I'll keep Mrs. Niebuhr informed of the progress of the case, so I suggest you stay in touch with her if you want to keep abreast of developments." He pushed back his chair and stood up.

"Wait," said Ted Valmont. "Can't you tell me anything now? Who found the car? Did anyone in Angwin see Niebuhr?"

"A couple of tourists riding around on their bicycles found it, so there's nothing there. And, no, no one in Angwin saw him."

Ted Valmont stood up. He put his palms on the table and leaned over it. "How about letting me look at it?"

Olken frowned. "The car? I don't see the point of that. Besides, it's against department policy."

"Were there any items found inside it? I could tell you if something stands out—or if anything is missing. I know as much about Niebuhr as anyone. And I'm already here."

Olken stared at Ted Valmont and drew in a deep breath. He looked down at his watch. "All right. I'm only on for another hour so there's no way we're getting Mrs. Niebuhr up today. The car is in the impound shed behind the main building. We've got a couple guys sifting through the effects right now, so we can go back and look at what they've found. But stay out of their way, and don't handle anything unless I tell you to. Got it?"

"Certainly, Deputy."

Olken escorted Ted Valmont out the back of the building to a fenced parking area. At the rear of the lot was a tin shed whose large roller door was pulled wide open. A dusty, dented Citroën DS of 1970s vintage was parked in the middle of the floor, and in front of that, two uniformed officers stood by a wheeled table with a disorganized jumble of luggage, Taco Bell wrappers, paper cups, computer disks, electronics and evidence bags stacked upon it. The hatchback and all four doors of the car hung open, and as Ted Valmont approached, he could see that the items stacked on the table represented only a fraction of the total volume of flotsam and jetsam to be scavenged from the Citroën.

"How's it going, Pete?" asked Olken of the older of the two officers, a balding man with sad eyes.

Pete held his arms out wide in front of the table. "Beats me. Look at all this crap we've tagged—and we're not even halfway done. It's like combing through a dumpster."

His partner, a hulking kid not two years out of school, said, "We found some blood, though, Norm. In the back."

Olken and Ted Valmont walked around to the back of the car and looked into the hatchback. A patch of dark blood about the size of a quarter had dried on the carpet there.

"Can you find out if it's from Niebuhr?" asked Ted Valmont, his voice becoming suddenly hoarse.

"Yep," said Olken casually. "If there's another sample on file that we can match his DNA to. If not, we should at least be able to check the blood type. I wouldn't be too concerned about it yet. That's not enough to indicate a serious wound."

Olken walked around to the side of the car, and peered into the back seat. "Is this what his car usually looked like? All this garbage and such. Or could somebody have trashed it?"

Ted Valmont swallowed and licked his lips. "This is pretty much standard operating procedure for Warren. Everywhere he goes—his house, his car, his office—eventually ends up looking like this."

"That's nice," said Olken. "But it's going to make it just that much tougher to figure out what's significant and what's not." He pawed through the trash on the table to select a Der Wienerschnitzel cup, then squirted a ribbon of tobacco juice into it.

"Hey," objected Ted Valmont. "What about not touching anything?"

Olken gave him a long, patient stare. "You might have something there, but I wouldn't push it. This isn't the O.J. Simpson case." He set the cup down and pulled on a pair of rubber gloves he took from the table. "There. Feel better? Now let's take a quick look at the stuff they've tagged. If you want to examine something more closely, let me know and I'll hold it up for you."

Ted Valmont came up to the table and stood by Olken. He had Olken shift several of the items to one side, and asked to examine a thick binder that became uncovered. When Olken opened it and flipped through several of the pages, Ted Valmont identified the contents as proceedings from the conference. "You might want to go through it and see if Warren took any notes," he said. "As I mentioned, he's got a history of running off with colleagues he meets on business trips. He might have jotted down someone's name and contact information."

"Okay," said Olken, "that's a good thought. Anything else occur to you?"

Looking down at the table, Ted Valmont rubbed the back of his neck. "Have you found any other suitcases or bags?"

"No," said the sad-eyed officer from the other side of the car. "We got all the big stuff out. We're down to papers, trash and other miscellaneous crapola."

"In that case," said Ted Valmont, "I'd have expected Warren to have a laptop computer, and also a cell phone and some kind of PDA."

"PDA?" asked Olken.

"Personal Digital Assistant."

Olken grinned and the wad of Skoal under his lower lip showed like a furry black caterpillar. "Sounds like a vibrator to me. What kind of kinky stuff was Niebuhr into?"

The other cops chuckled and the younger one came up to the table and leaned down to pick up two plastic bags from the bottom shelf. They contained a laptop and a cell phone. "These fit the bill?" he asked.

"Yeah," said Ted Valmont, "they do. But he'd still have the PDA. Warren is never separated from that."

"Seeing how neither man nor machine is here, it looks like you're right," said Olken.

"What about the suitcases? Maybe he left it in one of those."

The sad-eyed officer grunted. "No personal digital assistants there. Just a lot of wadded up, smelly clothing."

"Okay," said Olken. "That's enough for today, Mr. Valmont. I appreciate your help, but we'll have to have Mrs. Niebuhr for the rest. I'll take you back out front."

"Wait," said the younger officer. "If you know this guy, I've got a question for you."

"Shoot," said Ted Valmont.

"See that writing on the dust in the back window. '*Lavez-moi.*' What does that mean?"

Ted Valmont snorted. "That's French for 'wash me.' French car, French dirt, I guess."

Olken leaned over to spit in the Der Wienerschnitzel's cup again. He wiped his mouth with the back of his hand. "Great. That'll be the clue that breaks this case wide open. Come on, let's go."

Olken and Ted Valmont retraced their steps across the parking lot, into the building and through to the main lobby. As Olken reached over to shake hands, Ted Valmont asked, "So what will you do next?"

Olken sighed and dropped his hand to his side. "Talk with Mrs. Niebuhr, like I said. Finish with the analysis of the car and its contents."

"What about interviewing the hotel staff and the conference attendees?"

"At this point the amount of manpower it would take to track down all those people isn't justified. We're much better off trying to find people locally who might have seen him. Hell, he's probably camped out at some bed and breakfast, sipping on chardonnay."

"You really think it's that simple?"

"Jesus, man, I don't know." Olken turned to walk away. "Save your worrying until later," he called over his shoulder. "When and if there's reason to justify it."

Ted Valmont stared at his receding figure for a moment and then went out the lobby door. He got into the Jaguar and brought it back onto Highway 37, heading south towards the Bay Area. As he drove, a wooden expression settled on his face, his eyes appearing depthless and vague. Then slowly, without a precipitating change, his face began to soften and a light came into his eyes. At the southern edge of the valley, he passed a flower shop and abruptly tromped on the brakes, skidding a dozen yards into the shoulder of the road. He wheeled the car around in a U-turn and zoomed back into the shop's parking lot.

Inside, he ordered a dozen French tulips for delivery to Gabrielle Maitland. He wrote on the card:

> Gabrielle,
> Thank you for a magical evening. You are a beautiful, giving young woman and I look forward to seeing you again soon.
> yours,
> Ted

When he finished, he read what he had written and then tore up the card in frustration. Finally, he wrote:

> *Gabrielle,*
> *Thanks for a great evening.*
> *If you're ever down my way,*
> *be sure to get in touch.*
> *-Ted*

Placing his business card in the envelope, he passed it back to the sales clerk for delivery with the flowers.

Ted Valmont returned to his home in Woodside at 7:12. Long, dark shadows stretching across the lawn obscured the fact that the mailbox pole at the curb had been knocked over by an automobile. Harder to obscure were the deep tire tracks in the otherwise flawless green turf that led from the fallen mailbox to the front porch, where red paint was splattered over the door and the surrounding woodwork. "Leave her alone!" was written in dripping, foot-high letters on the glass of the front window.

Ted Valmont brought the Jaguar to an abrupt halt in the middle of the drive and jumped out to run to the porch. He touched the paint on the door and window in several places, and each time his finger came away dry. He stood by the door for a moment, breathing rapidly through a slack mouth, then yanked out his cell phone. He punched in the digits 911, but stopped just short of hitting the "talk" button. He sighed and brought his hand up to massage the familiar place just below his sternum.

Grimacing, he cleared the number from the cell phone and used the built-in browser to order a six-pack of liquid antacid for delivery from a web-based delivery service.

FINCOM FOLLIES

"Running out of cash in an otherwise really good company is like running out of gas in an otherwise really good helicopter."
—Unknown

TED VALMONT HAD BEEN SITTING WITH FOUR of Basis Ventures' most senior general partners in the company's largest conference room for 20 minutes before Larry Breen walked in. Dressed in his shirtsleeves, he carried a tremendous bowl of popcorn and a laptop computer. He plunked both down at a spot at the head of the table and wheeled out a special, high-backed chair to sit down. "Please excuse the delay," he said cheerily. "My fetching ex-wife Beth continues to make trouble on the settlement." He picked up a copy of the meeting agenda that had been placed on the table in front of him. "So, who's up first? Mary and her toilet flushers?"

Mary Wong, sitting across from Ted Valmont, made a face. "Yes, Larry," she said in an exasperated tone. "But I wish all you overgrown adolescents would quit making cracks about this technology."

Wong passed out stapled copies of her funding proposal. Breen's copy sat unmolested in front of him while he filled his mouth with popcorn, but the other partners made at least a cursory pass through the document. Wong continued:

"I believe we've worked through the problems with this deal since the last time I pitched it. We're calling for a ten million dollar investment in conjunction with Kirchner Perry."

Breen licked salt from his plump fingers. "The issue isn't how much money we're putting in. The issue is how big a slice of the pie we're getting out."

"The full 50 percent. I did as you suggested and approached Roger about cutting his partners out of the equation—"

"And he dropped them like an amputated leg."

Wong grimaced. "No, Larry. He said he'd walk before he sold them out. But it was clear he'd never considered anything other than an equal split among them. In the end, he brought them down enough for us to get what we needed—but he didn't drop them entirely."

Breen chuckled. "Just wait until the first dilution."

The group voted to approve the financing, subject to Kirchner Perry's acceptance, and two other funding proposals—an initial round for a pharmaceutical company and a late stage or "mezzanine" round for a wireless e-mail company—were discussed and approved. Ted Valmont then launched into his pitch for NeuroStimix.

He summarized the bad state of the balance sheet and acknowledged that product development was behind schedule, but pointed to the big potential returns if the stimulator technology could be perfected for commercial use. He was not, he said, asking for a new round of funding because he realized the current position of the company was not tenable. However, he asked that the committee fund a bridge loan of $1.5 million in order to get NeuroStimix through the quarter and give him time to get things back on track.

Tillman Cardinal looked up from the handout that Ted Valmont had distributed, frowned, then wheeled his chair back to where his briefcase rested against the wall. He pulled out a quartered section of the *San Jose Mercury News*.

"I almost missed the connection," he said. "There's an article on—what's his geek, Niebuhr—right here. It says his car was found abandoned in Napa."

"Niebuhr's an eccentric," said Ted Valmont. "He's taken these little sabbaticals before."

"Does he always bleed all over the back seat of his car before he goes?" Cardinal held up the paper. "This can't be good for the company. The technology is pretty much all his doing, isn't it?"

"There's no question," said Ted Valmont evenly. "If something serious has happened to Warren Niebuhr, then NeuroStimix will hit the windshield."

"But, Ted," said Mary Wong softly, "something serious has happened to Warren Niebuhr."

"She's right," said Breen, pushing aside the now empty bowl of popcorn. "And I know from my contacts at NeuroStimix that Niebuhr has bitched up more than his relationship with the CEO. The whole R&D department is in revolt against the man."

Ted Valmont stared over at Breen, his nostrils moving in and out with his breathing. "You went around my back?"

Breen held his hands up in a "so what" gesture. "Does that surprise you? I told you I wasn't going to support this. The point is, even if Niebuhr returns, the product development effort is in serious jeopardy. We simply can't pour any more money into this deal."

Ted Valmont started to say something, then clamped his jaw shut. His face became pale and hard.

"Hold on," said Jay Curio, a clean-cut, serious-looking man sitting to Ted Valmont's right. "Bridging NeuroStimix does make sense. No question. But only to sell it and recoup some of the investment. Including the $1.5 million, we'd have put in—let's see—about $13 million total. If we got five or six for the company, we'd have almost half that back. That's pretty good for a loser, Ted. You remember my last dog, Blue Gopher Software, cost us $17 million and we never saw a penny of that again."

Tillman Cardinal laughed in a forced way. "Ha!" he said. "Blue Gopher. Talk about night of the living dead."

Jay Curio smiled in response, but Ted Valmont ignored the wisecrack. "Listen to me, damn it," he said earnestly. "We have an obligation to society to fund this company. If we can make this work, the amount of good we can do for para- and quadriplegics would be enormous. Not to mention stroke and multiple sclerosis victims. This would be akin to finding the cure for cancer—or better."

There was a long, uncomfortable silence. Ted Valmont glanced around the room, but no one would meet his eyes except Larry Breen. Breen smiled in a jovial way, seemingly immune to the others' embarrassment. "Now you've done it. You've gone and acknowledged a motivation other than greed. But isn't that just code for the obligation you feel to your brother? You do understand that we can't make critical business decisions involving millions of dollars merely to allay your feelings of guilt, don't you?"

Ted Valmont's eyes knifed into Larry Breen's. His lips barely moved as he hissed, "You leave my brother out of this."

Breen shrugged hugely. "As you wish. I think we've talked enough. I'm going to defer decision on the bridge loan for NeuroStimix until you work up a credible plan for getting the company sold, including some preliminary discussions with potential buyers. When the plan's done, we'll review it and reconsider the loan. Otherwise, we're simply not going to fund."

Ted Valmont stared down at the papers in front of him, saying nothing.

"Hey," said Mary Wong suddenly, "we can sell it to Life Science Associates!"

"Yeah, right," said Cardinal. "Just how many times do you think we can pull that trick? There've been too many drive-by shootings in that neighborhood already."

As the group laughed at Cardinal's comment, Ted Valmont gathered up his things and walked stiffly out of the conference room door.

Chuck DeMarco flinched as Ted Valmont came through the door of his private office without knocking. He brought his arms down from an awkward position in front and behind his head in a vain attempt to conceal what he was holding: a pair of pocket mirrors.

"How's the Minoxidil working on the old bald spot there, Chuck?" Ted Valmont asked in a snide tone.

"Fuck you, Valmont," said DeMarco and hastily shoved the mirrors in his desk drawer. "What's the idea of barging in like that?"

Ted Valmont dropped into a visitor's chair. "I thought I'd institute a surprise VC inspection."

"You didn't get the money, did you?"

"No. No money. It gets worse if you'd like the full dose."

DeMarco got a pained look on his face. "Am I—am I out?"

Ted Valmont laughed. "Give it time, Chuck. The bigger news is they—or should I say, we—are cutting the whole thing loose. The company's going to be sold."

"Bastards. How can they expect me to make a legitimate run at the business if they don't even try to back me?"

Ted Valmont looked at DeMarco with an amused expression. "Actually," he said, "I hold myself to blame."

"Why's that?"

Ted Valmont began to count on his fingers. "First, I let you drag out the search for a new VP of Sales. Second, I let you bring in an unqualified crony to run Customer Support. Third, I let you alienate the Engineering organization in general and Warren Niebuhr in particular. Forth, I let you waste money on unneeded corporate marketing activities. And fifth, I let you bungle the last new product introduction." He wriggled the fingers of one hand at DeMarco. "I've got another hand and two feet if you'd like me to go on."

"Give it a rest," said DeMarco and carefully patted the back of his head. "You're just pissed that the finance committee turned you down and you're taking it out on me."

Ted Valmont fell back in his chair with feigned surprise. "Why Chuck, I do believe that's the most perceptive thing I've ever heard you say."

"So what are we going to do?"

"I'm going upstairs to talk to Niebuhr's secretary."

"Julie Hempel?" asked DeMarco. "What's the point of that?"

Ted Valmont stood up. "I've got to find Warren Niebuhr before they find a buyer—it's the only way to turn things around."

DeMarco shook his head and smiled. "Go get 'em, tiger. If you were on the Titanic, you'd have spent your last moments rearranging the deck chairs."

"Maybe. But if you were on it, you'd have been steering," said Ted Valmont and went out of the room.

He walked a short way to an open stairwell and went up the stairs two at a time. On the second floor, he steered a course through a warren of cubicles to the perimeter of the building and strode along a row of window offices. Reaching a cubicle by the corner office, he pulled up sharply. A plump woman with thick glasses and a pinched nose sat inside, perusing a virtual makeover site with her web browser. When she noticed Ted Valmont standing over her, she lunged for her mouse, clicking frantically until she managed to close the program down.

"Oh, hello, Ted," she said in a chagrined voice. "I was just—well, I...the thing is, with Warren gone, there hasn't been much to keep me occupied."

Ted Valmont grunted. "Today's my day for surprising people around here. I just walked in on your president."

"I don't want to know what he was doing."

"No, you probably don't. You mind if I sit down, Julie? I wanted to ask you some questions about Warren."

"Of course." Hempel pushed back from her desk and pulled over another chair from the corner of the cubicle. As Ted Valmont moved to sit, she wove her hands together in her lap. "What would you like to know?"

"Can you tell me if Warren seemed out of sorts or depressed before the conference?"

"Warren? I don't think he ever gets depressed. He certainly wasn't before the conference. He lives for those things. Rubbing elbows with his colleagues and finding new techie things to get enthused about—that's his idea of heaven."

Ted Valmont swung a leg over a knee. He nodded. "Yeah, you're right. He always has been annoyingly upbeat. What about his home life? Any signs of stress or anxiety from that quarter?"

"As far as I know, everything was fine. He certainly dotes on his kids. Doesn't talk about his wife much, though."

"You haven't, ah, known him to show interest in other woman, have you? You, for instance?"

Julie Hempel smiled and pulled off her glasses. Her eyes appeared small and weak looking without them. "Warren Niebuhr is the most asexual man I've ever met. I've often wondered if his kids were conceived by artificial insemination—the thought of Warren making love to a woman is so preposterous. I don't have a problem envisioning other men in that activity, though." She batted pale eyelashes at Ted Valmont, who flushed and took a sudden interest in the tassel of his shoe.

"Okay. Right. Let's shift gears a bit. Did he have any unusual appointments, phone calls or correspondence before he left? I mean with people you weren't familiar with?"

"Not that I'm aware of. But I don't have access to his e-mail. His voice mail, yes. But not his e-mail."

"And nothing funny's come in since he's been gone?"

"No. Nothing."

Ted Valmont leaned forward and fixed her in an inquisitive stare. "You would tell me if you'd been in touch with him, wouldn't you Julie? This has reached a serious stage. Warren can't just come waltzing home like he has all the other times."

Hempel ran an anemic tongue across thin lips. "I know it's serious, Ted. We heard about his car being found. I would certainly tell you if I knew something more."

Ted Valmont sighed. "Sorry. I didn't mean to doubt your word." He lingered for a moment, then rose, yawning and stretching. "Do you suppose I could have a look at his office? I don't know what I expect to find, but I feel like I have to give it a shot."

"No problem," said Hempel getting to her feet. "Assuming we aren't buried in an avalanche when I open it."

They crossed to the corner office, where Hempel unlocked the door. She flipped on the light switch, said, "Happy hunting," and returned to her cubicle.

Compared to Warren Niebuhr's office, his car was a model of order and purity. On a substructure of desk, table and file cabinet, the occupant had erected towers of books, papers, floppy disks, computer tapes and empty diet soda cans. Scattered about the floor were paper cups, donut boxes, computer software packages and worn, smelly gym clothes. Large white boards covered with a dense pattern of text, equations and diagrams covered every square inch of the walls, and computers from three manufacturers, as well as an empty Palm computer docking station, were nestled among the towers of debris. Finally, a mélange of wires, cables and circuit board components covered every horizontal surface and—where they found purchase—many of the vertical ones.

Assaying this scene from the doorway, Ted Valmont said, "Fuck me" with undisguised awe.

He maneuvered around the desk to the chair, where he brushed aside a pile of chaff from a hole-puncher along with a healthy portion of the ubiquitous computer parts, and gingerly sat down. He pulled an in-tray with a foot-high stack of papers towards him and began fishing through it. He went slowly and diligently at first, reading each paper carefully and placing it in a neat pile to one side, but gradually his technique degraded to the point where he was riffling through papers a fistful at a time and cavalierly tossing them aside. He stopped entirely when he came upon a half-eaten candy bar in the middle of the stack.

He pulled open all the drawers of the desk and poked through them, but found nothing to interest him except an old picture of himself and a pasty-faced man with wispy hair standing in front of a fraternity house. The other man was dressed as a gigantic bee, complete with bobbing antennae and cardboard wings. He stood in profile to the camera, reaching around his back to menace the photographer with the barb of a sharp, foot-long stinger that sprung from his butt. His teeth were gritted in a fierce, exaggerated expression. Ted Valmont, on the other hand, was dressed as Zorro, in black from head to foot. He looked smooth and handsome, and he, too, menaced the photographer with the point of his fencing foil. In contrast to other man, he had a relaxed, whimsical expression on his face.

Ted Valmont smiled and lingered over the photograph for a moment, then returned it to its place among a stack of four-year-old technical magazines and moved to the filing cabinet. There he had even less luck. The lowest drawer was filled completely by a partially deflated basketball. The second contained a plastic trash bag full of wrinkled dress shirts with a note from Niebuhr's wife asking him to take them to the dry cleaners, and the top drawer—which was very heavy and jammed when Ted Valmont first attempted to open it—contained a glass fish tank, filled to the brim with spare change.

Ted Valmont cursed and started to walk away without closing the drawer, but its weight brought the whole cabinet forward and he had to jump back to prevent it from toppling down. He jammed the drawer closed and leaned up against it, glancing around the office. Eventually his eyes came to rest on one of the computers, which had a screen saver program running on its display. He jiggled the mouse and a small prompt for a password appeared on the screen. Ted Valmont cursed again and typed in some random characters, but the computer did not accept them. Checking the remaining two computers, he found them similarly protected.

He walked out of the office and returned to Julie Hempel's cubicle. This time she was busy filing purchase orders. "Any luck?" she asked when she noticed him.

"Who knows? I might have stared at a dozen hot clues in the face without knowing it. I swear he's gotten worse over the years."

"Probably. Most people just become more concentrated versions of themselves over time."

"Not me. I feel pretty diffuse these days, I'll tell you. Do you know if Warren took his Palm computer to the conference? I noticed it's not in the docking station."

"Oh, yeah. He took it. He can hardly even go to the bathroom without it."

Ted Valmont tugged on an earlobe. "I tried the computers in the office and they are all password protected. Is there any way to get into them? You said you didn't have access to his e-mail."

"No, I can't help you there." Hempel picked up a pencil and chewed on the eraser. "The only person who might be able to is Chris Duckworth. He's the network administrator."

"Let's have him, then. Lead on."

Hempel took Ted Valmont into the thick of cubicles behind her desk. She stopped by one with a picture of Barbra Streisand taped at the entrance. "Knock, knock," she said as she rapped on the metal casing of the partition. "There's an evil venture capitalist to see you, Chris."

A slight, waif-like man with short blond hair stood up. He had china blue eyes, a small pug nose and a sensuous mouth. He wore jeans and a short-sleeved shirt made of clingy, synthetic material that emphasized the slightness of his torso and arms. "Oooh," he said. "I've never met one of those. Does he have cloven hoofs and a tail?"

Ted Valmont hesitated a beat before extending his hand. "I'm Ted Valmont," he said in voice that did not quite sound like his own. "No hooves or tail. But you won't find my reflection in the mirror, either."

"Why would I want to? When the original is so nice."

Ted Valmont flushed a deeper crimson than he had when Hempel had batted her eyelashes at him. She smiled now at his discomfort. "I'll just leave you two boys alone," she said, and walked in the direction of her desk.

Duckworth crossed the aisle to an empty cubicle and pulled a chair from it into his own. He placed it by a round table that had a set of yellow Post-its with to-dos written on them laid out in neat rows. He dusted off the fabric of the chair and gestured towards it. "Please have a seat, Ted. What can I do for you?"

Ted Valmont lowered himself slowly into the offered chair, as if he was getting into a bath of cold water. "I'm on the board here at NeuroStimix," he said, "and I'm looking into Warren Niebuhr's disappearance. I noticed all the computers in his office are password protected. Julie suggested you might be able to get around that."

Duckworth plopped down in his own chair and wheeled up within six inches of Ted Valmont's. He smiled. "For anyone else in the office but Warren, the answer would be yes. I have the 'superuser' password for the Unix network and that lets me access any account I like. The problem is Warren keeps all of his network files encrypted using a routine he developed himself. So, even if we got into his account, we wouldn't be able to read anything. There's one computer in his office that isn't on the network, but he's got that protected with special security as well."

"You can't hack it in some way?"

"No, not Warren's routines. He's a genius. I'm just a fairly clever *ingénue*."

Ted Valmont arched his brows and nodded uncertainly. "I see. What about e-mail? Isn't that kept on a central server? Could you look at the messages on the server that are for Niebuhr?"

Duckworth brought his index finger to his lips and pressed it there, thinking. "Yes, we could look and see what's left on the server. Warren always downloads his e-mail to his notebook computer. But we could check the messages queued up since the last time he logged in to get them."

"Which would have been the day he left for the conference—unless he logged in remotely. Correct?"

"That's right. We do have remote access facilities and Warren makes regular use of them, so my bet is he's checked his e-mail since he's been gone."

"That's perfect. If he's been reading his mail all this time, that means nothing bad has happened to him — he's just gone off to enjoy another of his little delectations."

"Oh, good SAT vocabulary word," said Duckworth and wheeled over to his computer. He opened a terminal window and typed some commands into it. "Okay, I've logged onto the mail server and I'm dumping out the headers for the e-mail that's queued up for Warren."

Ted Valmont rolled his chair forward to get a better look at the screen. "What date did the conference start?" asked Duckworth. "Do you know?"

"Ouch. I guess I never got a precise date, but everyone's been telling me it happened about two weeks ago. That would make it the last week of May."

Duckworth pointed at a line on the screen. "The farthest any of these messages goes back is Friday, May 31st."

"That's probably the day he checked out. Looks like he read his mail at the conference but stopped after he left. Nuts. That doesn't tell us anything positive. How about the messages themselves? See anything unusual?"

Duckworth cupped his chin in his hand and looked at Ted Valmont coyly. "What do you mean unusual? He's got over 800 here. He gets a ton of mail—mostly from internal distribution lists."

"All right. I withdraw the question. But maybe you could collect the mail from external addresses and print it out for me to review later."

Duckworth turned back to the screen. "Sure," he said vaguely. "We could do that." A long moment went by. "Wait a minute—there is something funny here. A lot of these messages have been read. Looks like someone's accessed them but left them on the server."

"I thought you said that Niebuhr always downloaded his mail."

"Yes, he does. It's a user selectable option, though. You can keep them on the server if you want."

Ted Valmont made a pumping motion in the air with his fist. "Which means that he must have logged on since the conference."

"That, or somebody else hacked his account."

Ted Valmont frowned and unclenched his fist. "Seems unlikely given all your protestations about superior security. How do we find out for sure?"

"Easy enough. I can check the system logs to see the last recorded login for his user id." Duckworth opened another window and typed in a command. The computer responded with a long string of text including several dates. "May 31st," read Duckworth.

"What? Then somebody else did get into his e-mail? That means we can't even be sure it's all here. I mean, his messages might just as easily have been deleted as read, mightn't they?"

Chris Duckworth puffed his out cheeks and poked at them with his fingertips. Rude noises and air leaked from his lips with each poke. "Right again, handsome," he said when all the air was gone. "I suppose we could compare the delivery logs on the server with the mail that's in his queue to see if anything's missing..."

"What about back-ups?" said Ted Valmont shortly. "Could you go to the back-up tapes for the server and recover old correspondence?"

Duckworth cocked his head and smiled at Ted Valmont. "More than just handsome. Smart too."

"Yeah, and I make a great cup of coffee. Lay off, will you? Here's what I want from the back-ups: any messages that have been deleted from the 31st forward and all messages from outside for the last three months. I want to see if Warren planned to meet with anyone after the conference."

"Sure. I can do that, but it'll take some time—and it will also draw me away from my other duties."

"Do it," said Ted Valmont emphatically. "Do it on my authority. I'll clear it with DeMarco." He extracted a business card from his silver case and handed it to Duckworth. "Give me a call at that number when you've pulled it together."

"Aye-aye, sir."

"Thanks," said Ted Valmont and stood up. He negotiated the gap between Duckworth's chair and his own and stepped nimbly out of cubicle into the aisle.

"Wait," snapped Duckworth, standing to catch Ted Valmont's eye.

"What is it?"

Duckworth bit his lower lip. "Well, I was wondering how the search for Warren is going—apart from all this."

Ted Valmont massaged the back of his neck. He exhaled heavily. "If you've been reading the papers, you know as much as I do."

"Do you think—I mean, are you happy with the job the police have been doing?"

Ted Valmont flicked his eyes up and down Chris Duckworth's face. "No offense, Chris, but aren't you over-stepping your bounds just a little?"

Duckworth held up his hands in a placating gesture. "I'm sorry. I'm not trying to be nosey. I just wanted to ask if you had considered hiring a private investigator."

"You moonlighting?"

Duckworth laughed nervously. "No, not me. A friend of mine. Someone very qualified and experienced."

Ted Valmont raised an eyebrow.

"You don't understand," Duckworth put in quickly. "He's not that kind of friend. I was involved in a case he worked on and that's how I know him. You might have heard about it: the thing with Edwin Bishop—that big shot game software entrepreneur."

"Yeah, I heard about it. We funded one of Bishop's first companies."

"Well, this friend of mine—August Riordan—he pretty much solved that case. And he's got a lot of other experience with investigations in the high tech industry."

"I appreciate the suggestion, but I really don't see the benefit to bringing in a private investigator. They're certainly not the most reputable people in the world."

Duckworth smiled. "No, nothing like vulture—I mean—venture capitalists. Why don't you take his card just in case. I've got it in my Rolodex."

Without waiting for a response, Duckworth pulled opened a drawer in his desk and brought out a perfectly organized card file. He flipped to the R's and selected one of a half dozen identical business cards filed in the middle of the pack. "Here you go. It can't hurt to talk to him, anyway."

Ted Valmont took the card and examined it briefly. He shoved it in his breast pocket and then narrowed his eyes at Duckworth. "You know, you test pretty high on the insubordination scale there, Chris. You better tone it down or it's going to get you into trouble."

"Oh, it has. It already has—believe me."

"Well, let's not let history repeat itself, shall we? Now, get going on gathering that e-mail."

Duckworth flashed a shit-eating grin. "Yes, mastah."

Ted Valmont turned and walked away, shaking his head as he went.

RIORDAN RIDES IN

"We see 3,000 business plans a year, and we only make between eight and 20 investments…[A] lot of people go away unhappy. There's a simple answer for those people: You didn't measure up."
—Mark Achler, founding principal, Kettle Venture Partners

TED VALMONT STEPPED THROUGH THE DOOR OF his Woodside home at 7:05 pm. After carefully draping his jacket over the study sofa, he went to the roll-top desk in the corner and fell heavily into a leather-bound chair. He pushed open the roll-top to reveal a PC and brought up a program to download and read his e-mail.

The program informed him there were over 50 new messages. He sat with his chin in the palm of his hand and watched as the title and sender of each message appeared on the screen. He scrolled through them listlessly—not selecting any to read—until he noticed an e-mail titled "Thank you!" from gmaitland@grapevine.net. Sitting up in his chair, he clicked on the header. The body of the message read:

> Ted,
>
> You're a darling! Thank you for the lovely flowers. They're in a vase

on the table across from me as I
write this message.

I only recently got up on the
Internet, and when I saw the e-mail
address on your card, I couldn't
resist sending you an electronic
thank you. I hope you don't find
it too impersonal; it seemed an
appropriate way to communicate
with a Silicon Valley Titan such
as yourself.

It just so happens that I'm coming
down to San Francisco tomorrow to
do some shopping. I'm staying overnight at the St. Francis, so I was
wondering if you would be free to
join me for dinner, etc., etc. ;-)

I do hope you can make it. Please
give me a ring at 707-555-1122 and
let me know.

    —Your Gabby

Ted Valmont highlighted the words "It just so happens" in the text of the message and chuckled. He took a cordless phone from its base and dialed the number from Gabrielle's message. "Is this my Gabby?" he said into the receiver a moment later. He chuckled again. "Yes, it's me... It's nice to talk with you too... Well, you're lucky. I have it on good authority that tomorrow night's episode of *America's Funniest Home Videos* is a repeat...No, of course not. I'd walk across Death Valley in August to see you. You said you were staying at the St. Francis, right?…Okay, how about I meet you downstairs at the Compass Rose bar at 7 and we'll go across the street to Farallon…Yes it's excellent…Don't worry, I've got connections. They feature our wine, after all…Sure, wear something nice. I'll try to keep pace…Great. Looking forward to it. See you then."

Ted Valmont dropped the connection and pressed a button on the phone to dial a pre-set number. After a long wait, he said, "Jack?… It's Ted. Sounds like you're busy…Yes, much better than the alternative. How would you feel about me calling in a favor? I've got a date tomorrow night with a young lady who is destined to be the future Mrs. Ted Valmont—" He laughed. "Didn't I tell you I believe in polygamy?…Well, around 7:15 if you can swing it, and I'd like a booth in the back…Yeah, right under one of those plastic sea anemones or whatever it is you've got hanging from the ceiling…Don't be so touchy. I didn't actually compare it to Red Lobster this time…Okay, great. One last thing: can you pull a bottle of the '95 Chardonnay and the '93 Cab for us?… Perfect. Thanks Jack— I owe you one. Bye."

Ted Valmont put down the phone and snapped his fingers crisply in the air. "All right then," he said to the computer screen. He got up from his chair and walked to the exercise room at the back of the house. There he shed his work clothes—taking special care not to wrinkle his dress pants and tie as he laid them on the hanger—and padded over to a doctor's scale along the near wall. Standing naked on the scale, he moved the large counterweight to the 150-pound mark and tapped the smaller one along the top rail until it reached the 24-pound mark and equilibrium. He grunted and stood on tiptoes while he stretched his arms above his head. Taut, well-defined muscles rippled in his back and legs as he strained upward.

He stepped off the scale and went back to the locker where he had undressed. He took swim trunks, socks, leather shoes, two rolls of rough cotton wraps and a pair of 10-ounce boxing gloves from the locker. He stepped into the trunks, then sat down on a bench to lace up the shoes and carefully wrap each hand. Finally he pulled on the gloves, using his teeth to tug the second one into place, and punched them together with a loud pop.

He worked on the speed bag in the corner first—awkwardly, without a steady rhythm—then switched to the heavy bag. There he showed better coordination, slinging sets of jabs, hooks, and uppercuts with right and left hand and mixing them in two- and three-punch combinations. He ended the session with a terrific right hook that sent the bag skittering along the wall where it added to an existing scuff mark.

With shaking arms, he wrenched off the gloves and yanked at the Velcro fasteners to unwind the wraps on his hands. After toweling off thoroughly, he pulled off his shoes and went out a door to the back yard. He walked along a flagstone path to the fenced olympic-sized swimming pool, dove smoothly into the water—and with a competence that far surpassed his efforts at boxing—swam ten laps each of butterfly, backstroke, breaststroke and freestyle.

Once more he toweled off. He returned to the house with the towel wrapped around his waist and went into the kitchen where he opened the ice box, pulled out an ornate china plate covered in plastic wrap and slid it into the microwave. When the oven chimed, he retrieved the plate, gathered a napkin, silverware and a charged wine glass, and carried them all back to his study.

Unwrapped, his dinner proved to be chicken *à l'orange* and snap peas on a bed of mashed potatoes. He ate it greedily while reading and replying to e-mail. As the last of the sunlight faded from the study windows, he responded to voice mail and began to wade through a stack of business plans. At 12:30 he threw down in disgust a plan from a company that sought to develop commercial pharmaceuticals from plants in the South American rain forest. He switched off the light and went to bed.

When he next entered the study, Ted Valmont was showered, shaved and dressed in a smart, three-button olive green suit. He picked yesterday's jacket off the sofa and rifled the pockets to transfer his wallet and silver card holder. Doing this, he came upon the card for "August Riordan, Private Investigator" that Duckworth had given him at NeuroStimix. He stared down at the card, rubbing his fingers over the ink and paper stock as if to gauge its quality. He walked to the wastepaper basket near his desk and hovered. He shifted his weight and tugged on his earlobe. Then, making a face, he reached abruptly for the phone and dialed the number on the card.

"Yes," he said into the receiver. "I'd like to speak to him, please... Oh, I see." He glanced down at his watch. "Would it be possible to make an appointment then?... Sometime this afternoon—near the end of the day... Yes, that would be ideal...The Flood Building? Yes, I know where that is...Great. Thank you. I'll see you at five."

Nearly seven hours later— at twenty before five—Ted Valmont pulled his Ferrari Spider into the valet parking zone in front of the St. Francis hotel. When the valet on duty inquired if he was staying the night, he smiled and said, "Yes, that's the plan, anyway."

He got out of the car and walked down Powell towards Market Street. He threaded through the crowd of tourists at the cable car turn-around, turned left on Market and walked past the line of street vendors and old men playing chess. A short ways up the street, he came to the cavernous entrance of the Flood Building and pushed through the lobby doors.

He paused at the building directory, looking up at the names listed under R, and then caught an ascending elevator to the 12th floor. Riordan's office was in a suite he shared with an insurance agent. The agent—fat, white-haired and quick with a phony smile of large capped teeth—was engaged in an animated phone conversation when Ted Valmont walked in. The agent covered the mouthpiece of the phone with a plump hand, winked, and said, "Be right with you, chief."

Ted Valmont frowned and would have said something, but a handsome young woman with cornflower blue eyes, luxurious auburn hair and an unusually narrow waist came up to him. She said, "Please ignore him, Mr. Valmont. In spite of copious evidence to the contrary, he cheerfully assumes that everyone who comes up here wants to buy insurance."

"Can't blame him for trying, I suppose," said Ted Valmont.

"I certainly do," she said, and smiled. "August is in the back office. He's been expecting you."

The young woman led Ted Valmont down a short corridor to an office with an old-fashioned pebble-glass door. She knocked lightly on the door and pushed it open. "August," she said to the occupant, "Mr. Valmont is here to see you."

August Riordan got up from his chair and walked around the desk to shake Ted Valmont's hand. He was over six feet tall, but his heavy musculature made him appear shorter—especially in contrast to Ted Valmont's willowy stature. His forehead and jaw were square and his mouth was a crooked line that seemed fixed in a sardonic grin. A crookeder scar traced a route from the corner of his mouth to the edge of his jaw. He had brown eyes and tousled brown hair that he had not invested over ten dollars to have cut. His suit—with puckered seams and lapels that would not lay flat—was poorly made and its fit on his heavy frame was bad. His nose had been broken at least once.

"Nice to meet you, Mr. Valmont," he said in a low voice. "Chris told me you might be getting in touch." He gestured at one of the hard-looking metal chairs in front of the desk and resumed his place in an old swivel chair that squeaked loudly as he sat down.

Ted Valmont slid into his chair and glanced about the room. It was dusty, bare, and with the exception of two black and white photos of jazz bassists, devoid of decoration. "Pardon me for saying this Riordan, but you're not the sort of friend I would expect Chris Duckworth to have."

Riordan further loosened the already loose knot of his tie. "Well, you would be more his type."

Ted Valmont stiffened. "That's not what I meant."

Riordan nodded. "No, what I think you meant was you were having second thoughts about coming here. Don't let first impressions fool you. I don't make boatloads of money, and I don't work off flashes of inspiration like some kind of detective psychic, but I do my job and I do it competently. I have plenty of references you can check if you want—including people familiar with the Bishop case. Chris said you knew of that."

Ted Valmont grunted. "Maybe I'll do some checking later," he said. "But I want you to get started now. Can you give this your full attention?"

"Virtually. You better tell me more about what you want done, though. I've talked to Chris of course, and I've read a little about Niebuhr's disappearance in the papers, but I'd like to be sure you're hiring me to do something I can deliver on."

Ted Valmont smiled grimly. "What? You mean you won't work for a flat sum contingent on his return?"

"Hardly. Tracing missing persons isn't really a one-man job. If you hire me, you hire me because you want to augment the efforts of the police and improve the percentages."

Ted Valmont picked his tie off his chest and turned it over. The short end had come out of the retaining loop on the back. "I understand," he said, rethreading the tie through the loop. "As it happens, I have some specific things I want you to look into. Things that the police are unwilling to undertake."

"Oh yeah?" said Riordan uncertainly. "What kind of things?"

"First, I want you to interview the conference organizers and the staff at the hotel in Yountville."

"I'm sure the police could be counted on to do that much."

"You haven't met the individuals assigned to the case. The guy in Napa is a tobacco-chewing redneck and the detective in Los Altos doesn't have the brains God gave a swizzle stick."

Riordan pulled a warped yellow legal pad from his desk and picked up a blunt, three-inch length of pencil. "It's the Appellation Inn in Yountville, right? Who organized the conference."

"The Porter Group ran the conference. And, yes, it was held at the Appellation Inn."

Riordan noted this down in a childish scrawl, his large hand almost completely obscuring the short pencil. "Okay, what else?"

"I want you to get hold of the attendee list of the conference—there were only about fifty—and try to interview as many of them as possible. I want to find out if any of them spent time with Niebuhr or heard him mention what his plans were after the conference."

Riordan cleared his throat. He rolled the pencil between his hands, a heavy class ring from UCLA making a clicking noise as the pencil moved up and down. "That it?"

"That's enough, isn't it?"

Riordan smiled and his mouth and the scar beside it became even more crooked. "Yes, it's more than enough. And that's the problem. These things might have been good to do right after Niebuhr's disappearance, but you won't be getting the most bang for your buck if I tackle them now. The attendees are widely scattered, and they may not remember any interactions they had with Niebuhr. And if they do know something significant, the coverage in the papers and TV will encourage them to come forward anyway."

Ted Valmont swung a leg over his knee. He flicked at a speck of lint on his sock. "What would you suggest, then?"

"I'd say let me talk with the cops on the case, see where they are with things, and then figure out where I could use my time most profitably."

Ted Valmont shook his head. "No," he said flatly. "That's just a plan to make a plan. I don't have time to screw around with this. If you want the job, then it's got to be as I described. Talk to the staff, and find conference attendees and interview them. Period."

Riordan took a large folding knife out of the desk drawer, opened it deliberately and whittled on the business end of the stubby pencil. The shavings settled onto the desk blotter and floor but he made no attempt sweep them up. "It's your dime, Mr. Valmont," he said without looking up. "I make five hundred a day plus expenses. On a job like this, I'd need at least a three thousand dollar retainer."

Ted Valmont pulled a business envelope from the breast pocket of his suit. He dropped it on the desk. "That's a check for five thousand drawn on the Basis Ventures' account. My card's in there too. I'd like daily status reports."

Riordan reached across the desk to retrieve the envelope and extracted Ted Valmont's card. He examined it carefully and ran his thumb over the top of it—much like Ted Valmont had done with his own card. "Okay. You'll get daily reports—both written and verbal. I'll start with the hotel staff and conference organizers since I'll need them to get the list of the attendees anyway."

"Makes sense," said Ted Valmont and stood up. He put his hand out to Riordan across the desk. "Thank you. I'm looking forward to good results in short order. And sorry I got a little dictatorial just now. I'm used to having things my own way."

Riordan stood up and took Ted Valmont's hand. "That's okay," he said. "I'm inured to tragedy."

With a distinctly unsettled look on his face, Ted Valmont walked out of the office.

PARNASSUS PUZZLE

"Visitors to our office are greeted by 'Vamoose', a 2-foot-high wooden sculpture of a vulture perched on a 4-foot-high road sign in our reception area…"

—Frederick J. Beste III, Venture Capitalist, Mid-Atlantic Venture Funds

SITTING AT THE OAK BAR OF THE Compass Rose, Ted Valmont had just knocked back his second Campari and soda when Gabrielle Maitland came up. She was 45 minutes late. He stood to greet her, wrapping her in a hug whose ardor seemed to surprise her. "Just where have you been, young lady?" he said into her ear. "I was beginning to worry that you stood me up."

She put her arms around his neck and beamed up at him. She wore an elegant black crepe dress, a pearl necklace and matching pearl earrings. Her hair was swept up in a formal style. "The hair salon was running terribly late," she said. "And I had a devil of a time with these pearls. I just could not get the silly little clasp to fasten."

Ted Valmont laughed and reached down to resettle the pearls. "It's well worth the bother. They look lovely. You look lovely."

"You look pretty yummy yourself, Monsieur Valmont."

Ted Valmont put out his arm for Gabrielle. "Well, we better get going or Monsieur Jacques, *maître d'* at Farallon, is going to give our table away—regardless of our how yummy we are."

They went out the Post Street side of the hotel, crossed the road and walked a short distance to the shell-like awning that covered the restaurant entrance. Inside they came into a space that was a mix of *20,000 Leagues Under the Sea* and the lost city of Atlantis. Sculpted pink and purple jellyfish lamps dangled from the ceiling, oversized pillars of kelp—illuminated with golden light from within—swelled from the corners and muted seascapes covered the shell-encrusted walls. Overhead, an elaborate design of bathing beauties graced the arched ceiling.

Ted Valmont took Gabrielle up to the reception podium—one of the few furnishings that failed to sustain the undersea motif—and greeted a rotund man with curly black hair and a full beard. He wore a tuxedo and a pair of half reading glasses and broke into a broad grin when he saw the couple.

"Valmont!" he said in a booming voice. "We gave your booth away to a pair of visiting nuns, but I've saved a cozy spot for you between the bus station and a very outgoing family of six from Fresno. They're here to see *Phantom of the Opera* and I mentioned that you've already seen it ten times. They're dying to discuss it."

Gabrielle giggled and held out her hand to the *maître d'*. "You must be Jack," she said easily. The curly haired man bowed and took her hand. "I'm sure we will be very happy wherever you seat us," she continued, "but you mustn't blame Ted for our being late. It's entirely my doing."

Jack took a pair of leather-bound menus from the stand. "That puts things in a different light," he said in a mock-serious tone. "I'm throwing the nuns out on their ear. Come with me."

He led them past the bar, up a sweeping staircase studded with iridescent blue lights and across the mezzanine floor to a large booth against the back wall. It was upholstered in plush maroon fabric and a chandelier in the shape of a gigantic sea urchin hung overhead. Ted Valmont and Gabrielle sat side by side—their knees touching under the table—and before leaving, Jack poured each a glass of chardonnay from a bottle that was chilling in a gold bucket.

"This is wonderful, Ted," said Gabrielle. "I'm so glad you brought me here. And I love your friend Jack."

"He is a card," said Ted Valmont and gestured for a toast with his glass. "To our first real date."

Gabrielle hesitated a moment, then picked up her glass and clinked it with Ted Valmont's. "To our first date," she agreed. She took a modest swallow.

Ted Valmont frowned. "I hope I didn't say something wrong. Saturday night was very special. I didn't mean to trivialize it. I just meant that this was the first time we planned to be together."

Gabrielle looked at him with amusement and shook her head. "There was nothing wrong with the toast, silly. I'm just not a big drinker is all. But I like what you said about Saturday night. Tell me more about how special it was."

Ted Valmont swirled the wine in his glass. "Its specialness is exceeded only by my desire to relive the occasion."

"Oh, no. That won't do. I wanted poetry and confessions of undying love. Still and all, I'd say you were on track for a return engagement. And I did mention that I have a very nice room at the St. Francis, didn't I?"

He reached over to squeeze her hand. "Well, what do you know? That must be the reason I parked in the St. Francis garage. But I've got a question for you. Why in the world are you studying to be a winemaker if you don't like to drink?"

Gabrielle brought his hand up to her lips and kissed his fingers. "It's not a matter of not liking, it's more a matter of not be able to. Sometimes it makes me ill."

He caressed her cheek in a perfunctory way and pulled his hand back to his lap, as if embarrassed by the show of affection. "It makes me ill too," he said stiffly. "If I pour it down my throat through a funnel. Besides, this is Val du Grue—truly a nectar of the gods. Ninety-seven points from *Wine Spectator*. No one ever got sick from drinking it."

Gabrielle's eyes followed Ted Valmont's hand. She smiled wanly. She picked up her glass and gulped down some chardonnay.

"Whoa, wait a minute," he said. "That's too much like the funnel approach. Slow down or you will get sick."

She nodded almost imperceptibly.

He turned to face her. "Really. It's no skin off my nose if you don't like our plonk. Don't feel pressured to drink it. Okay?"

"Okay," said Gabrielle softly. "I do like it though, Ted. It's a very nice wine."

"Naw, it's overrated. What the hell do those *Spectator* people know anyway?" He drew in a deep breath and let it out heavily. "Look, let's not trip over our own feet here. Relax. Be yourself. I'm not keeping score."

"I—I want you to like me, Ted."

"And I want you to like me. Sounds like we might have the basis for something there. What's the closing line in *Casablanca*? 'This could be the start of a beautiful friendship?'"

She grinned. "They dubbed that line in after they were done filming you know."

Ted Valmont started to respond but a pony-tailed waiter came up to tell them about the specials for the evening. He refilled both wine glasses and went off to put in Ted Valmont's order for smoked salmon and caviar.

"Enough with the serious talk," said Ted Valmont after he had gone. "Let's get down to some real chit-chat. Did your jolly, happy-go-lucky uncle tell you I ran into him on Sunday morning?"

Gabrielle blanched and took another swallow of wine. "No—no he didn't"

"No offense, but a conversation with that guy is about as comfortable as a Nuremberg cross-examination."

"He can be rather severe," she said, and drank some more wine.

Ted Valmont looked at her thoughtfully. "We are having our troubles finding a lighter tone, aren't we? I'm sorry. Did I get you in trouble with him? An odd thing happened at my house that I couldn't help thinking was related."

Gabrielle stared down in her lap and shook her head. "You didn't get me into trouble. It's just that our relationship is rather strained at the moment. He's also wondering about my decision to study enology, and I would rather not provoke him. I'm not sure what you mean about your house, but he didn't say anything about seeing you on Sunday."

Ted Valmont reached over to pull her chin up. "Cheer up, kiddo. If you think getting caught by your uncle is bad, wait until you hear this." He launched into a long, convoluted tale from grade school about being trapped after hours under the desk of the librarian when she returned unexpectedly.

A distracted, uncomfortable look settled on Gabrielle's face as she listened. But as Ted Valmont described the contortions he went through to avoid detection when the librarian sat down at the desk, her mood seemed to lift, and at the end, she smiled and asked, "And just how did you get into the library in the first place?"

He shrugged. "Picked the lock."

"Picked the lock? In grade school? Where did you learn to do that?"

He licked his lips, suppressing a grin. "From a book in the library."

"You little criminal!"

Gabrielle was still smiling when the waiter came back with the caviar and salmon. Neither the appetizers nor the remaining wine lasted long, and soon the couple was talking in a less self-conscious way about their respective childhoods and families.

Gabrielle had just finished the story of her first kiss to an awkward, red-haired boy who had a habit of wearing mismatched socks, when she relaxed back in the booth and reached for her water glass.

Abruptly, a tremor ran through her arm, knocking the water glass over. A flash of terror convulsed through her features and her eyes became wide, glassy and dreadful. Her arm jerked again. She cried, "No, not this!" and the tremors spread to both arms. Her upper torso became enveloped in spasms. Her head whiplashed and her eyes rolled back in her head. She slid down the side of the booth, bucking violently as she went.

Ted Valmont gaped as Gabrielle dropped below the table. He clutched at her and caught the neckline of her dress, tearing it away. She fell to the floor, flopping grotesquely like a fish on a stringer. Her head, arms and legs pounded the booth and the center post of the table.

Ted Valmont yelled, "Help!" and crawled crabwise out of the booth. He grabbed the edge of the table and pulled it aside. Dropping to his knees, he lunged for Gabrielle's flaying arms, receiving several blows to his face and neck for his trouble. He managed finally to capture a wrist, and only with the full force of both arms, was able to pin it to the floor. The pony-tailed waiter rushed up and dove into the blurry windmill of limbs, reaching for the other wrist. But there was little point: the seizure ended as suddenly as it began.

Gabrielle lay in a tumbled, bag-of-bones position, her hair fallen down, her arms and legs cut and bruised and her dress pulled over her waist. Saliva dribbled out of her mouth and her panty hose were wet with urine. On their hands and knees, Ted Valmont and the waiter blinked at each other like the only survivors of a disastrous battle. "Is she—is she okay, man?" said the waiter in a trembling voice.

Ted Valmont made no reply but brought two fingers to her neck and searched for the artery with nervous, clumsy movements. He blew out his breath with relief. "Her heart's beating. Her heart's beating," he said like a mantra.

He turned to the waiter. "What the hell are you waiting for? Go call an ambulance!"

The emergency room doctor at Parnassus Hospital was a petite Asian woman with dark circles under her eyes and long hair pulled back in a ponytail. She wore blue scrubs and had a stethoscope around her neck. "Dr. L. Zhou," read her name tag.

Ted Valmont stood in front of her in the waiting area, holding his elbow with one hand, tugging an earlobe with the other. "What happened then?" he asked.

"I can't say for sure," said the doctor. "But from your description, it was most likely an epileptic seizure. We'll keep her under observation for the remainder of the night and run more tests in the morning. Are you aware of any history of epilepsy?"

Ted Valmont dropped his arms to his sides and slipped a hand into his pocket. He rattled his change impatiently. "No, I only met her last week."

"I see. Then I don't suppose you know anything about her neck."

"Actually, I can help you there. She had a horseback riding accident when she was younger and fractured her neck. She told me the doctors wired the damaged vertebrae in place to help them heal. She said everything was fine now and she was going to have an operation to take the wire out."

Dr. Zhou's looked carefully into Ted Valmont's face. She shook her head. "No. I don't know precisely what's on the back of her neck, but it's got nothing to do with stabilizing vertebrae."

"What do you mean? Is it something that shouldn't be there?"

"Please don't concern yourself, Mr. Valmont. There are many reasonable explanations—I'm just not enough of an expert to know which is right. If I had to wager, I would say that it is an implant to treat the epilepsy. There are new devices that can detect seizures when they occur and send electronic impulses to the brain to interrupt them. It strikes me that your description of the abrupt end of her fit seems consistent with that explanation." The doctor sighed and massaged her temples. "It's too bad she wasn't wearing a medical ID bracelet. This is exactly the sort of situation where they can be of benefit."

"She might have been too embarrassed for me to see it."

Dr. Zhou pressed her lips together in an expression of disapproval. "Yes, many young women do unhealthful things for the sake of appearance. Do you know her next of kin?"

"Only her uncle. Up in Napa."

"I need to get back to my other patients, but I would appreciate it if you informed the receiving clerk of the uncle's name and phone number so that we can notify him. We may also need his permission for other tests."

"I gave them what information I had when I first came in. I also left my own name and home number."

"Very good." The doctor flashed a lukewarm smile. "I'm sure everything will be fine, Mr. Valmont. She's resting comfortably now, so you should do the same: go home and get some sleep. You can check in with her tomorrow."

Ted Valmont nodded and thanked the doctor. He watched as she returned to the trauma care room through a pair of swinging doors and then went over to sit down in a chair. He took out his cell phone and punched in a number. It rang for a long time. "Bruce," he said finally. "It's me, Ted…Yes, I'm sorry, but something bad has happened. I was having dinner with Gabrielle Maitland in a restaurant and she had some kind of seizure…They think she's okay, but she still hasn't regained consciousness…Yeah, epilepsy was what they guessed…No, down in San Francisco. Look, I called the number I had from Gabrielle, but it must be her private line because no one picked up and her voice was on the recorder. Do you have Maitland's direct line? I've got to notify him…Good, I'll wait." Ted Valmont got up and went to the reception desk to grab a pen and clipboard with a receiving form. He sat back down again. "Okay …7-0-4-5. Got it…No, it's not the same. Thanks. I'll call him now. Let me know if you hear anything from your end…Right, bye."

Ted Valmont pressed a button to drop the connection and dialed the number he had written on the receiving form. He waited while the phone rang and then frowned, his eyes flicking back and forth as he listened to a message. "Douglas," he said into the phone. "This is Ted Valmont. I had dinner with Gabrielle tonight in the City. She had some kind of seizure at the restaurant and passed out. They took her to Parnassus Hospital on Parnassus and Third. They think she's okay, but she still hasn't regained consciousness. Dr. Lin Zhou is the admitting doctor, and she's eager to talk to someone who's familiar with her medical history. Please call the doctor as soon as you get this message at—" He read the number for the hospital, then gave his own home and cell phone numbers with the request that Maitland call him, too.

He punched the button to drop the line and sat staring at the phone, as if willing it to ring. At last, he roused himself, folded up the phone and returned to the reception desk to give the clerk the new number for Maitland. Rubbing his face vigorously with both hands, he walked out the automatic doors and into the dark, cold night.

The clock on Ted Valmont's study desk said 3:21 when he threw his jacket down in a heap next to the carefully folded one from the day before. He went to the kitchen, returning to the study with a cut glass tumbler and a bottle of bourbon. Standing in the middle of the room, he poured himself an inch of bourbon and downed it in one go.

The message light of his phone flashed at him. He walked over to his desk and set the glass down next to the phone, pouring himself another drink as he pressed the button to play the messages.

"Message one," said the phone in a metallic voice. "2:45 am. 28 seconds." Another voice came on—a female voice with a slight Chinese accent. It sounded strained, on the edge of panic. "Mr. Valmont. This is Dr. Zhou from Parnassus Hospital. I need to talk with you urgently. Please page me at 415-555-0804 as soon as you get this message. Thank you."

Ted Valmont set the bottle of bourbon down with a thud, and not bothering with the phone on the desk, took out his cell phone and began to punch in the number Dr. Zhou had left. The desk phone continued to the next message. "Message two," it said. "3:17 am. 13 seconds."

"Ted," said the plaintive voice that followed. "It's Gabrielle. Don't let them do this to me. Please come get me. Help."

Ted Valmont froze with his finger over the pad of the cell phone. He threw it aside and replayed the message with the volume louder. It was the same: no mention of where Gabrielle was, how to reach her or who was doing what to her. He retrieved the cell phone and finished entering the doctor's pager number. He listened at the earpiece, then typed his own number into the phone and broke the connection.

He spent the next few minutes pacing up and down the study with the bottle of bourbon in one hand and the glass in the other. The bottle was several inches lower by the time the phone rang. He rushed to the desk and depressed the speaker button. Leaning over the phone, he said, "Valmont," with a combative, drunken tone.

"Oh, Mr. Valmont. This is Dr. Zhou I'm so glad you got—"

Ted Valmont pounded on the desk. "What have you done to that girl, Dr. Zhou?"

There was a stunned silence. The sound of the doctor's rapid breathing came over the speaker. "I—we haven't done anything. All I know is she's not in her room and no one can account for her whereabouts. We were hoping you knew what happened to her."

"What are you talking about? How could she get out of the hospital without being seen?"

Dr. Zhou cleared her throat. "The nurse on duty was paged to another room. When she returned to check on Ms. Maitland, she was no longer in her bed."

Ted Valmont fell into his desk chair. Bourbon came up from the glass and splashed his tie. "She called me after you did. Left me a message." His voice had lost its edge, bewilderment replacing anger.

"I'm not sure I understand. What did she say?"

"She asked me to come and get her. To make someone leave her alone. I assumed she was upset about something you guys were doing to her."

"We haven't touched her since we transferred her upstairs. I did not even know she had regained consciousness. What time did she call you?"

"Like I said, after you did. My machine said it was about 3:20."

"I see." A beat. "That would have been after the nurse reported her missing."

Ted Valmont put the bottle and glass—which were still in his hands—down on the desk. He yanked off his tie and threw it across the room. "Did you ever get hold of her uncle?" he asked. "I left another number for him at the desk."

"No. We left several messages for him, but we haven't been able to reach him."

"All right. I'll try again. I can call the hotel she was registered at as well. Maybe she went back there. I mean, could she have gotten up and gone on her own?"

Dr. Zhou made no reply for a moment. Then she admitted flatly, "I've no idea."

Ted Valmont growled with impatience. "What about the police? Have you called them?"

"They're already here. I need to go now to talk with them. I will let them know what you've told me."

Ted Valmont said good-bye and hung up. Over the next several hours he drank bourbon, dialed and redialed the numbers for the St. Francis hotel and Douglas Maitland. He never got hold of either Maitland or his niece. At 5:45, he passed out with his head on the desk, saliva from his gaping mouth soaking into a bill from the utility company that lay nearby.

BREAKFAST AT BUCK'S

"We're going to lift ourselves out of the doldrums one pancake at a time."

—Jamis MacNiven, owner of Buck's (the famed Woodside eatery where venture capitalists often meet to discuss deals), commenting on his plans to deal with the economic downturn

THE HARSH RINGING OF THE TELEPHONE BELL inches from Ted Valmont's ear woke him the following morning. He groaned and lifted his head. The utility bill was stuck to his cheek and there were creases in the skin of his face that matched the topology of the desk. Squinting through a single bloodshot eye, he stabbed at the speakerphone button with a trembling finger.

"What?" he croaked in a voice with more phlegm than vocal cords.

"Ted? Is that you, Ted?" said a male voice over the speaker.

Ted Valmont pulled the utility bill off his face and cradled his head in both hands. "Yes it's me," he said to the desktop, eyes squeezed tight against painful light. "Or what's left of me. Who's this?"

"It's Bruce. I've got some news about Gabrielle Maitland. I called your office, but they said you hadn't come in yet. Are you—is there anything wrong?"

"I'm swell. What about Gabrielle?"

"She's okay, Ted. She's resting at home."

Ted Valmont hoisted his head upright and leaned back in his chair, eyes still closed. "Bruce," he said heavily, "something screwy is going on here. The doctor at the hospital said she disappeared without checking out. They didn't know if she left on her own power or was taken away. Later I got a phone call from her begging for help. She said someone was trying to hurt her."

"When did all this happen?"

"After I called you. I had a message from the doctor and Gabrielle on my recorder when I got home from the hospital."

"Hmm," said Crane. "I don't know about that. All I know is I called Forest Hawley this morning to see what was up and he told me that some servants brought Gabrielle home late last night and now she's resting in bed. Apparently she's had these kind of attacks before."

Ted Valmont blinked open his eyes and stared at the phone. He cleared his throat savagely. "That's not the way you handle things. The hospital has notified the police for Christ's sake. What the hell did Maitland think he was doing?"

"Beats me. Like I said, I'm just telling you what I know." Crane paused for a moment. When he spoke again, his voice had a softer, more persuasive tone. "Ted, I wouldn't let yourself get wrapped around the axle on this one. Maitland probably blames you for what happened to Gabrielle, and while you and I both know you had nothing to do with that, she is only 22 years old. You two aren't playing the game by the same rules."

"What exactly is that supposed to mean?"

"It means that it's not a relationship between equals. It means that you ought to lay off, Ted."

"Bruce?"

"Yes?"

"Go barrel-age your brains." Ted Valmont pounded on the button to break the connection. He wheeled back in the chair and sat still and frowning, looking down at his feet. Eventually he came out of the trance to check his watch—which read 8:20—and scooted back to the desk to dial another number. The ringing of the phone came over the speaker and then a female voice answered:

"Ted Valmont's office. How may I help you?"

"Carrie, it's Ted. I'm not coming in today. I've got some personal business to take care of."

"Boss, you've got two deal review meetings and Breen wants to talk with you this pm. He said it's important."

"He says everything is important. Tell him I'm sorry, but I can't do it. I've got to take care of this. Now I'll talk to you later, okay?"

"Okay," said Carrie skeptically.

Ted Valmont cleared the line again and got up to stretch. He rubbed his neck and lower back and hobbled out of the study. He stood in the shower under hot water for a long time, shaved and dressed in khakis and a polo shirt. By the time he walked out to his garage, many signs of the hard night were gone, but his face was pale and tiny lines around his eyes—such as those that beset a man in his early thirties—seemed deeper and better defined.

He yanked the cover off the Ferrari and fired up the motor. Driving less than a half mile to a cluster of shops near the intersection of Woodside and Canada Roads, he parked in a lot full of other expensive cars and walked into a restaurant called Buck's to take a booth by the front window.

He pounded down two cups of coffee and made a fidgety, half-hearted attempt to read the morning paper while waiting for his order of fried egg and toast. When the food came, he sniffed at it warily, grimaced, then covered the gleaming yellow eye of the egg with his napkin and pushed the plate to one side.

The waitress returned with the coffee as he drained his third cup. "My, what a big caffeine craving you have, grandma," she said.

"The better to kill a hangover with, my dear," Ted Valmont said with forced cheeriness. "Say, Ruth, would you bring the check? I'm in a rush."

Ruth nodded and lifted a corner of the napkin to peer underneath. She was a sturdy, college-age blonde with freckled forearms who looked as if she would swing a mean field hockey stick. "And maybe a few Rolaids, too," she said. "Your ulcer's going to love this diet."

He straightened in his seat and brought his hand to his sternum. "Better bring the whole roll," he agreed.

As Ruth turned to go, there was the screech of car tires followed by the blast of a loud horn. Ted Valmont glanced up to see a BMW stopped in the middle of Woodside Road in front of a man in a bulky windbreaker. While the man in the windbreaker continued serenely across the street, the BMW driver leaned out of his window to shout, "What the hell?!"

Ted Valmont watched as the man threaded through the cars parked in the lot, then looked back to Ruth as she returned with the check and a roll of antacids. "Here ya' go, cutie. Hope the head and the tummy feel better."

Ted Valmont reached to take the tray Ruth proffered, but his hand closed on empty air as she shrieked and flung the tray to one side. "Look out!" she yelped.

The plate glass in front of Ted Valmont's booth shattered with a tremendous crash, and the man in the windbreaker came flying through in a hailstorm of shards to land on the table with a punishing thud. There was a moment of eerie, stunned silence, then the restaurant was flooded with the sound of dropped silverware, scraping chairs and frightened, bewildered shouts.

Amidst the pandemonium, Ted Valmont and the man made eye contact. A clean-cut, professional type in his early thirties, his face was cut by glass, he was hyperventilating and tears streamed down his cheeks. He struggled to open his mouth and barely croaked out the words:

"Run—run away from me."

Ted Valmont launched out of the booth—tackling Ruth as he came—and propelled them both several yards from the table. They rolled as one across the floor, behind a half wall that separated the dining area from the entryway.

The man on the table snaked a hand under his jacket and suddenly the table and the area around it blossomed into a roaring fireball.

As the cloud of wood chips, plaster, glass and burning bits of cloth settled around the area like an evil precipitation, Ruth could be heard to wail, "That's his hand. Holy Jesus. That's his hand on the floor!"

Ted Valmont stood next to a patrol cop on the sidewalk in front of Buck's. Police cars, emergency vehicles and television vans crowded the small lot, many of them parked with their front wheels over the curb.

There was a bandage over Ted Valmont's eyebrow, his face was white as lime and both knees in his khaki pants were torn, but otherwise he appeared unharmed. He shook his head angrily. "I've told you everything I know," he said to the patrol cop. "I need to go. Call me at the office if you have more questions." The spinning yellow light from a fire captain's car swept across both men's stomachs as he spoke.

The patrol cop pushed his cap further back on his head and sighed. He was an older man, and tendrils of damp gray hair were plastered to his forehead above the line where the cap had ridden. "All right, Mr. Valmont, I can't make you stay. But you're being very foolish. You should go with the girl to the hospital and have yourself checked over. There's no telling what injuries you have. Shock is a very funny thing."

"I'm not in shock," said Ted Valmont flatly, and shouldered his way past the officer to a bench in front of the restaurant where Ruth sat wrapped in a blanket, drinking tea from a mug that she cradled against her chest like a baby kitten. She watched him approach with frightened eyes and then burst into tears when he touched her shoulder. "Oh, Ted," she half-whispered.

Ted Valmont sat down on the bench and pulled her close in a sheltering embrace. They sat that way for several long minutes while cops, paramedics and firemen crunched over glass on the sidewalk and pavement in front of the restaurant. At last Ted Valmont pulled back from the girl, sought her hand under the blanket and gave it a firm squeeze. "I have to go now, Ruthie."

She blinked back more tears and nodded almost imperceptibly. Ted Valmont kissed her chastely and then stood to negotiate his way through the boiling cataract of men, vehicles, equipment, hoses and cables to the far end of the lot where his car was parked. He grabbed a loitering paramedic and shouted at him to move the ambulance that was blocking the Ferrari and then yanked open the door to fall behind the wheel with a heavy groan.

After a lot of back and forth, he managed to get the car out of the stall without hitting anything and inched it forward towards the exit. At the mouth of the lot stood a KTVC station truck and cameraman—and beside them, standing squarely in path of the Ferrari—Amelia Crenshaw with her too-red lipstick. Oblivious to Ted Valmont's car, she was speaking rapidly to the camera in the middle of a "hot roll" back to the station:

"There's no indication of any linkage to the September 11th attacks. Except for the bomber himself—who police believe was a software entrepreneur whose company recently filed Chapter 11—there are no serious injuries. Police credit quick thinking on the part of Basis Ventures partner Ted Valmont for foiling the bomber's plans and speculate that the motivation for the attack was resentment against the venture capital industry for its role in the dot-com meltdown. Mr. Valmont has not been available—"

With the nose of the Ferrari inches from the back of Amelia's legs, Ted Valmont mashed down the horn. The reporter jumped a good six inches—her luxuriant mane convulsing in an auburn wave—and dropped her microphone and story notes. The cameraman stepped forward to pull her out of the path of the car, and Ted Valmont wheeled rapidly out of the lot. Catching sight of the "Valmont" vanity plate as the car accelerated past on Woodside Road, Amelia shook her fist at him and yelled, "That's twice now!"

Ted Valmont drove north on Highway 280. He made good time to San Francisco, cut through Golden Gate Park and crossed to Marin County on the Golden Gate Bridge, but just a few miles from the span he pulled off the road and rushed to a place at the back wheels to retch violently. His face reddened from the effort and tiny beads of sweat popped out from his forehead, but he produced nothing more from his gut than a thin stream of bile flecked with blood. He returned to the car to huddle white-faced and shivering against the callous black leather of the bucket seat.

He sat this way for close to twenty minutes with the oppressive roar of traffic permeating the interior of the Ferrari and the occasional concussion of air from passing big-rigs shaking the car to its springs. It was the passing of a tractor-trailer hauling a construction crane that finally jolted Ted Valmont out of his huddled cocoon. As the turbulence from the passing truck buffeted the Ferrari, he cursed and grabbed at the steering wheel to steady himself. He pulled himself up to stare at his still-pale face in the rearview mirror, then said grimly, "No, officer. I am not in shock. Not one little bit."

The shaking hand he brought to the ignition key might have put the lie to his words, but he managed to start the car and merge back onto the freeway without incident. He covered the remaining thirty-plus miles to Napa in a little over a half hour. By the time he pulled onto the winding drive of Douglas Maitland's estate, the sun had yet to reach its zenith, but the valley fog had burned off and the temperature was climbing fast.

He parked in the cul-de-sac in front of the house and walked swiftly up to the granite-columned portico. He mashed down the doorbell and—getting no immediate response—pounded with the brass knocker for good measure. Presently the sound of a lock being disengaged came through the heavy oak door and it swung open to reveal a Latino woman dressed in the pink uniform of a maid. She looked stone-faced at Ted Valmont and said dully, "Yes? Can I help you?" with a thick Mexican accent.

"I'm here to see Mr. Maitland."

"You are expected?"

"If I'm not, I should be. I'm Ted Valmont."

The pronouncement did not seem to carry much weight with the maid. She dipped her head slightly, then stepped back to push the heavy door closed. The lock snicked into place.

"Hey!" said Ted Valmont. "Tell Maitland I'm here, God damn it."

A long minute went by. Ted Valmont paced back and forth on the porch, and then attempted to look through a curtained window to the entryway. As he brought a hand up to shade against the reflection, the door pulled open again and a cadaverous looking man with sunken cheeks and long, disjointed limbs stepped through. "What are you doing?" he asked.

"What's it look like I'm doing? I'm trying to see into the window."

The cadaverous man harrumphed. "This is a private residence. It's not part of the winery. If you are interested in a tour, you must go back out on the main road and take the next exit to your right. You'll find the Maitland Vineyards sales and tasting room there."

Ted Valmont snorted. "I'm not interested in a tour. I'm here to see Douglas Maitland."

"Mr. Maitland does not have any appointments scheduled for this morning."

"Come on. You know perfectly well who I am and why I'm here. I want to talk to Maitland about Gabrielle. If you take his phone messages you know I've left at least a dozen in the last twenty-four hours."

The cadaverous man tilted his chin up and looked at Ted Valmont along his nose. "Ms. Gabrielle Maitland is ill."

Ted Valmont stamped his foot. "I know that," he said forcefully. "I was with her when she threw her fit. I need to talk to Maitland about what happened at the hospital. Now will you drop the haughty servant act and take me to see him?"

The cadaverous man drew back. He rubbed his bony hands together in an agitated way. "Mr. Maitland does not like to be 'talked to' much by anyone."

"Take me to see him," Ted Valmont said through clenched teeth.

This last directive, uttered as it was like a cold imprecation, seemed finally to break the man's resistance. Slowly, like a snail pulling in its horns, his combativeness faded. "Very well," he said limply. "You can wait in the library. I will speak with Mr. Maitland."

He gestured through the open doorway and led Ted Valmont to a room at the front of the house, just off the entryway. It was a library of the old style with walls of leather-bound books, heavy, leather-bound furniture and dark wood paneling. Ted Valmont sat down on a brown leather couch and picked up a book from the coffee table in front of him. It was titled *Manufacturing in the 1990s: Shop Floor Automation Comes of Age*. He thumbed through it listlessly for several minutes until Douglas Maitland stepped through the library door.

He was dressed much like their prior meeting, in overalls and a work shirt. His black eyes glittered darkly and the deep lines that ran from his nose to mouth seemed liked fissures in a marble slab. "My brother tells me you were very high-handed just now, Mr. Valmont," he said in his reedy voice.

Ted Valmont seemed nonplussed. "Brother…Gabrielle's father? Why does he call you Mr. Maitland?"

"Gabrielle's father is my younger brother. This is my older one—but he's also my secretary. And as my secretary, he is expected to address and refer to me as any secretary would his employer."

"I guess you really like to keep things in the family, don't you Maitland?"

Maitland gave no indication that he had heard the question. He went over to the coffee table and sat down in a wing chair across from Ted Valmont. "Please return the book to the table. I didn't give you permission to examine it."

Ted Valmont tossed the book on the table without ceremony. "Hope you don't mind me breathing your air."

"If I could prevent it—short of committing a crime—I would. Now what are you doing here?"

"I came to find out what happened to Gabrielle."

"She had an epileptic seizure. Sometimes callously referred to as a 'fit' by those who enjoy belittling people with disabilities."

Ted Valmont flushed. "I meant what happened to her at the hospital. She was asleep in her room and someone took her out of there against doctor's orders—and without notifying the hospital staff."

Maitland smiled slightly, drawing the lines on his face even deeper. "There's more, isn't there? You're also going to tell me that she called you and asked for help. Aren't you, Valmont?"

"I sure as hell am. Now what is going on?"

"It's really none of your affair. There's no reason for me to explain myself to you."

"Maitland! I'm involved—"

"Except," Maitland put in hastily, "to end these displays of righteous indignation."

"Let's have it then. What happened?"

Maitland pulled the book across the table and squared it with the corner nearest him, out of Ted Valmont's reach. He folded his hands in his lap. "Gabrielle has been afflicted with epilepsy since her early teens. The doctors think it was triggered by a blow to the head she received in a horse-riding accident. As far as last night goes, she regained consciousness in her room and called me to take her out of the hospital. She has had a phobia about hospitals since the time of her accident. Rather than driving down myself, I found it more expedient to have one of my employees in San Francisco pick her up. While he probably should have followed procedures for checking her out, he was under instructions to get Gabrielle home as quickly as possible—and he knew there was little or nothing the hospital could do for the girl."

Ted Valmont leaned forward. "Nothing they could do for her? They hadn't even started treatment. They were waiting to hear from you about her medical history."

"Her medical history would be beyond their knowledge. She has an experimental implant to stimulate her brain whenever she has a seizure. It works as a kind of circuit breaker. When it goes off during an episode, it stops the seizure and brings on unconsciousness. A few hours later, she wakes up and is fine—except for being tired and somewhat disoriented."

"That's not what she told me. She said the wires under her neck were to brace a cracked vertebra. She didn't say anything about epilepsy."

Maitland unfolded his hands and made a temple out of his fingers. His fingers, like his brother's, were long and bony—with curiously splayed tips. But unlike his brother, Maitland had dirt under his nails. "She wouldn't say anything about the epilepsy," he said patiently, like a parent lecturing a child. "She's embarrassed by it. She doesn't want others—particularly romantic interests—to know anything about it."

"What about her calling me then? She said that she wanted help. That someone was hurting her."

"You've dramatized that, Valmont. She called you on the car phone on the way home. She never said anyone was hurting her. As I mentioned, when she wakes up after an episode she is disoriented. She didn't understand exactly what was happening because she wasn't familiar with the employee who I assigned to bring her back. It's as simple as that."

Ted Valmont fell back against the couch. His frown conveyed incredulity. "What do you take me for? There's something else going on here. I still haven't heard a legitimate reason for her to have been whisked out of the hospital like that. And the hospital agrees. I know for a fact they've informed the police."

Maitland twitched his head no. "We've cleared all that up. Neither the hospital or the police are concerned with the matter any longer."

"Very convenient. Then tell me why you didn't return my calls. If this is all so innocent, why didn't you let me know what was going on?"

"As I've suggested before, I didn't judge it to be your concern. You've caused more than enough trouble for the girl already. Do you know what triggered the seizure? It was the wine you fed her. She's not allowed to have more than one drink a day. You had already taken advantage of the girl sexually. Did you need to get her drunk to insure a second engagement?"

Ted Valmont jumped up from the couch. He held his arms rigid by his side with fists clenched. "I want to see her. I want to talk to her now."

Maitland met Ted Valmont's eyes calmly, showing no outward sign of concern over his threatening stance. "You're acting like a spoiled teenager—which isn't far from the truth. You punks who luck into millions from Silicon Valley start-ups make me sick. It comes so easily that you never gain the maturity and experience that ought to go hand-in-hand with the money." He looked Ted Valmont up and down with obvious disdain. "I'll ask you to go now."

Ted Valmont landed heavily on the coffee table with an outstretched palm. He shot the other hand over to grab Maitland by the shirt. "I don't care what you think of me or my life—something fishy is going on here, Maitland. I want to see the girl alone or I'm calling the cops."

Maitland did not flinch or draw back from Ted Valmont's grasp. He turned his head to one side and yelled, "Ramos!"

The stocky foreman came running into the room, muscles protruding from a white cotton tank top, still wearing the backwards baseball cap. In keeping with the baseball motif, he carried a short aluminum bat.

"Take your hand off me and leave the premises immediately," said Maitland coldly, "or Ramos will beat you to within an inch of your life."

Ted Valmont screwed up his eyes and wrinkled his forehead, looking first at Maitland and then at Ramos. He released Maitland's shirt and straightened up. "You people are incredible," he said in a tense voice.

He walked towards the door. As he passed, Ramos put his thumb to the bandage on Ted Valmont's forehead and mashed it in. "*Adios, cabrón*. If you want to see something really fuckin' incredible, just come back here again."

LIFTED LAPTOP

"Q: How do you get a dot-com CEO off your front porch? A: Pay him for the pizza."
—Unknown

TED VALMONT WHEELED INTO THE LOT OF the Napa County Sheriff's office, skidding to a stop by a parked cruiser. He jumped out of the Ferrari and doubled-timed it up to the entrance. Inside, the coffee machine still had the "Out of Order" signed taped on it, but there was a different clerk on duty. Ted Valmont walked up to the reception desk and addressed the middle-aged black man behind it:

"I'd like to report a crime."

The officer pulled a form from a stack beside him. "All right, sir," he said with pen poised above paper. "Let's start with your name."

"Ted Valmont. That's spelled V-a-l-m-o-n-t."

"What's the crime then, Mr. Valmont?"

Ted Valmont looked down at the form. Check boxes for burglary, robbery, assault, rape and murder stood out in bold print below the area where the clerk had written his name. "Right," he said slowly, "the crime." He tugged at his earlobe. "Look, officer, I've changed my mind. May I just speak with Deputy Olken?"

The officer drew his heavy features into a frown. He pointedly clicked the retraction mechanism of his ballpoint pen. "Does he know you?"

"Yes, he does. We spoke over the weekend. I believe he'll agree to see me."

The clerk grunted noncommittally and eased himself off his stool. He walked to the phone behind the reception desk and talked for several minutes. When he returned, his features were drawn into an even deeper frown. "He's coming right out," he said shortly. "Wait here."

Ted Valmont barely had time to say, "fine" before Deputy Olken stepped through the swinging half door behind the reception counter. He put his hand out for Ted Valmont to shake and then led him by the elbow to the interview room from the day before. "You've had a busy day," he said after they had sat down.

Ted Valmont raised his eyebrows slightly. "What do you mean?"

"I mean the business in Woodside. Anything that smells even remotely like September 11th puts all the police departments on alert." Olken looked blankly at Ted Valmont.

"Something else been keeping you busy?"

"That's enough, isn't it?"

"More than enough." Olken smiled lopsidedly, making clear the Skoal had stayed in the can in his hip pocket. "In fact, I'm surprised to see you here at all. But Officer Johnson said you came in to report a crime."

Ted Valmont moistened his lips. He thought a moment, then shook his head, smiling. "Yeah, well, that was something different—something I decided not to pursue. It was more of a personal disagreement than a crime, I guess."

Olken nodded vaguely. "I see. Why ask to talk to me, then?"

"More of the same: to get an update on Niebuhr. I wondered if you had learned anything else from his car."

Olken made a fist and pressed it into the palm of his other hand. Knuckles cracked loudly. "I'm really not obligated to tell you anything more about the case. You understand that?"

"Yes, I know."

Olken leaned over and pressed his hand flat on the table. He ran it across the scarred Formica surface. "We've identified the blood in the back of the car. It's Niebuhr's."

"Jesus," said Ted Valmont. "I'd convinced myself it wasn't his. Wouldn't there be blood in the front seat if he was hurt?"

"Blood in that location is consistent with situations where a victim has been placed in the trunk." Ted Valmont started to say something but Olken waved him off. "Like I told you before, there's not enough blood there to indicate a serious wound. And there are plenty of other explanations for its presence besides Niebuhr being held in the trunk."

Ted Valmont grimaced as he massaged his stomach with two knuckles. "Anything else?"

"A little. Dusting for fingerprints, we found a bunch of Niebuhr's and others that belong to the family. We also found four that we couldn't identify. We're running these through the fingerprint computers, but no matches so far."

"What about all the junk in the car? Did you find anything of significant there?"

"Apart from the volume, no."

"How about the conference proceedings? Any names or numbers jotted down?"

"Nope. Nothing like that."

"And you didn't find any other notes or letters that seemed important?"

Olken gave his armpit a good scratching, looking at Ted Valmont all the while. "That your way of asking if we found a suicide note?"

"The thought crossed my mind."

"There wasn't any note. And I wouldn't expect one. People usually write them—when they write them at all—right before they kill themselves. Which means if you don't have a body, you usually don't have a note. Or more accurately, if you find a body, that's where you'll find the note—if there is one."

Ted Valmont nodded with slow emphasis. "All right," he said after a moment. "I've shot my wad. I can't think of anything else."

"Really? A high tech guy like you?"

Ted Valmont's eyes probed Olken's face. "I guess I'm stupid today. What else should I be asking?"

Olken ran his hand over the table again, then dug his thumbnail into a depression from a cigarette burn. "I might have asked if we found anything on the laptop computer. Unless I already knew the answer."

"Of course. That was stupid of me...But what do you mean unless I already knew the answer?"

Olken dug out a piece of charred Formica and flicked it across the table. He looked over at Ted Valmont. "I appreciated how you were able to identify items missing from the car the other day."

"Like the Palm computer."

"Yes, like the Palm computer. And the cell phone and the laptop."

"Sure. But as it turned out, you did find those last two in the car, whereas the Palm computer is still missing."

"The laptop is missing too. Someone broke into our property locker and stole it."

Ted Valmont frowned. "What are you saying exactly? That I took it?"

"It's curious that you came here to report a crime. And both you and Niebuhr's wife have told me he was an important contributor at NeuroStimix. Could be you decided the information on the laptop was needed there."

Ted Valmont shook his head angrily. "That's ridiculous. I agree the information on the laptop might be valuable to NeuroStimix. But had I thought of it, I would have asked to have it released or requested permission to copy the contents onto another computer. I wouldn't have stolen it out of a police locker."

"May I ask where you were last night?"

"San Francisco, followed by Woodside. And, no, I don't have witnesses to vouch for the whole time. What makes you so sure that a sheriff's department employee didn't steal it?"

Olken folded his arms across his chest. "It's possible. I wouldn't like to think it, but it's possible."

The two men stared at each other across the table, not saying anything for a long moment. When Olken finally broke the silence, his tone was conciliatory. "Assuming neither of us is responsible—and by that I mean neither you nor someone from the department—then who would take the damn thing?"

Tension went out of Ted Valmont's shoulders. He sighed and rubbed more at his gut. "I don't know. A NeuroStimix competitor, an employee or—for a real stretch—how about Warren himself. I'll tell you one thing, though. They had another incident involving computers there recently."

"What exactly?"

"Someone hacked the NeuroStimix computer network and read—and possibly deleted—Warren Niebuhr's e-mail."

Olken moved his hand over the table again and returned to his excavation of the cigarette burn. He said idly, "What would be the point of that?"

"To get information valuable to NeuroStimix—as you suggested earlier."

"Uh-huh. But my assumption was that you took the laptop to return information to NeuroStimix. This would be to take it away."

"Yeah, I guess so."

Olken looked up. "I don't think this is getting us anywhere." He rose and opened the door. "I've got an appointment with the Sheriff over in Calistoga. Let's remember our commitment to keep each other informed. All right, Mr. Valmont?"

"Of course."

Olken nodded, stepped out of the room, but then pivoted sharply to lean his head back in. "And, Mr. Valmont…no more of these crimes that you almost need to report."

Late that afternoon, Ted Valmont walked into the bar of a popular St. Helena restaurant. Bruce Crane and Forest Hawley, the winemaker from Maitland Vineyards, were waiting for him at a table with olives, salami, bread and glasses of pilsner beer.

Crane jumped up when he saw Ted Valmont. He hesitated for a moment, then stepped forward to wrap him in a hug. "I was worried about you, buddy," he said, pounding him on the back.

Ted Valmont laughed and eased out of the embrace. "Thanks, Bruce. I was worried about me too."

The two men went back to the table, where Forest Hawley greeted Ted Valmont with a nod and a flash of his crooked, tobacco-stained grin. "I'll take on rain check on my hug," he said wryly.

"That's good because a bomb and a hug from Bruce are my limit."

"Don't joke about it," said Crane. "You were very lucky. I still don't understand the point of it."

Ted Valmont reached for a hunk of bread with a trembling hand and took an enormous bite out of it. He held up a finger in a give-me-a-moment gesture while he chewed and then gulped the food down. "Sorry. I don't think I've eaten in 24 hours." He took a sip of beer from Crane's glass. "I assume you're talking about the bomber."

Crane nodded. "Of course."

"One of the other VCs in the restaurant—Pranav Hingorani— recognized the guy when he came through the window. His name was Sullivan. He was the CEO of a start-up that ran out of cash. They had a signed term sheet for their next round, but the dilution of employee shares was so bad that Sullivan backed out of the deal. He said he'd rather have the company go out of business than have the vultures take everything they'd worked years for."

"So he suicide bombs a restaurant full of VCs to get even," said Crane. "That's a pretty extreme way to extract your revenge. Who was his investor?"

Ted Valmont hurried the pit of an olive from his mouth and dropped it onto a bread plate. "Can't you guess? Hingorani. He was sitting one table over. I just happened to be in the way."

Hawley made a whistling noise between his teeth. "You've a knack for picking your spots. From what Bruce tells me, you're right in the middle of it with the Maitlands as well."

"I gave Forest a run-down on what happened last night and this morning," Crane put in quickly. "I told him you were concerned about Gabrielle and would appreciate a chance to talk the situation over."

"That's right," said Ted Valmont, glancing from Crane to Hawley. "I just hope you don't get in trouble for meeting with me."

Hawley scratched the back of his head while squinching up one side of his face. "Oh, I'm too old to let anyone dictate who I can talk to," he said in a near drawl. "Besides, I haven't heard word one about this from anyone but Bruce."

Ted Valmont stabbed at a hunk of salami with his fork. "I was so mad this morning that I drove to the Sheriff's office with the intention of filing a complaint. But when I got there, I realized there wasn't anything criminal in what Maitland had done—with the possible exception of threatening to sic Ramos on me. Even so, I didn't think it would help matters any to involve the law."

Hawley grunted. "Hardly."

Ted Valmont held up his fork and treated the salami to a thorough inspection. "To be honest, I'm not sure what the hell I expect to gain from talking with you," he said listlessly. "Maybe some kind of assurance that Maitland really does have Gabrielle's best interests in mind and that he wasn't lying about taking her out of the hospital."

"That's it," said Crane. "You need to feel comfortable letting this drop. To know that you don't have an obligation to protect Gabrielle from her uncle."

"I think you guys are setting the bar a little high," said Hawley. "All I can do is tell you what I know about the situation and give you some idea of what I think. You'll have to draw your own conclusions."

Ted Valmont had popped the salami into his mouth. With one cheek bulging, he said, "Fair enough," in mumbled tones.

"Right," said Hawley, and took a swallow of beer. "I already told you some about Maitland. He's a retired industrialist. A self-made man who worked his way up from the factory floor. I believe he still owns a lot of companies involved in manufacturing—many of them overseas. As far as his relationship to Gabrielle goes, she's the daughter of Maitland's younger brother. The brother is sick, though, so Maitland has taken on the job of guardian. It's hard for him—hard because he has no children of his own and hard because he's not used to Gabrielle's freewheeling ways. I told you before she's the only bone of contention between us. My opinion is that he lets her get away with way too much."

Ted Valmont drew himself up in his chair self-consciously. He dusted bread crumbs off his lap. "Maybe I'm the thing that's prompted the new get-tough policy."

Hawley looked directly at Ted Valmont. "Look. I don't know you that well, so I may be a bit out of line with this, but I think you should hear it. As an individual, you would hardly be the reason for a get-tough policy. While you're a little old for Gabrielle, you're well-educated, successful and, as far as I can tell, a pretty decent guy."

Ted Valmont inclined his head towards Hawley. "But?"

"But as one of a long line of waiters, field hands, motorcycle gang members and all kinds of other riff-raff, you could be the straw that broke the camel's back. I hate to be so blunt, but that girl gets around. She's slept with half the male population in the valley."

Bruce Crane had been paying close attention to the bottom of his beer glass as Hawley spoke. Now his eyes shifted to look at Ted Valmont.

His friend paled and rubbed his hand over his mouth. "That bad, huh?" he said in a soft voice.

Forest Hawley pulled a pack of cigarettes out of his breast pocket and shook one out. "Damn," he said abruptly. "I keep forgetting you can't smoke in bars." He rolled the cigarette between his thumb and forefinger and licked his lips. "I'll tell you a little story—and then I think I'll shut up. I was over at the dining room at Meadowood and I heard two waiters talking. Evidently Gabrielle had been in there recently. The first guy—older, and better looking—said that he had barely been able to serve her dinner without being raped. Then the second guy—a tubby kid with pimples—says naively, 'Are you saying she's a nymphomaniac?' The older guy looks off across the room like he's remembering something and says slowly, 'She would be, if they quieted her down a little.' That about sums it up."

Ted Valmont nodded gloomily and bit a fingernail. "Okay. I get the message."

Crane leaned forward over the table. "I don't want to belabor this, Ted, but do you get the message? Do you see what you've got to do here? Nothing. You've got to let this drop. Maitland is a bit of a bastard, all right, but he's got more than he can handle with Gabrielle and you're only adding to it. Now promise me you're not going to make any more trouble for him—by going over to his place, or talking to the cops or whatever."

"Okay. I promise," said Ted Valmont in an exasperated tone.

"And no more Gabrielle. You can have your pick of women, Ted. You don't need to be fooling around with someone like that."

Ted Valmont laughed sourly. "Yeah, right. You see the irony in what you just said? I can have my pick of women and that's just fine. I'm admired and envied by other men, even. But if a woman does the same thing, it's quite another story."

Crane looked at Ted Valmont soberly for a moment, then burst out laughing. "I never thought of it that way."

An embarrassed smile crept over Ted Valmont's face. He looked at Crane and then Hawley and self-consciously combed his fingers through hair. "All right. Drop it. What's a guy got to do to get some beer around here, anyway?"

Crane slapped him on the back, said, "That's more like it," and signaled a waitress. The men spent another hour in the bar talking about wine, then Hawley excused himself to go home. Crane and Ted Valmont stayed for dinner and later retired to Crane's cramped quarters in Oakville, where Ted Valmont slept 12 hours straight on Crane's living room sofa. Gabrielle and Maitland were not mentioned again.

THE EMPEROR HAS NO STOCK OPTIONS

"There are going to be a lot of disappointed iguanas who have to stay home."

—Paul Ziv, recruiter, commenting on dot-commers who are laid off or defect to more corporate environments and can no longer bring their pets to the office

TED VALMONT STOOD ON THE PORCH OF his brother's house, looking through the screen door at his brother's male nurse. Dressed in chinos like before, Archie had traded his black sweater for a camouflage tee shirt. He pulled a pair of reading glasses off his nose and let them fall around his neck, suspended by a white shoelace.

"Where have you been?" he said in low tone. "I've been trying to reach you for the last two days."

Standing with his hands in his pockets, Ted Valmont shifted his weight from one foot to the other. "I got your messages, but with the bomb thing and some business I had in Napa…" He let his voice trail off. "How's he doing? Is he up yet?"

"No, he's not up. He's sleeping off another drunk so keep your voice down."

"Still upset about Christy?"

Archie unlatched the screen door and stepped out, forcing Ted Valmont to give ground. "For Christ's sake, Ted. Just because he's in a wheel chair doesn't mean he can't read."

"What do you mean?"

"Did you think he wouldn't hear about Warren Niebuhr's disappearance? The guy you've promised is going to make him walk again? The least you could have done is called and told him about it yourself. The only thing he lives for now is NeuroStimix and the miracle cure."

Ted Valmont looked down and nervously rattled the change in his pocket. "What an idiot. Of course he would find out," he said to his feet. He looked up to study Archie's ruddy features. "I don't know what the hell I'm doing any more. Let me talk to him. I'll put the best spin I can on it. Tell him no one thinks anything serious has happened, the police have some good leads, etc."

Archie frowned and rubbed his hand speculatively over the top of his blond crew cut like he was gauging the nap of a carpet. "Now you've got me confused. You haven't heard that Niebuhr's okay? I thought that's what you meant when you said you had business in Napa."

Ted Valmont yanked both hands out of his pockets and took an eager step forward. "Who says he's okay?"

"The wife—Lori or Laura or whatever her name is. They interviewed her in today's *Merc*. She says it's all a mistake and that her husband is fine. He's off on a sabbatical. I was reading the article when you pulled up."

Ted Valmont's face became flushed and he took several rapid breaths through an open mouth. "Let's see it."

Archie grunted and went back through the screen door to retrieve the paper. He passed a quarter-folded section to Ted Valmont, pointing at the headline with a well-bitten fingernail.

Ted Valmont scanned the article briefly and then shoved the paper back into Archie's mid-section. Archie slapped at it, pinning it to his stomach. "I've got to go see Laura Niebuhr," said Ted Valmont in a rush. "Tell Tim I'll be by later."

The sound of Laura Niebuhr's greeting came over the speakers in Ted Valmont's car as he barreled south on 280. Her voice had a crisp, confident tone.

"Laura," said Ted Valmont from behind the wheel. "It's Ted. What's this I hear about Warren contacting you?"

"Oh, Ted, I meant to call. I got a letter from him."

"A letter?" said Ted Valmont in a hard, ringing voice. "Why a letter?"

Laura Niebuhr chuckled. "I've no idea, Ted. You know better than to ask those questions."

"What'd it say, then?"

"Basically, it says he's fine and he's coming home soon."

"Where is he?"

"He doesn't say exactly. Somewhere in the Napa Valley."

Ted Valmont drew his lip down over his front teeth and chewed on it. "Laura, that's ridiculous. How can you even be sure it's from him?"

"It's definitely from Warren," said Laura patiently. "And it's postmarked from the Napa Valley."

"Look. I'm on 280 headed your direction. Can you wait to go into work until I get there? I'd like to take a look at it."

"All right, but make it soon. I've got a 9:30 appointment."

"I'll be there in 30."

Ted Valmont beat his ETA to the Los Altos home by a good ten minutes. He parked in the circle drive and went up to the porch to knock on the door. The dead plants and the recycling bin full of computer parts were still there, but this time there was no sound of dogs panting in the entryway.

Laura Niebuhr pulled open the door, juggling a very full mug of coffee. She wore a simple A-line cotton dress, and while her unruly hair would need a great deal more attention to be considered "styled," she had at least achieved a measure of symmetry. She said:

"Hello, Ted. Dogs are in the back. I figured I'd spare you a return engagement."

Tension seemed to go out of Ted Valmont's shoulders. "Thanks," he said. "I appreciate it—not that they were a problem or anything."

Laura Niebuhr laughed merrily. "Oh, come on. You are the most fastidious man I know. Let's go in the kitchen. I made a pot of coffee."

Ted Valmont followed her through the dining room to a narrow kitchen behind a swinging door. They sat at heavily shellacked oak table near a window that looked out on the back yard. Amidst a plastic napkin dispenser shaped like a barn and a pair of salt and pepper shakers in the shape of pigs, a coffee maker gurgled on the table. Laura Niebuhr poured coffee into a mug with a rooster painted on it and passed it over to Ted Valmont.

"There's cream if you want it," she said, and held up a cow creamer by its curved tail.

He sniffed at his coffee, and staring at the fantastic "O" of the cow's mouth where the cream poured through, shook his head. "Ah, I think I'm good for now."

Laura nodded and put the creamer down. "So you want to see the letter, then?"

"Yes, please."

She pulled a folded business envelope from a pocket on the side of her dress and passed it over to Ted Valmont. He took it eagerly—examining the outside of the envelope to see the Napa postmark and lack of return address—and pulled out the two sheets of ruled paper and newspaper clipping it contained. Written in a juvenile scrawl with a dull pencil, the letter read:

Dear Laura,

I expect by now you are probably very upset and worried over me. There's no need to be concerned. I am safe and healthy and in no danger of any sort.

I'm sorry to have caused all the trouble, but after the conference the need to get away and rethink my life became too pressing. As you know, I've felt for some time that the research on Functional Electronic Stimulation I've been doing for Neurostimix wasn't going anywhere, and the discussions I had with colleagues at the conference only reinforced this conclusion.

This, coupled with the responsibility of being Chief Scientist and chairman of the board for a company whose president I no longer respect, made it very difficult for me to go back and face the music after the conference ended. I decided, therefore, to take some time off to consider new research directions, and with them, new career options.

I'm staying at a small place in the Napa Valley, making occasional use of the Internet to access technical data, but for the most part I'm not doing research or work in the traditional sense. I'm simply using the time to get my head clear and ponder what I want to do with the rest of my life. Im nearly 33 years old, and as I approach what I hope to be my most productive years, I want to be sure that the work I do is as impactful and beneficial to science and society as it can be.

I realize the way I've gone about this is not very mature, and I know it's put an unfair burden on you and the children, to say nothing of the few friends and associates at Neurostimix who I do respect. In my defense, I can only say that I didn't select this approach for meditating on my future intentionally. Rather, it came about as a consequence of a minor automobile accident.

The details aren't important, but the result was I was forced to abandon my car and walk some distance to get assistance. It was during this walk that I determined to get away for a time, and so rather than getting help for my car, I elected instead to check in to a small hotel and begin my retreat.

I know there has been a lot of publicity about my disappearance, but I'd like to ask you to put the police inquiry to a halt. I promise I

wil' be home soon, but I need another week or
two to work things through.

Do what you think is best as far as informing
the NeuroStimix executive team and board
about my whereabouts and my intentions.
(I'm sure Ted Valmont for one will be very
upset!) Give my love to Sarah and Jenny
and Tom, and I promise when I get back I
will make this up to you all.

Your loving, but harebrained, husband,

Warren

P.S. See the enclosed clipping. I cannot believe
the amount of coverage this has gotten!

Ted Valmont passed from the letter to the clipping. It was an
article from the Sunday *San Francisco Chronicle* describing Niebuhr's
disappearance. Included were quotes from Deputy Olken and Cassia
Price, Vice President of Marketing at NeuroStimix. There was a
plea to the public to assist with the search, and a publicity still of
a serious looking man in a dark suit with the caption, "Warren
Niebuhr, Ph.D." The man in the photo was a slightly older version
of the pasty-faced college student from the picture Ted Valmont
had found in Niebuhr's office. There was some difficulty, however,
in discerning this as the clipping photo had been crudely amended
with a mustache and beard. "Look, Mom! I'm famous!" had been
written beside it.

Ted Valmont sighed, refolded the notepaper and clipping and
returned them to the envelope. He handed it back to Laura Niebuhr.
"The writing looks as bad as I remember. But you're certain it's his?"

"Oh, yes. It's his."

"What in the world possessed you to call the *Mercury* before telling me or the rest of the board?"

"Truth is they called me. The reporter seemed to know I'd heard from Warren. Since Warren had requested it anyway, I didn't see the harm in telling the paper he was okay. I didn't give out any details. Just that he was on sabbatical and would be home soon."

Ted Valmont traced a finger down the tip of his nose and gazed out the window to the back yard. "Is the writing on the newspaper clipping the same as on the letter?"

Laura frowned and flexed open the envelope to peek inside. "Yes, that's Warren's too," she said in a puzzled tone. "Why do you ask?"

Ted Valmont took a sip of his coffee and tried unsuccessfully to cover the sour look that came over his features. He reached for the cow creamer and poured a good half-inch of cream into his mug. "Only because it proves that Warren wrote the letter subsequent to the time he disappeared. It rules out the possibility—" Ted Valmont faltered and broke eye-contact with Laura. "Well, it means that he was still alive as of Sunday morning."

"Jesus, Ted. Way to reassure the jittery wife."

He held up his hands in a placating gesture. "I'm sorry, Laura," he said quickly. "But I'm really having trouble accepting this. It's too far-fetched—even for Warren. If he's staying in Napa, why hasn't someone reported seeing him by now?" He paused. "What if he's being held against his will? What if he was made to write the letter to stop the search?"

Laura exhaled sharply and stared at Ted Valmont open-mouthed. "I know you are disappointed by what he says about NeuroStimix," she said forcefully. "I know you had high hopes for what the technology might do for your brother. But you're just going to have to live with the fact that it's a non-starter. Warren is simply not going to waste any more time on it. You know him. He's the most optimistic guy in the world. If he says it's time to throw in the towel, then it really is."

Ted Valmont started to reply, but was distracted by a muffled buzzing noise. He pulled his cell phone off his belt and opened it up. Then: "Hello…Yes, this is he…Oh, Chris. How did you get this number?— No, that's all right. Look, I'm in a meeting right now. Are you going to be at your desk for a half hour or so?— Layoffs? That can't be. I'm sure you misunderstood— Yes, I promise. Whatever it is, we'll deal with it… Okay, good. Talk to you shortly." He put the phone back and glanced up at Laura. He shook his head. "I'm sorry. That was a strange call. Where were we?"

She looked at him from under her lashes while sipping at her coffee. She smiled. "I was just exorcising your delusions."

Ted Valmont pressed his palms against his temples. "I guess you're right: what I said before was pretty far-fetched."

"That's more like it," she said in an upbeat tone. Then, as if she was extracting a promise, "And you're satisfied about the letter?"

Ted Valmont scowled. "Satisfied is not the word I would use. But I suppose it's not beyond the pale for Warren to do something like this. And at least it explains what happened with the car."

"Yes, and the blood too. Assuming he hurt himself in the accident."

"Well," he said hesitantly, "I don't know about that. If there really was an accident, why wasn't there any damage apparent to the car?"

Laura Niebuhr brought her lips together in a thin line. "Don't you start this again."

Ted Valmont bowed his head. "Okay. I withdraw the comment." He reached for his coffee mug. "So what will you do now?"

"What he asked. Call off the police and sit tight. And I expect you to do the same."

He swallowed hard, evidently not finding the doctored coffee any more to his liking. "All right, Laura," he said in a grave voice. "I'll accept that. But I hope you'll let me know first if you hear from Warren again."

"Of course, Ted."

Ted Valmont nodded in a distracted way. He stood up. "I need to get going. Thanks for letting me read the letter."

She smiled mischievously. "And for the yummy coffee?"

"Yeah…for that too."

Ted Valmont hurried out to the Ferrari, started it, and with the motor idling called NeuroStimix on his car phone. He asked to speak to Chris Duckworth, but succeeded only in getting his voice mail. He called twice more with the same result. Frustrated, he zoomed out of the Niebuhrs' driveway, flattening the head of a disrobed Barbie doll in the process, and drove to NeuroStimix as fast as the clogged residential streets would permit.

Inside the building, he greeted the receptionist with a curt nod and went directly to the open door of Chuck DeMarco's office. DeMarco stood by his only office bookshelf, shoveling its meager contents into a cardboard box. Red-faced and winded, he was in his shirtsleeves—his tie thrown over his shoulder. A trickle of sweat ran down his temple. "What in the heck is going on here?" asked Ted Valmont as DeMarco met his gaze.

"I'll give you a hint," said DeMarco with a sullen voice. "I'm not donating books to the Junior League Rummage Sale."

Ted Valmont advanced into the room. "Cut the crap. I heard there were layoffs. Who initiated them?"

DeMarco smiled malevolently. "You're on the board. You ought to know."

"Well I don't. Enlighten me."

DeMarco held a paperback copy of *Swim with the Sharks* in his hand. He stabbed with it at Ted Valmont as he spoke, his voice rising. "Breen told me I was out. He said the investors aren't putting up the bridge loan with current management and head count. He said you're bringing in a new CEO and cutting the work force by 40%. Preparatory to a sale, he said."

Ted Valmont's jaw became hard and lumpy. "When did you talk to Breen?"

"Late yesterday afternoon. Just after we got the good word on Niebuhr's sabotage."

"What?"

DeMarco laughed and tossed the paperback into the box. "Oh, you didn't hear about that either, eh? I figured since you had Duckworth checking into it, he would have told you by now. It turns out that nut cake Niebuhr sabotaged the computer system before he left."

"You mean the e-mail system was sabotaged."

DeMarco brought his bicep up to his temple to blot the sweat. "No," he said, looking at Ted Valmont through his one unobscured eye. "Whole damn thing. He erased all the research data on the stimulator from the computer disks and got rid of the back-ups. I'm told it'll set product development back by months or even years. Not that it matters."

Ted Valmont abruptly turned heel and walked out of the office. As he went down the hall towards the stairwell, DeMarco called after him, "I told you we were better off without Niebuhr!"

On the second floor, Ted Valmont pounded up the aisle to Chris Duckworth's cubicle. Duckworth wheeled to face the sound of his heavy tread. "I guess what I told you about the layoffs was right," said Duckworth meekly.

"Yes, damn it. Why didn't you answer your phone when I called you back?"

Duckworth shrugged his narrow shoulders. He put down a carefully wrapped oddment into a box full of carefully wrapped, neatly arranged oddments. "I think they must have already cut off our phone service. I know my last official act was to block network access for all the people that were being laid off—myself included."

Ted Valmont crossed his arms and exhaled through his nose. "Who'd they get?"

"Uh—you want to know the names?"

"No. Just give me a feel for what departments got hit and how hard."

Duckworth was wearing a black nylon shirt with a chrome zipper and a pull ring. He tugged nervously on the pull ring as he answered, unzipping and zipping the front of his shirt. "Marketing's all gone—so's all the engineering group that was working on the stimulator. I guess the rest of it was general thinning: some people from each department."

Ted Valmont's face became vague. "What I figured," he said almost to himself. Suddenly his expression sharpened. "What's this about sabotage then?" he said in a too loud voice, startling Duckworth.

Duckworth's hand clenched around the pull ring. "I'm sorry I didn't get a chance to tell you sooner. The engineers figured it out about the same time I did."

"Well, tell me about it now, damn it."

Duckworth dipped his head in acknowledgment. "I was looking through the backup tapes for Niebuhr's e-mail like you requested. The first one I checked was erased—or corrupted was what I figured at first. Then I pulled another and that was bad too. Same with the next one. Finally, I went through them all methodically and every single one was erased."

"But DeMarco said the live data was gone too."

"Yes, that's right. The engineers discovered that gradually as they tried to access it. Everything associated with the stimulator research is gone. That includes databases, documents, source code, hardware design diagrams, you name it."

Ted Valmont brought his hands down to his hips, arms akimbo. He pinned Duckworth in a stare. "And you think Niebuhr did this?"

Duckworth got fidgety and yanked on the pull ring again. "It had to be someone who had unrestricted access to the computer system. And someone who knew the research well enough to find all the files related to it. Even in other engineers' directories. No one but Warren fits that bill."

"Can you tell when the data disappeared?"

"The live data must have been zapped over the weekend. The backup tapes could have been done earlier, but even the ones from last Friday are gone, so at least some of them must have been done around the same time."

Ted Valmont glanced down at the cubicle partition. He picked at the Scotch tape holding up Duckworth's picture of Barbra Streisand. "Last time we talked you couldn't find any record of Niebuhr logging on to the computer since he left the conference. That still true?"

"I'll take Barbra down, thanks," said Duckworth peevishly. "The answer to your question is no. I still can't find any record. But I thought about that after we talked. I'm sure if Warren wanted to, he could cover his tracks. Make it look like he hadn't been on the system when he had. For that matter, he may even have other user ID's I don't know about."

Ted Valmont pounded on the top of the partition, rattling the metal frame. Duckworth flinched. "This isn't making any sense. Niebuhr's wife got a letter saying Warren is holed up in a hotel in Napa. And what about the laptop? Who took that?"

Duckworth placed his fingers delicately along his cheekbone and blinked at Ted Valmont. "I don't get the part about the laptop, but I heard you hired August. Maybe you should talk to him."

Ted Valmont's eyes ranged up and down Duckworth's face. Duckworth reddened under the scrutiny and stepped back to lean against his desk. "Maybe," Ted Valmont said finally, his thoughts apparently elsewhere. Then: "Breen's got some explaining to do. Let's have your home number in case I need to get in touch with you."

Duckworth smiled coquettishly and produced a card with lavender print that Ted Valmont shoved in his hip pocket. He made no reply to Chris Duckworth's "Great seeing you too," as he rushed out of the building.

Larry Breen held a curious U-shaped device in his hands. The inner circumference was made of polished aluminum, the outer of plastic. The legs of the U were hinged so that they could be adjusted closer or farther apart and there was a vented protrusion at the base with the words "Air Intake" written above it. "Look at this, Valmont," said Breen as Ted Valmont stepped into his office. "It's a personal air conditioning system. Keeps your head up to 20 degrees cooler than the ambient air." He put the device around the back of his neck, opening it wide to accommodate his ample collar size.

Ted Valmont gave no indication of having heard or absorbed what Breen had just said. Standing less than a foot from his desk, Ted Valmont glared down at him with a frigid intensity. "Where do you get off making NeuroStimix board moves without my involvement?" he demanded hoarsely.

Breen adjusted the air conditioner on his neck and slid a switch forward. There was a faint whirring noise. "Glad to see you're still in one piece after the incident at Buck's," he said pleasantly. "But to your point, someone had to act to salvage the firm's investment. And you were nowhere to be found…Ah, that feels cooler already."

Ted Valmont's faced darkened with anger. "Will you stop playing with your toys for one God-damned minute and listen to me? You are not a board member. With me absent and Niebuhr missing, there can't even be a quorum. You cannot fire the CEO of the company, and you cannot institute layoffs. It's that simple."

Breen smiled in a condescending way. "That's curious, Ted. We seemed to have done exactly that. Go ask DeMarco if he thinks he still has a job. Ask the employees who are busy pulling down their Dilbert cartoons and copying their resumes to floppy disks."

"You can't do it," Ted Valmont repeated doggedly. "It's not—"

Breen cut him short. He spoke in a commanding voice, quite unlike the genial tone he had employed until now. "Shut up, Ted. I won't debate this any further. The fact of the matter is you are screwing up. You're letting personal relationships and personal problems cloud your business judgment. We discussed the NeuroStimix situation at Fincom and you knew what to do. You failed to do it. Even in the face of evidence that Warren Niebuhr had sabotaged the company's R&D effort."

Breen paused to lounge back comfortably in his chair. When he continued, his tone was softer, more matter-of-fact. "As of today, you're off the NeuroStimix board. Tillman's taking your place. I'm giving you the rest of the week off and I expect you to come back with your head screwed on straight or you're fired." Breen adjusted the air conditioner again and sighed contentedly.

"Now, go have a nice vacation, Ted. And please close the door behind you."

Much as he had done with DeMarco, Ted Valmont turned abruptly and charged out of the office. He reached for the doorknob as he went by and swung it closed with a slam that reverberated throughout the building. Minutes later, as he raced down the fast lane of Highway 280, the needle on the Ferrari's speedometer crept past the 120 mph mark and continued climbing.

LEAVE HER
ALONE
OR THIS IS
WHAT
WILL HAPPEN
TO YOU

PENILE PROJECTILE

"Question of the day: if you wear the Pets.com sock puppet while masturbating, is it bestiality?"
—Posting on an Internet news group

TED VALMONT STEPPED THROUGH THE DOOR OF his Woodside home carrying a speeding ticket for three hundred dollars. He went immediately to the exercise room, where he shucked off his clothes—not bothering to fold or hang any article—and changed into his boxing gear. He walked up to the heavy bag and regarded it with a ruinous gaze. He swung—then swung again. The heavy bag danced on its chains like a demented puppet. Ted Valmont expelled a roaring noise from deep within his chest and leaned into the bag to deliver a ferocious combination of punches that tattooed it to the wall.

The punching frenzy went on for a long time. When Ted Valmont could barely muster the strength to lift his gloves, he ended it with a rubbery left uppercut and fell into the bag, his chest heaving as he hugged the stitched leather to retain his balance. "Bastards!" he yelled at the top of his lungs. In the comparative silence that followed, the chime of the front doorbell could be heard.

Ted Valmont frowned at the insistent ringing—someone was working the button like pinball flipper—and stumbled out of the room. The knob of the front door was hard to manipulate with his gloved hands, but after jiggling it ineffectually for several moments, he managed to pull it open. August Riordan stood on his porch with a stout Latino woman whose gray-streaked, iron-colored hair was pulled back in a tight bun. She wore a shapeless dress of rayon with black polka dots on a field of green, industrial strength hosiery of a too-dark brown and clunky shoes that needed polish. She smiled uncomfortably at the panting, half-naked young man who appeared before her.

Riordan grinned unabashedly. "Whoa," he said in mock surprise. "Been sparring a few rounds with a Campfire Girl?"

Ted Valmont brought a forearm up to wipe his cheek. "Shut up, Riordan," he said harshly. "Unless you want to go a few yourself."

Riordan arched his eyebrows. "Pretty feisty today, aren't we? Someone put Ben-Gay in your jock?"

"Lay off. What are you doing here?"

"I called your office repeatedly. First you were taking a day off, then the whole week. Pretty cushy for you."

"Cushy? I don't call being attacked by a suicide bomber cushy. My question stands. What are you doing here?"

Riordan gestured to the Latino woman. "Meet Mrs. Salaiz, formerly employed as a maid at the Appellation Inn. Since you were so keen on speaking to hotel staff, I thought I would bring her over here directly."

Ted Valmont pinned one glove under his arm and yanked out his hand. "Formerly employed?" he said in a disinterested tone. "Where'd you find her then?"

Riordan ran a broad tongue between his lower lip and teeth. "Look, Valmont, did you hire me or did I dream it? And weren't you the guy that wanted daily status reports? Why don't you show a little common courtesy here and ask us in?"

Ted Valmont blew air through his lips. He looked alternatively at Riordan and Mrs. Salaiz. "Sorry," he said resignedly. "It's been a bad week—a bad month. Nice to meet you Mrs. Salaiz. Please come in. I do appreciate your making the trip."

The maid nodded without speaking and Ted Valmont stepped clear of the doorway to let her enter. Riordan followed part way, but lingered at Ted Valmont's shoulder to say in a low tone, "By the way, you appreciate it so much you're giving her a hundred bucks—up front."

Ted Valmont acknowledged the comment with a quick nod, and while Riordan and Mrs. Salaiz got settled on his living room couch, excused himself and hurried out of the room. When he returned he was wearing a snazzy nylon warm-up and carried a business envelope in his hands. He passed the envelope to Mrs. Salaiz with the comment, "To thank you for your trouble," and fell in a modern looking chair of Italian design across from the couch.

Mrs. Salaiz glanced at the money in the envelope and then beamed at Ted Valmont. "Thank you very much, Mr. Valmont," she said in heavily accented English. "You are very generous."

Ted Valmont smiled back politely. "So, Mrs. Salaiz. If I may ask, where did you go after you left your job at the hotel?"

Mrs. Salaiz put the envelope in a pocket of her sturdy purse. She sat with the purse balanced on her lap, both hands griping the clasp. "My mother got sick. I went back to her house in San Jose to be with her. To help her get better."

"Oh," said Ted Valmont uncertainly. "I hope she is better now."

Mrs. Salaiz nodded eagerly. "Yes. She is."

Ted Valmont rubbed at his knuckles, which were reddened from the boxing. He scratched behind his ear and crossed his legs. An awkward silence permeated the room.

"So what's the program here, Riordan?" he said finally. "What's Mrs. Salaiz going to tell us?"

Riordan shrugged his heavy shoulders. "You're the one who wanted to interview the staff."

Annoyance flickered across Ted Valmont's face. He uncrossed his legs and leaned forward in his chair, looking at the Latino maid. "Mr. Riordan told you we were interested in one of the guests who stayed at the hotel?"

"Yes, he said you wanted to talk about a guest who stayed in room 304. Mr. Niebuhr. I cleaned his room."

"I see." Ted Valmont thought a long moment. "Did you...did you notice anything unusual among his belongings?"

A doubtful look came into Mrs. Salaiz's eyes. "Unusual?"

Ted Valmont leaned even further forward. "You know. Something you don't typically see in guests' rooms."

"I'm sorry, Mr. Valmont," said Mrs. Salaiz, shaking her head. "I don't know what you mean."

"How about a Palm computer, then," Ted Valmont said coaxingly. "Did you see a Palm computer in his room?"

Mrs. Salaiz hugged her purse to her chest. Her face took on the look of someone who doesn't want to disappoint. "I—I don't remember. Maybe there was a computer. There might have been one in a bag. I can't say for sure."

Ted Valmont squeezed his eyes shut with his fingers and lapsed back in his chair. He looked over at Riordan. "Okay, wise guy. I said to interview the staff. I didn't say to bring them over to my house one by one to waste my time."

Merriment came into Riordan's eyes. "Relax, chief. You were right and I was wrong. You just need to ask better questions." He addressed Mrs. Salaiz. "Did you happen to see Mr. Niebuhr with anyone else?"

Mrs. Salaiz smiled and nodded, relieved to be of help. "Oh, yes. One morning I came up to do the cleaning and I knocked on the door to see if anyone was there. Mr. Niebuhr, he opened the door.

He said to come in—that he was going. Then I saw another person. There was a young woman in the room with him."

"Do you remember what she looked like?" asked Riordan.

"Yes, I think so. She was thin. She had long hair that was red, not dark red. It was...*como se dice*...strawberry. Yes, it was strawberry. Mr. Niebuhr, I think he called her Gabby. When I came into the room, he said, 'Come on Gabby, let us go downstairs to the coffee shop.'"

A stupid look came over Ted Valmont's face. His head drooped forward. "Did she have dimples?" He brought his index fingers up to his cheeks. "You know, little places on her cheeks when she smiled?"

Mrs. Salaiz thought this over. "Yes, I think so. *Ella era muy bonita*. She was very pretty."

Ted Valmont tugged on his earlobe. He looked off to the corner of the room and then his gaze snapped back to Mrs. Salaiz. "Did she spend the night with Mr. Niebuhr?"

She avoided Ted Valmont's eyes. A tinge of pink was visible under her dark complexion. "I could not say. I thought she was a nice girl."

Riordan grunted and shifted on the couch. "Was her hair wet, Mrs. Salaiz?" he asked in no-nonsense tone. "Did the bed seem like it had been slept in by two people? Was she wearing clothing that was more appropriate for the evening?"

Her hands fluttered around her the back of her head, prodding nervously at the hairpins in her bun. "No, I do not think any of those things are true. She was wearing jeans and a shirt."

Riordan frowned and looked over at Ted Valmont, who seemed lost in thought. "So you know this girl, Valmont?"

The answer was a long time in coming. "Yes," he said slowly. "Yes, I think so."

"You think Niebuhr was having an affair with her then?"

Ted Valmont made no response.

"Hello," said Riordan loudly. "Somebody cut the telegraph wires to Fort Valmont? Dot-dot-dash-dash. Are you receiving?"

Ted Valmont cocked his head and looked at Riordan with an exasperated expression. "I don't know if Niebuhr was having an affair. I'm still not one hundred percent certain the girl is the person I'm thinking of. There's no reason for Niebuhr to know her, except that she happens to live in the Napa Valley."

Riordan stared at Ted Valmont for a moment and then pulled a cheap lighter out of his coat pocket. He flicked it idly, causing it to spark but not to light. "Okay, you don't know for certain it's her. But what does it mean if it is?"

Ted Valmont opened his mouth to answer, but before any words came out, there was a thud followed by a loud crash at the front of the room. The drapes on the front window billowed out as glass rained down on the carpet behind Ted Valmont's chair. A long, flesh-colored object tied to a stone flopped to a halt by his feet.

Mrs. Salaiz screamed something inarticulate in Spanish and wrapped her head in her arms. Ted Valmont flinched and dove forward to land under the coffee table. Only Riordan kept a measure of his equanimity. He flicked his lighter once more, surveyed the wreckage thoroughly and said:

"Must be one of those micro-climates you read about. It's hailing severed penises in Woodside."

"That's not the least little bit funny, Riordan," said Ted Valmont heatedly from his spot under the table. "Are you sure it's not a bomb?"

Riordan got up from the couch and crunched over broken glass to Ted Valmont's chair, where he snatched the flesh-colored object from the floor. It was a larger-than-life rubber penis, crudely painted with red finger nail polish at the base of the scrotum to simulate blood. Apart from the stone, a folded piece of yellow notepaper was affixed at its midpoint. Riordan pulled out the paper and opened it. "Penis-gram," he announced. "Penis-gram for Mr. Valmont."

As Ted Valmont backed out from under the table, cursing both the private detective and the broken glass, Riordan tucked the penis under one arm and stared down at the note. "I can't make this out. The letters are screwy."

Ted Valmont stood up, his face going from indignation to wonder to limited recognition as he took in the tableau. "It's Graffiti," he said slowly. "That's why."

Riordan glanced up to find Mrs. Salaiz gawking at the rubber phallus under his armpit and quickly released it to the floor. He cleared his throat. "What do you mean, graffiti? Like the stuff kids spray paint on walls?"

"No, not that. It's a simplified alphabet developed to make handwriting recognition easier on Palm computers."

Riordan frowned, and self-consciously wiped his hands on the front of his shirt. "What's the point of that?"

"To make clear that the person who sent the message knows high technology."

"Oh, sure. That and a rock through the window really screams high technology." Riordan shoved the paper under Ted Valmont's nose. "So can you read it?"

Ted Valmont looked down at the paper and raised his eyebrows. "I can, but it doesn't fit. It says, 'Leave her alone or this is what will happen to you.' I can't believe Maitland would do something this crude."

"Maitland? Who's Maitland?"

Ted Valmont shook his head noncommittally. He nudged Riordan in the direction of the couch and returned to his seat. "Maitland is some kind of big shot industrialist. He owns a winery up in Napa and I think the girl Mrs. Salaiz saw in Niebuhr's room is his niece, Gabrielle Maitland, but I need to be sure. See if you can find a photo of her in the files of the local paper. Maybe from a social event. Have Mrs. Salaiz look at the photo and confirm that Gabrielle was the woman she saw. If she is, I want you to check into her background and tell me all you can find out. Then I want anything you can dig up about her Uncle, Douglas. He ought to be easier."

"Okay," said Riordan skeptically. "But wouldn't it be better to talk with the niece and see if she knows Niebuhr? Find out if she knows where he is?"

"No," said Ted Valmont. "Don't approach either of them. That's important."

Riordan flicked his lighter impatiently. This time it lit and he blew out the flame with an angry burst of air. "Don't approach 'em. Check. You still want me to follow up with the conference attendees? See if someone else noticed Niebuhr with the girl—maybe heard them talking?"

"Yes, please do that, but start with the identification and background checks on the Maitland's."

Riordan leaned over to return the lighter to his jacket pocket. The butt of a gun flashed under his coat and he moved. He looked at Ted Valmont levelly. "You know, Valmont, it would be a heck of a lot better if you would give me some idea of what's going on. Just a few hints, like who's launching rubber dildos through your front window and how you know this girl. Things like that."

Ted Valmont's face became sullen and his eyes slid from Riordan's down to his necktie and from there to a spot on the wall beyond. "You're giving me too much credit. I'm afraid I have no idea what's going on. Just humor me and do what I ask."

Riordan regarded the younger man. "All right," he said in a calm, weary voice. "It won't be the first time I operated in the dark." He patted the area of couch between himself and Mrs. Salaiz. "Well,

Mrs. Salaiz, I think that's our cue. I'll take you back to your mother's house in San Jose."

Mrs. Salaiz looked from one man to the other. She licked her lips, nodded and stood up anxiously. She covered the ground from the couch to the front door in a near trot. Riordan followed with a more leisurely stride and Ted Valmont brought up the rear, head bowed, hands in pockets.

In the entryway, Riordan stopped and punched Ted Valmont lightly on the shoulder. He said, "Sorry I rode you so hard earlier. I'll be in touch. Take it easy now, okay?"

Ted Valmont nodded slightly. "Yeah, okay. Thanks."

Riordan exited and pulled the door closed. Over the sound of her heels clicking down the sidewalk, Mrs. Salaiz could be heard to say, "Oh, Mr. Riordan. What a terrible thing to do to nice Mr. Valmont. And do you think Gabrielle is his girlfriend? *Dios mio*, I hope not."

WHAT THE DETECTIVE DRAGGED IN

*"It's easy for the press to say that we spent $135 million on Concordes
and Champagne, but we only drink vodka."*
—Ernst Malmsten, co-founder of failed fashion e-tailer Boo.com

TED VALMONT PASSED OUT OF THE AUTOMATIC glass doors of
the Palo Alto Medical clinic to the sidewalk in front of the
building, gripping a small square of paper in his right hand. The
paper had been torn from the prescription pad of Dr. Geoffrey
Pettibone and bore a scribbled prescription for Zantac.

He was dressed casually—jeans, sweatshirt, DKNY baseball cap
and Nike tennis shoes—and the bandage above his eyebrow had
been replaced by a smaller butterfly closure. As he moved beyond
the jagged shadow projected by the tile roof, a loud hiss followed
by "Hey sailor" in a stage whisper emanated from the shrubbery to
the side of the entrance.

He wheeled to face August Riordan coming out from behind
an oleander bush with a thoroughly smug expression on his face.
"Seaman in the dick navy?" asked Riordan.

Ted Valmont frowned. "What are you babbling about?"

Riordan gestured at the baseball cap. "Dick Navy. That's what
DKNY stands for, right?"

"It's a designer brand, you moron."

"Oh," Riordan intoned, "my mistake."

Ted Valmont crammed the prescription into his hip pocket. "What the hell are you doing here?"

Riordan brought his hand from his side, balancing a gleaming black automatic in his palm. "Nothing much. Just stopping the owner of this from pumping a few rounds into your unappreciative hide."

Ted Valmont leaned forward to stare at the gun. "Is it loaded?"

Riordan closed his thick fingers around the automatic and deftly ejected the magazine. Sunlight glinted off the steel casings of the 9mm shells inside as Riordan waggled the full magazine under Ted Valmont's nose. "Oh yeah. It's loaded. But it's a French-made Beretta—a designer handgun, if you will—chocked full of French ammo. Maybe that doesn't scare you."

"You know damn well that Valmont is a French name—don't try to bait me. Besides, the French make the Exocet and that seems to work just fine. Now where'd you get the gun?"

Riordan grinned and slipped the magazine and automatic into the hip pockets of his suit coat. He nodded towards the parking structure. "Come on. I'll show you."

Riordan led a tortured path through scores of late model SUVs parked in compact-only parking spaces, down three flights of stairs to a dusty, dented Ford Galaxy on the basement level with three out of four of its hubcaps missing. There were no other cars or people in the area.

Ted Valmont dabbed at the dust on the faded paint of the trunk. "Bitchin' car. But I had you figured for a Camaro with mag wheels."

"Yeah, and I had you figured for a Vespa scooter with a pinwheel on the handlebars."

"Ferrari F355 Spider, actually—among others."

"Yeah, I know. Now can we skip the conspicuous consumption and get down to it? I trussed her up pretty well with duct tape before I locked her in the trunk, but there's no telling if she's worked loose since then. You better stand back."

Muffled shouting and a dull pounding that visibly rocked the heavy sedan issued from the trunk. Whoever was inside was apparently aware that others were nearby.

Ted Valmont gasped and jumped back from the car. "You don't mean to tell me you've got somebody locked inside there? That's kidnapping, Riordan."

Riordan seemed not to hear Ted Valmont. He pulled a heavy ring with over 20 keys from his pocket and sifted through them deliberately to find a silver, oval-shaped key with a well-worn Ford emblem.

"Are you listening to me? You can't go around hog-tying people and throwing them into your trunk."

Riordan jabbed at Ted Valmont with the trunk key. "If you don't like kidnapping, then maybe you'd prefer first degree murder."

Ted Valmont let his mouth drop open in a phony way and shook his head. "Just why are you so sure I was at risk?"

"That's easy. I've been following you around since you left your house this morning." Ted Valmont leaned forward to object, but Riordan cut him off. "Did you really think I was going let you steer me around by the nose without any idea of what you were up to? About half way between breakfast at Hobee's and your stop at the window repair place, I noticed someone else was following you: a young woman driving a Jeep. She stayed with you to the medical center and parked in the space next to your Jag. She was sitting in her car with the Beretta in her lap waiting for you to return when I surprised her."

Ted Valmont's eyes widened. "It's not the girl that we talked about last night? Gabrielle Maitland?"

Riordan jangled the key ring. "See for yourself." He jammed the key home, turned it sharply and drew back as the trunk yawned open.

Lying on the greasy, matted carpet of the trunk, her forehead blackened from contact with the nearly bald spare tire, was a shapely young woman with dark hair, dressed in black jeans and a clingy black tee shirt made of synthetic material. Her wrists and ankles were bound with duct tape and a strip of it covered her mouth. She squinted in the stark fluorescent light, shouted incomprehensibly through the tape and raised her feet to kick at Riordan.

Riordan dodged out of the way and reached down to place restraining hands on her hips and ankles. "Simmer down," he said through clenched teeth. Then, twisting back to address Ted Valmont, he said, "Anyone we know?"

Ted Valmont's face lost all expression. "It's Odile," he said dully. "Esme's girlfriend, Odile." Then, more sharply: "Get her out of there. Take off that tape."

Riordan scowled. "Odile. I've not heard one word about an Odile—or an Esme for that matter. And I don't think it's a good idea to ungag her. I know from experience."

"Take off the tape," repeated Ted Valmont doggedly.

"You would have it." Riordan lifted the struggling girl out of the trunk and sat her upright on the bumper. He took hold of the tape covering her mouth and yanked it off.

A loud, angry torrent of rapid-fire French erupted from the girl. Riordan ducked his head to one side and put a finger in his ear. Ted Valmont stood his ground, listening as she yelled and gestured with her bound hands for nearly a minute. Finally the exigencies of breathing and crying overcame her and she sagged forward with her elbows on her knees, sobbing.

Riordan put a steadying hand on her shoulder to keep her from toppling over. "Guess that cleared the air, huh? What'd she say?"

Ted Valmont pressed his lips together in a neutral expression. "The net-net is she's going to cut our balls off and feed them to her dog."

Riordan nodded. "Seems I get a lot of that. So she's the one who put the rubber novelty through your window last night?"

"Yes, and she also knocked over my mailbox and splashed my house with red paint."

Riordan put a foot on the Galaxy's bumper to pull a one-piece stainless steel knife from a rig on his ankle. He squatted down to cut the tape off the still sobbing girl. "Mind telling me why?"

Ted Valmont grimaced at the sight of the knife, but he made no comment. "She thinks I'm trying to steal her girlfriend," he said.

Odile brought her head up to stare at Ted Valmont with stricken, red-rimmed eyes. "You are trying to steal her," she said hoarsely. "You are."

Both knees popped as Riordan straightened up. "Hold out your hands, Odile," he said in a gravely gentle voice. Then, in a more business like tone, "So this has nothing to do with what you hired me for?"

Ted Valmont tugged on his ear and watched as the gleaming blade bit through the duct tape around Odile's wrists. "No, it doesn't. I thought so last night, but I was wrong."

Riordan returned the knife to the rig and took Odile by the elbow. "Think you can stand?"

Odile yanked her elbow away from Riordan's grasp and stumbled forward. Ted Valmont caught her under the arms and pulled her upright. She thanked him for his trouble by slapping him twice in quick succession. He blocked the third attempt and said something low in French. When she failed to respond, he spoke more French to her, emphasizing his words with a shake of her shoulders.

She shrugged out of his grasp and stood defiantly just out of reach. "Why should I believe you?"

Ted Valmont turned his palms out in an appeasing gesture. "Because it's true. Look—I promise to stay away from Esme, but you've got to stop harassing me. There's nothing to be gained by it except trouble. Come have coffee with me. We'll talk it through."

Odile looked down to pick at the duct tape on her wrists. "Maybe," she said sullenly.

"Okay, Riordan," said Ted Valmont. "Odile and I are going to work this out. I appreciate your help, but I need you looking into the items we discussed last night."

Riordan reached over to the Galaxy trunk and slammed it shut. A heavy whump reverberated through the garage. "Are you sure about that? Don't forget she had a loaded gun."

"I'm sure. What I need to know now is whether the girl with Warren Niebuhr was really Gabrielle Maitland."

Riordan looked at Ted Valmont and then at Odile and then back to Ted Valmont. He shook his head. "What a life, Valmont. I really do hope you know what you're doing."

Ted Valmont and Odile stood to one side as Riordan got into the Galaxy and backed it out of the parking space. They watched while he rumbled up the exit ramp and then rode the elevator together to street level, where they walked to the corner Starbucks.

OAK TREE RENDEZVOUS

"It's unbelievable how many cars I got from that lot—100 cars easily."
—James Kevern, Silicon Valley Repo Man, commenting on the headquarters for Apple Computer, Inc.

T HE CLOCK ON TED VALMONT'S JAGUAR SHOWED 8:20 pm. The car was parked on the side of a country road that bordered the Maitland estate. In the front seat, Ted Valmont said, "Replay message."

August Riordan's deep bass worked the subwoofers of the car's stereo system. "That's the girl, chum," he reported simply. "Mrs. Salaiz picked her out of a photo from a winery opening. I'm going to start digging into the family background. I'll keep you posted."

Ted Valmont switched off the ignition and hoisted himself out of the low-slung seat. The sun had sunk behind the Mayacamas Mountains, and while there was still a faint glow of dusky light, crickets in a nearby culvert had already begun their nightly chorus of chirping. Ted Valmont wandered down the side of the road, his eyes on the cluster of buildings that made up the Maitland residence, more than a half mile away. After glancing about to ensure he was not observed, he stepped briskly off the shoulder and into the adjoining field. He ducked between the strands of a barbed wire fence and jogged to the cover provided by a trio of gnarled, aging oak. He dodged through the trees—spooking a rabbit from the mouth of its burrow—and came into the open again for a fifty yard run to the edge of the vineyards surrounding the main house.

Bending forward to stay below the tangle of grape-laden vines, he followed a zigzag course up a row, down a tractor path and finally up another row and into the front yard. He sprinted around the side of the house and down the flagstone path that led to Gabrielle Maitland's cottage. Bounding onto the porch, he knocked urgently on the door. There was no answer. He tried the knob, but found it locked. All that could be seen through the window was the darkened sitting room with no hint of light or activity in the bedroom beyond.

The sound of a barking dog caused him to sink down against the singled wall of the cottage. Resting on his haunches on the dark porch, his breath came in a shallow pant and sweat ran down the side of his face. His hand shook as he wiped at it. He looked across the yard in the direction he had come. Lights were burning in the rear of the main house—and less than a hundred yards to the left—in the window of a low cabana that was situated between the tennis court and pool.

As the barking of the dog subsided, another sound became audible. The nasally, New York-accented voice of Donald Fagan drifted out from the cabana, chanting as much as singing the lyrics of Steely Dan's "Two Against Nature." Ted Valmont glanced at his watch and then back at the cabana. He stood up, crept down the wooden porch steps, ran over the open ground, across the concrete decking that surrounded the tennis court and up to the back of the cabana. The sound of the music was louder here, and light streamed from a window just above eye level. He searched for something to stand on, and eventually took a folded wooden chair from where it rested against one of the posts of the tennis net. Setting the chair beneath the window, he inched himself up to peer over the ledge.

The room he looked into ran the full length of the building. Pool toys and chemicals were stacked in one corner, but the majority of the space was taken by exercise equipment of various types, including free weights, a treadmill and a stationary bicycle. Donald Fagan's voice issued from an oversized boom box in the middle of the floor. Next to that, working a flossy new rowing machine in time to the music, was Gabrielle Maitland. She wore tight, black shorts made of Lycra that ended at mid-thigh and an abbreviated Lycra top that showed her sinewy back and midriff to good advantage. Her hair was pulled back in a ponytail.

She rowed at a blistering pace with almost mechanical precision. Her breath came like the huffing of a steam locomotive and her ponytail described a wild arc as she exploded from a contracted to an extended position again and again. Ted Valmont watched with an awed expression as she continued the performance through the remainder of the CD and many minutes beyond. Finally, with no sign of fatigue or even recognition of the effort she had expended, she abruptly stopped rowing—and after struggling to disentangle her feet from the rowing machine—rose crisply and walked to a stand of weights. There she rubbed herself vigorously with a towel and picked up a pair of thirty-pound dumbbells.

She carried them to the far wall, and with her back flat against it, began to do curls. Once again, her form was flawless, and even as her biceps bulged hugely from the increased flow of blood, she showed no signs of tiring or slowing down. Ted Valmont silently mouthed a count of repetitions. Somewhere around forty, he stopped counting and brought his hand to his mouth, benumbed.

Then something changed. As Gabrielle curled her left arm to her shoulder, it trembled violently. She let the arm fall, hammering her thigh with the weight, and attempted to bring up her right. It, too, began to spasm. The dumbbell slipped from her grasp to the floor, where it hit her foot on the second bounce. She gave this no notice, but extended her still trembling arm to stare at it coldly—as if it had failed her. She jettisoned the other dumbbell in disgust and returned to the weight stand to use the towel once more.

Her next stop was a mat in front of the sliding glass door that opened out on the pool. She lay on the mat with her legs extended and began to do sit-ups. These were executed with the same degree of precision and tirelessness, but given his vantage point at the window, Ted Valmont had to stand on his tiptoes to see her. He watched from the awkward perch for a long time—longer even than the rowing had lasted—then said aloud, "What the hell?" and jumped off the chair.

He stumbled around the back of the dark cabana and up to the well-lit entrance, where he jerked open the sliding glass door. Although he was less than three feet from her, Gabrielle did not stop or turn her head until after he had called her name. Even then, she spared him only a darting glance, and continued through several more sit-ups before finally relaxing onto the floor—like a watch winding down. "Ted," she said at last, twisting around to look at him. "What are you doing here?"

Ted Valmont opened his mouth to respond, then bit back his words. He looked at her with a bewildered expression and got down on his haunches. "I came to see you," he said finally. "I was worried about you. It seems silly to ask this now, but are you all right? I want to understand what happened in San Francisco."

Gabrielle reddened under his gaze. She looked down at the mat. "I'm fine," she said quietly. "I shouldn't have drunk the wine at the restaurant." She reached up for his hand. "And you shouldn't be here. My uncle doesn't want me to see you anymore. He blames you for everything."

Ted Valmont took her hand in both of his. "He's got plenty to account for himself. Just what was going on when you called me that night?"

Gabrielle pressed her lips together. A worried look came into her eye. "Don't be concerned about it. I was confused." She squeezed his hand. "Now please go. You could get into trouble being here. They can see you from the house if they happen to look out."

He shook his head angrily. "I don't give a damn about that. And I have to ask you something. You were seen with a friend of mine at a conference in Yountville several weeks back. His name is Warren Niebuhr. He's missing and I need to find him."

Gabrielle's face took on an unsettled appearance. She struggled to smooth her features into an impassive expression, but her eyes betrayed her: there was a twitchy look of suppressed fear in them. "Yes, I—I did meet a guy named Warren in Yountville. I had dinner with some friends at the California Cafe and he was having a drink at the bar. He was such an odd, lonely-looking guy that we took pity on him and invited him over to our table. He turned out to be very funny in an off-beat sort of way." She pulled her hand out from between Ted Valmont's and sat up. "Not that I was really interested in him. I mean, he was married and all—and he's nothing like my type. Besides, that was before I met you."

Ted Valmont drew in a ragged breath and stood up. He crossed arms under his chest and stared pensively at Gabrielle. "Setting aside whether Warren's your type and exactly what your interest was, what did you two talk about? Do you have any idea of where he went?"

"Ted, please. It was all very silly and innocent. We talked—" Gabrielle stopped suddenly and her eyes went wide. Douglas Maitland and Ramos appeared behind Ted Valmont on the patio of the cabana.

"You've crossed the line now, Valmont," Maitland almost shouted.

Ted Valmont spun on his heel and tried to say something, but Maitland gave him no opening. "Shut up," said Maitland, and slammed his palm against the glass of the sliding door. It made a terrific whack and rattled the door to its rollers. "You're trespassing.

I'll ask you to leave immediately—immediately!" He turned to Ramos. "Get him out of here."

Ramos came up to Ted Valmont and grabbed him roughly by the arm, just beneath the shoulder. Ted Valmont tried to shrug him off, but Ramos only laughed, tightened his grip and took a fistful of Ted Valmont's shirt with his other hand. "Go ahead, *pendejo*. I'd love to pound the crap out of you in front of *la Señorita*."

Gabrielle gave a strangled cry. "No, don't. Ted, please go. It's better for everyone."

Ted Valmont turned to look at Gabrielle, but said nothing. A beat went by, and then Ramos yanked him forward by the shirt. Ted Valmont stumbled into a slow walk and let Ramos escort him around the pool, off the decking and onto the lawn between the main house and Gabrielle's cottage. As he went from Gabrielle's view—still without saying a word—she called out to him, "I'm sorry, Ted. Don't be angry with me. It's not like it seems."

Ramos chuckled at this and imitated Gabrielle in a high wavering voice, "Oh, Teddy, it's not like it seems. I only slept with your buddy Warren a couple of times."

Ted Valmont froze in his tracks and then turned on Ramos to launch a wide, looping punch at his head. The shorter man ducked it easily—white teeth flashing as he bobbed out of the way—and pushed Ted Valmont headlong onto the grass. As Ted Valmont struggled to his feet, Ramos reached round his back and pulled an automatic pistol from under his waistband. He shoved the gun into Ted Valmont's side. "I'm tired of pulling and pushing. Now, I'm just gonna steer."

"Wait a minute," said Ted Valmont in a strained voice. "You don't need that. I'm going."

"Going's not good enough. You had your chance to go yesterday, but you bounced right back. Now we got to have some—what they call it—negative reinforcement. We need a little trip to the barn."

"What's that supposed—"

"Shut up." Ramos slapped Ted Valmont on the side of the head. "Not another fucking word out of you."

Ted Valmont and Ramos came around the side of the main house and walked across the front lawn in the direction of the tractor barn. Ramos pushed Ted Valmont down a dark row of the surrounding vineyard and then guided him up the path that led to the building. A single floodlight shone from the apex of the roof, illuminating the yard with a cone of yellow light. Two Hispanic men stood in negligent poses under the light, smoking cigarettes and talking in low tones. One was older—thirty-five going on fifty—with a thin white scar down the middle of his nose and a long tuft of curling beard below his lower lip. The other was in his early twenties, had a tattoo of crimson flames on the side of his neck and was missing his left earlobe.

"*Escuche, zurramatos,*" said Ramos to the men. "*Vengan aquí y tomen sus brazos.*"

The men stubbed out their cigarettes on the soles of their shoes and came up to Ted Valmont and took him by the arms. They wrestled him to a spot in the middle of the yard. Ramos stepped back and put his gun down on a pair of sawhorses that were stacked nearby. Whistling a Mexican folk tune between his front teeth, he casually and unhurriedly rolled up the sleeves of his denim shirt. His wrists and hairless forearms looked enormous in the harsh light. Moths and other insects flitted about in a tight circle above the men, casting fluttery shadows over the ground and the men's hard faces. The faint noise of cars on the Silverado Trail—more than two miles away—was the only other human sound to be heard in the night.

Ramos hooked his finger under the tight roll of fabric on each arm and tugged on it in satisfied way. "Hey Valmont," he said genially. "You wanna know something funny? My little brother—he got a bad case of mono last year. You know, the kissing disease. Anyway, the interesting thing is it busted his spleen." Ramos came up less than a foot away. He leaned into Ted Valmont's face. "Imagine that. Somebody kissed him and it ruptured his spleen."

Without warning, Ramos drove his left fist into Ted Valmont's abdomen—just under his heart. Ted Valmont expelled two lungs full of air and crumpled back. Ramos immediately followed with a right uppercut that had even more weight behind it. The punch burrowed into Ted Valmont's gut and bent him in half. Ted Valmont sagged to his knees and made a retching noise. Ramos laughed and said, *"Bésame mucho, maricon."* He gestured for the other men to pull Ted Valmont back up.

Ramos took a mincing step forward and kicked Ted Valmont between the legs. Ted Valmont's piercing yell startled the men holding him. He strained to double over again, but they held him bolt upright, his chest bent forward like a sail. Ramos did not linger over more taunting remarks, but instead waded directly into Ted Valmont's mid-section with his head down and both arms working. Uppercut after uppercut connected with groin, stomach and chest. An expression of unmitigated agony formed on Ted Valmont's features and his skin took on a look of clammy, fissured marble.

At the beginning, the fall of each blow was punctuated with a stifled groan, but over time Ted Valmont ceased even to make a distinct noise. A steady, low-toned whimpering was all he could manage. Presently even this stopped and it became apparent from the lack of sound and the heavy sag of Ted Valmont's body that Ramos was beating an unconscious man.

The older man with the scarred nose yelled harsh Spanish at Ramos. Ramos slowed, took a final punishing shot at Ted Valmont's mid-section and staggered off to one side, reeling from the exertion. As the men sluiced Ted Valmont onto the ground like so much boiled spaghetti, Ramos reached a blue bandana out of his pocket and slowly mopped his face, hands and beefy arms.

"Jesus, Ramos," said the man with the tattoo, "I think you croaked him."

"Relax," said Ramos in a winded voice. "I massaged his spleen pretty good, but I didn't croak him. Go put the wagon on the John Deere and bring it out to the yard. Get Luis to help you. And Mario—" Ramos paused.

"What?" said the tattooed man.

"Let's have a bottle of that shit tequila I know you've got hidden in there."

Mario nodded and tugged on the shirt of the man Ramos had referred to as Luis. "*Vayamos. Alonso dice conseguir el alimentador.*"

Still breathing heavily, Ramos stood and watched as they went into the barn. He began a meandering pacing around the yard, but checked up suddenly when his eyes came to rest on Ted Valmont. He strode back to where he lay and turned him on his hip to extract his wallet. Tapered fingers with surprisingly well-manicured nails helped five hundred dollars in cash find its way from the wallet to Ramos's pocket. Ted Valmont's silver watch soon followed.

Ramos had pulled off one of Ted Valmont's expensive Italian shoes and was holding it up in the dim light to read the size marking when the sound of a tractor coughing to life rent the night air. He threw down the shoe and jogged over to the double barn doors where he helped Mario swing them full open.

Luis drove a dusty, green and yellow John Deere farm tractor into the yard, pulling a long wagon behind it. Ramos and Mario picked up Ted Valmont by the arms and legs and hefted him into the back of the wagon, setting him down none too gently among the smudge pots and reels of bailing wire that were already piled there.

Mario jumped onto the back of the wagon and Ramos stood on the rear axle behind the driver's seat to direct Luis on the ten-minute trip to the road where Ted Valmont had parked. When the light from the single tractor headlamp fell on the Jaguar, Ramos signaled Luis to stop.

He went around to the back of the wagon and pulled on Ted Valmont's legs. As his pockets came within range, Ramos reached into one of them and fished out the keys for the sports car. He tossed them to Mario. "Go pull the wires on the air bag. Teddy's taking a little drive."

When Mario returned from his errand under the Jaguar's dashboard, he and Ramos carried Ted Valmont over to the car and tried to shoehorn him behind the wheel. The low, narrow opening taken in combination with Ted Valmont's limp body made the going difficult, prompting Luis to laugh at their clumsy efforts. Ramos bristled and dropped Ted Valmont's shoulders, leaving him sprawled across the seat with his arms and upper torso hanging out the door.

"Fuck you, Luis," Ramos said loudly. "Come down off there and give us a hand." When Luis did nothing but stare back with a blank expression, Ramos yelled, "*Venga aquí, pelotudo!*"

Luis stiffened and jumped off the tractor. He and Mario grabbed handfuls of Ted Valmont's shirt and jerked him upright. While Luis pinned him to the back of the seat, Mario pulled the seat belt across his chest and snapped it closed. Ted Valmont lolled against the seat belt like a crash test dummy.

Ramos jogged back to the tractor to get Mario's bottle of tequila. He bulled Mario and Luis aside, and shook the bottle over Ted Valmont's pants, shirt and head like he was sprinkling water over a basket of laundry about to be ironed. When he was satisfied with the soaking, he threw the bottle onto the floor of the passenger seat and took hold of Ted Valmont's hair. He slammed his face into the steering wheel—then slammed it again.

Blood flowed out Ted Valmont's nostrils and a bright red welt formed immediately on the bridge of his nose. Ramos barked a short, derisive laugh. He turned to Mario. "Gimme the keys."

Mario passed the keys over to Ramos, who shoved them into the ignition. He reached his leg over Ted Valmont's body to the gas pedal and pumped it while turning the starter. The car jumped to life immediately and ran with a smooth idle. Ramos withdrew his leg and slapped Luis on the shoulder. He leered at him. *"Escœcheme, Luis. Entre en el coche y lo maneja hacia los robles. El salto fuera antes golpea."*

Luis frowned and inclined his head away from Ramos. *"No mames,"* he said.

"Hígalo," Ramos commanded.

Luis shook his head and mumbled to himself. He walked up to the car door, and using the electric gizmo, ran the driver's seat as far back as it would go. Then he gingerly lowered himself on top of Ted Valmont's legs. He put the car in gear and drove it straight toward the trio of oak—the door flopping open like a broken wing. The car hit the barbed wire fence between two posts and pulled both down, dragging a length of wire and one of the posts as it gathered speed on the open field. About ten yards from the nearest tree, Luis rolled out of the car leaving it to pile head on into the oak. Though he had done nothing to stick the throttle in place, the momentum of the car was enough to hold the speed at nearly thirty miles per hour when it hit. The collision killed the motor and badly damaged the front fender. The hood was crumpled open.

Luis brushed himself off and walked up to the wrecked car, where he used the electric gizmo to move the seat forward once more. Ted Valmont had been spared further injury from the extreme rear position of the seat, but his breathing through his injured nose was labored and a pool of blood had formed in his lap. Luis slammed the door shut on him and jogged back to the edge of the field where Mario and Ramos waited.

"What do you want to bet," said Ramos, laughing. "He's more pissed about the car than the rest of it."

HOSPITAL HANGOVER

"Like many Americans, I was disgusted with the way retired politicians—even presidents—cashed in on their celebrity status."
—Former Surgeon General C. Everett Koop, Chairman, drkoop.com

A PETITE NURSE ADJUSTED THE DRIP ON TED Valmont's IV. Her hip brushed his arm as she turned and he grumbled in response. His eyes fluttered open. There was tape covering his nose and his left cheek was badly bruised.

"Where am I?" he asked.

The nurse smiled down at him. She had a kewpie doll hair cut, dainty features and tiny, porcelain teeth. Kitty Flynn was printed on her name badge. "This is Valley Hospital," she said gently. "You were in a car accident."

Ted Valmont tried to lift his head. He grimaced horribly and slumped back on the pillow. "The hell I was," he rasped. "Get me Bruce Crane of Val du Grue Vineyards."

"I'm sorry," said the nurse. "Visitors come later. Right now you need your rest."

She went to the window and turned the Lucite rod that controlled the blinds, darkening the room. She pulled the door shut against the pneumatic closer.

When Ted Valmont next woke up there was a basket of fruit on the nightstand. He rang for the nurse. She came quickly into the room, a concerned look spilling over her delicate features.

"Are you having trouble with the catheter, Mr. Valmont?"

"No," said Ted Valmont irritably. "I mean, yes, of course I am. Does anyone not have trouble with the catheter?"

The nurse suppressed a grin. "No, I suppose not. Was there something else then?"

This seemed to take Ted Valmont by surprise. "What time is it?" he asked finally.

Nurse Flynn glanced down at her brightly colored plastic watch. "It's a little past five—in the afternoon. You can have some dinner soon if you're hungry."

"That'd be swell. I'll take some compacted sawdust in the shape of a Salisbury steak and overcooked vegetables with freezer burn. Oh, and gelatinous pudding with unidentified lumpy masses in the middle if you have it."

The little nurse crossed her arms under her chest. "If you think you're the first to make jokes about the food, you're wrong. It's actually quite good. I ought to know, I eat two meals of it every day."

"I'll bet that disqualifies you from the organ donor program."

"Please, Mr. Valmont. That's not a joking matter." She uncrossed her arms and tugged at the bed sheets. "While I'm glad you're feeling well enough to be rude, I do have other patients. Anything else?"

Ted Valmont brought a hand up to his forehead and closed his eyes. "I'm sorry. Who's the gift basket from?"

"It's from your friend—the one you mentioned before—Bruce Crane. He came by earlier. He said he'll be back this evening."

"And did you tell me that I was in a car accident—or did I hallucinate it?"

"You didn't hallucinate it. You're a very lucky young man. The air bag on your car failed, but you weren't hurt as seriously as you might have been. It's a good thing you were wearing your seat belt."

Ted Valmont took his hand off his forehead and scowled. "It feels plenty bad enough as it is, believe me. But who exactly says I was in a car accident?"

The nurse leaned over and pulled a quartered newspaper from a shelf in the nightstand. "Here," she said. "Your friend Bruce left this."

Ted Valmont took the paper and held it close to his face with a trembling hand. He squinted at the newsprint for a moment, then let his hand fall to the covers and blew out his breath. "Would you read it for me please? I can't seem to focus right now."

The nurse pursed her lips and retrieved the paper. "I'm sorry. Maybe this should wait until later. I shouldn't have suggested it."

"Just read it, will you?" Ted Valmont said hotly.

Kitty Flynn flinched, then read in a contrite voice, "Prominent Silicon Valley entrepreneur and venture capitalist Edward Valmont was involved in an early morning automobile accident near the Silverado Trail, Napa County Sheriff's deputies reported today. Valmont apparently lost control of his car, ran off the road and struck an oak tree in an adjoining field. He was discovered unconscious by a jogger at around 6:45 this morning. Valmont sustained moderate injuries and is resting comfortably in Valley Hospital in stable condition. Although the Sheriff's office refused to officially confirm the reports, unnamed sources in the department have suggested that alcohol was a contributing cause for the accident. Deputy Norman Olken said—"

"Enough," Ted Valmont snapped. "That's one hundred percent pure bullshit. I was not drinking and I did not have an accident. I was beaten up."

The nurse nodded slightly and returned the paper to the nightstand. She started to say something more, but stopped herself.

"What?" said Ted Valmont. "What were you going to say?"

"Don't be mad at me, but your car is wrecked. John Hibbert called to say that they towed it to his body shop. The whole front end is ruined. And when you came in…well, you definitely smelled of some kind of liquor. You'll see when you take your clothes out to go home."

Ted Valmont stared up at the ceiling and let out a long sigh. "Fine. Have it your way. Leave me alone now. And don't bother with any of the great tasting hospital food, either."

The nurse clicked her tongue and left the room. She poked her head back in twenty minutes later, but found Ted Valmont staring at the ceiling in almost exactly the same position.

When Bruce Crane came through the door at a little after seven, Ted Valmont's eyes were closed. The bruise on his cheek seemed to have darkened. Crane shook his shoulder lightly and said, "Hey boss, it's me."

Ted Valmont opened his eyes and gave Crane a weak grin. "Thanks for the fruit basket," he said softly.

"It was that or a potted plant," said Crane smiling back. "I told them there was no way I was sending flowers to a man. How are you doing?"

"I guess I'm okay, considering."

Crane nodded. "You've sure been through the mill lately. I didn't think those air bags ever failed. Went off when they weren't supposed to maybe, but never fail to go off when they were."

"This isn't about air bags failing," said Ted Valmont. "I snuck over to Maitland's house to see Gabrielle, and Maitland and his foreman Ramos caught me. Ramos and two other farm hands beat the living crap out of me. They must have dumped me in my car when they were done and faked an accident."

Worry mixed with skepticism shown in Crane's mien. He said nothing.

"You don't believe me, do you?"

Crane cleared his throat. "Well, Ted, it does seem a little far-fetched. Maybe with the head injury, you've got things a little confused. Maybe you started over there after you'd had a few to drink and you ran off the road and hit the tree. You were found not far from the property. Maybe that's the way it happened."

"For the love of God, Bruce. If you don't believe me, who the hell will? I did not have anything to drink last night. Did they do a blood test? There couldn't have been anything in my system."

"Yes, Ted," said Crane patiently. "They did do a blood test, but it wasn't until the morning after the accident. It was too late to show any booze in your system. But your clothes were absolutely reeking of tequila." Crane paused, then went on with a forced cheerfulness, "The good news is the cops don't have much evidence for bringing drunk driving charges. You've got to be thankful for that."

"That's like being thankful when your family picks a tasteful casket for your funeral," said Ted Valmont. He squeezed his eyes shut. "Buzz off, Bruce. We can talk in the morning."

The next morning Ted Valmont yanked all the tubes and wires out of his body and got out of bed to hobble to the bathroom. He shivered when he saw his bruised and disheveled reflection in the mirror, splashed water on his face and then pushed up his nose with a finger in an unappetizing attempt to see into his damaged nostrils.

Back in the main room, he found two arrangements of flowers: one from Basis Ventures and another from Gabrielle Maitland. He sat on the edge of the bed and tried to read the nearly indecipherable handwriting on the card from Gabrielle. Phrases such as "sorry about the accident" and "don't see me again" were legible, but it was impossible to decode the message in its entirety. He tore up the card and threw down the pieces in disgust.

It was then that the door to the room pulled open. Deputy Norman Olken stepped through carrying a manila folder and a clipboard. He looked down at the floor and then back at Ted Valmont. "Hello, Mr. Valmont," he said neutrally. "Is now a good time to talk?"

"Don't let them kid you," said Ted Valmont. "Those Hallmark people do not have the perfect card for every occasion."

Olken nodded and said, "I hadn't considered it," in a tone that suggested he wasn't going to consider it now. "I came by to complete the accident report. Your friend Bruce Crane tells me that you are a little confused about what happened."

Ted Valmont reached over his shoulder and yanked on the fabric of his hospital gown. He pulled it down across his chest and abdomen, revealing a welter of dark, greenish tinged bruises. "Does that look something you'd get from an automobile accident?" he demanded. "Aren't those the marks of a beating?"

Olken shifted the folder and clipboard in his hands. "I'm sorry. Those are exactly the kinds of marks you get in a car accident. I've seen it plenty of times. And there's no question your face went into the steering wheel because your blood's all over it." He paused, softening his expression. "Look, I realize you've had a rough time lately...the thing in Woodside...the situation with Niebuhr. But I know Douglas Maitland. He's a respected man around here."

Ted Valmont pulled on his gown self-consciously. "What am I? Phylloxera blight? I've been in the Valley longer than he has."

Olken frowned. "You're missing the point. Mr. Crane gave me your version of events, and I'm telling you it just isn't credible—regardless of how long you've been in the Valley. The way it stands now, the Sheriff will turn a blind eye to the drinking aspect of the accident, but if you start making false charges about Mr. Maitland he's gonna come down on you like a ton a bricks."

"I can prove—"

Olken cut him off. "How far do I have to spell it out for you? I'll give you one more hint. Who do you think served as chairman of the Sheriff's re-election campaign? It wasn't you, Mr. Valmont."

Ted Valmont took a moment to absorb this. He opened his mouth to speak, but before any words came out, August Riordan poked his head through the doorway behind Olken. Riordan held his finger to his lips and then mouthed the words, "lose him."

Ted Valmont frowned and closed his mouth. He licked his lips. "So," he said in a calmer tone, "if I go along with the accident story, you're saying the Sheriff will let things lay?"

"That's about the size of it."

Ted Valmont ran his hand through his hair. "All right."

Olken nodded and dug the edge of the clipboard into his gut. He took a pen from his breast pocket and made a notation on the attached form. "Then your official statement is that you lost control of your car and hit the tree?"

"Yes, but I wasn't drinking. I don't want any mention of drinking in the report."

"Check. You weren't drinking. That's the way I'll file it." Olken wrote some more and then passed the clipboard and pen over to Ted Valmont. "Sign at the 'X' at the bottom, please."

Glancing quickly over the form, Ted Valmont scrawled a hasty signature at the bottom and passed it back to Olken.

"Just a couple more things," said the deputy, clasping his hands behind his back as if he were standing at parade rest. "Do you know anyone who fits this description: male, around six feet tall, approximately forty years of age, facial scar, brown hair, heavy build, heavy features—possibly had his nose broken?"

Ted Valmont reached up to lightly touch his own damaged nose. "You don't mean me, right? None of that fits except the last part."

Olken snorted. "No, I don't mean you. This is someone we want to question about the Niebuhr doings."

"The answer to your question is no. I don't know anyone like that. But I didn't think you were investigating Niebuhr's disappearance any longer."

Olken shifted his weight a little awkwardly. "We're not. Apparently this guy—well, apparently this guy has been asking around about Niebuhr and I was curious if you knew him."

Ted Valmont pushed his head further back into the pillow. "Nope, I don't. What was the other thing?"

Olken brought a hand out from behind his back and rested it on his gun holster. The leather made a creaking sound. "Not to put too fine a point on it, I think after you get out of the hospital you would do well to stay out of the Valley for a while. I think you should stick to the high tech world down south. You understand, Mr. Valmont?"

"Is that you, the Sheriff or Douglas Maitland talking?"

"Does it matter? I think it would be best for all concerned."

Ted Valmont set his teeth on edge and stared into Olken's face. "Whatever," he said sullenly. "I'll lay low for a while. I'd like to get a little rest now. Is that it?"

"Yes, that's it." Olken scrunched up one side of his face while thoughtfully scratching his ear. "I hope you feel better," he said and went out of the room.

Less than two minutes later, while Ted Valmont was squatting down to pick up the pieces of Gabrielle's card, August Riordan and Chris Duckworth sauntered in.

MAITLAND FAMILY TREE

"We believe we are well positioned as our customers...continue [to] express themselves and connect with all of the important people in their lives."
—Jim McCann, CEO, 1-800-Flowers.com, commenting on the uptick in flower sales after the September 11th attack

"YOU LOOK LIKE SHIT," SAID RIORDAN by way of greeting. He held up a vase of flowers with another card attached. "We picked these up at the nurses' station for you."

Ted Valmont stood up quickly, trying in vain to keep his hospital gown from falling down at the shoulder where he had ripped it. "Put it over there with the others," he said testily. "What's with the pantomime in the hallway? Why didn't you want Olken to see you?"

Riordan advanced into the room and dropped into a chair beside the bed. Duckworth hovered in the space between Ted Valmont and the door, looking pale and concerned.

While the other men weren't looking, Riordan palmed the card from its plastic holder, then set the vase on the nightstand. "I usually make it a policy to avoid cops," he said, settling back in his chair. "That's the generic answer. As for that Deputy—what's his name, Olken—I think the people at the Appellation Inn might have got a little miffed with my questions about Niebuhr and all. I had to get a little heavy-handed with one assistant manager in particular."

Ted Valmont dumped the scraps from Gabrielle's correspondence on the nightstand and lowered himself with a grimace onto the edge of the bed. He yanked some of the bedding over to cover his legs. "No one's going to accuse you of having a light touch—that's for sure. Did you come out of the goodness of your heart or do you have something to report? And what's he doing here?" Ted Valmont gestured at Duckworth.

"We've both got stuff to tell you," said Riordan. "Go ahead, Chris."

Duckworth walked over to the IV at the side of the bed and picked up the dangling tubing. "I'm sorry you got hurt, Ted," he said in a subdued voice. "Please tell me you didn't take this out on your own. It's very important for trauma patients to avoid dehydration."

Riordan let out an exasperated growl. "Can it, Chris. Just tell him your news and stop playing Florence Nightingale."

Duckworth blushed. "All right, then," he said and went over to sit in a chair by Riordan. "Do you remember the first time you came to talk to me we discovered that e-mail in Warren Niebuhr's account had been read—and some of it possibly deleted?"

"Sure," said Ted Valmont. "I remember."

"You might also remember that I hoped I could go to the mail server logs and see what pieces of e-mail were delivered to him. Then, by looking at the list of deliveries and comparing it to what remained in the account, I would be able to tell if anything had been deleted."

Ted Valmont wrinkled his forehead. "Yeah, yeah I remember all that, but I thought you told me you disabled network access for all the employees that were let go—yourself included."

Duckworth straightened in his chair and smiled enormously. "Well, I might have left one or two little loopholes in the network security to wriggle through." He moved his hips sinuously. "Anyway, the important thing is what I found out. There were definitely messages delivered to Warren Niebuhr that have been deleted. At least five that I counted. And I can tell you who sent them—or at least the e-mail address of the person who sent them."

Ted Valmont inclined his head. "I'm waiting."

"All five messages came from lbreen@basisventures.com. That's the address for Larry Breen, isn't it? Isn't he one of the partners at your firm?"

"He's the freaking managing partner at the firm. What the hell would he be writing Warren for?"

Duckworth brought his knees together and rubbed his hands up and down his thighs. "I'm afraid I can't tell you. I only know that they were received and who sent them."

Ted Valmont waved his hand. "That was a rhetorical question. I just don't understand why Larry would write Warren...unless he was trying to figure out if it was time to pull the plug on NeuroStimix. Or maybe he told Warren he was pulling the plug and that sent Warren into his tailspin." Ted Valmont slapped the bed covers. "Damn it. You're certain there's no way to get those e-mails back?"

"Yes, I'm sure. The mail itself was deleted and all the back-ups were erased like I said before. It just so happens that whoever did the sabotage forgot about the mail server logs. It would be easy to do—they only record the fact that messages have been sent or received. They don't keep the actual text. But that reminds me: the logs also show that Niebuhr wrote back to Breen. They must have exchanged a number of e-mails."

"And something about that correspondence was important enough that Warren felt like he had to go back and delete the messages. Assuming it was Warren who did that and all the other sabotage."

Duckworth squeezed his kneecaps and studied the tips of his well-manicured fingers. "The engineers at NeuroStimix think he knew about the upcoming layoffs and about Basis not giving us the next round of funding. They think he did the sabotage out of revenge."

While the other two were talking, Riordan had discreetly opened the envelope from the vase of flowers. Now he held up the card and waved it at Ted Valmont. "I don't believe it. You got flowers and a gushy 'get well soon' note from that French lesbian who was going to cut your nuts off. Is there anything that walks on two legs that you can't seduce?"

Ted Valmont snatched the card out of Riordan's hand. "You should take the word puerile for a spin around the block. It suits you." He turned back to Duckworth. "I guess the net-net is I'm going to have to have a little heart-to-heart with my boss. But thank you for all that, Chris. It was very helpful."

Duckworth beamed and shifted his legs to one side in a distinctly girlish fashion. "You're very welcome, Ted," he said brightly.

Riordan snorted. "I can leave and come back later if you two want to warm up with some chamomile tea and give each other hugs."

"Relax, we're done. What have you got?"

Riordan gave a long, wolfish grin. "Dirt with a capital D—on the Maitlands. First off, Gabrielle ain't his niece as far as I can tell. Maitland had two siblings: an older and a younger brother. The older brother lives with him and has no children that I can find. I don't think he's ever been married even. The younger brother is dead. However, he was married and his widow lives in England. They had a daughter named Gabrielle, but she is considerably older than the Gabrielle staying at the Maitland estate and she herself is married and lives in the north of Britain—at least according to the detective agency I had to sub this out to. We're trying to get a photograph of the Gabrielle in Britain, but she lives a pretty reclusive life so it's gonna take some doing."

Ted Valmont stared at Riordan as if he were three blocks away. "Then who is the Gabrielle in Napa?" he asked hoarsely.

Riordan picked a shred of tobacco off his lip and shrugged. "Hard to say for sure, but my guess is she's Maitland's mistress. I think he uses the niece business as a cover. But you'll have to excuse me. I've been known to be a bit cynical about rich people and the shit they pull."

If Ted Valmont was put off by Riordan's judgment of the rich, he didn't show it. "That could explain what happened to me," he said slowly. "I went to see Gabrielle at Maitland's house and he had his foreman and two other farm workers beat me up. He must be jealous of Gabrielle seeing other men—but he sure doesn't seem to be able to keep very tight control over her."

"You got that right, chum," said Riordan. "She's slept with half the Valley, the way I hear it." Riordan stopped short, and pushing out his blunt jaw, rubbed the edge of it. "Sorry—maybe I should be treading lighter here. But back to what you said about Maitland. I thought you were in a car accident. You're saying the reason you're in the hospital is that Maitland had you beat up?"

"Yeah, yeah that's right," said Ted Valmont wearily. "And spare me the skepticism. I don't have the energy to argue about it any more."

Riordan shook his head. "To tell you the truth, it wouldn't surprise me at all, given what I found out about Maitland. He's a definite hard case. He started out as a factory hand in an automobile parts plant in Detroit. He worked his way up to the top of the company and eventually bought out the owner. And then he was launched. From there on, he made money at whatever he put his hand to: manufacturing mainly, in a variety of industries including textiles, lumber, automobile parts and even tennis shoes. But no high tech products for Mr. Maitland—he's strictly a meat and potatoes kind of guy.

"Most of his plants are overseas now because of the cheap labor. And for somebody who started out as a laborer himself, he's got zero compassion for the workingman. He's had dozens of labor disputes over the years—in the US and abroad—and he always comes down on them with an iron fist. Intimidation, beatings, union busting, lockouts, plant closures; he's said to have done it all. In fact, there's one small town in rural Tennessee that simply doesn't exist anymore because he closed his plant and moved the operation overseas. Yeah, if you're saying he roughed you up a bit, that would pretty much be a normal day at the office for Mr. Maitland."

Ted Valmont's eyes became narrower. "Then what's he doing in Napa Valley? That kind of background doesn't seem to go with the genteel art of winemaking."

Riordan replied carelessly, "It's anybody's guess, but I'd say that he's doing the retirement gig. He's getting up there—he's about 66—and he probably just wants have a nice hobby, earn the respect of the Napa Valley upper crust and sleep with an occasional 22-year-old. You know, live the simple country life."

Ted Valmont rubbed his gut with both hands and looked at Riordan with a pained expression. "Right," he said with irony. "But thanks. It's good information. The big question is how do Warren Niebuhr and the NeuroStimix world tie together with Gabrielle and Maitland? Just what was Niebuhr doing with Gabrielle?"

"Could she have been sleeping with him too?" piped up Chris Duckworth. "I mean, if she's got that kind of history."

Ted Valmont's face got lumpy and he pulled at a thread on the bed covers. "She says not," he said after a strained moment. "And everyone I talk to swears that Niebuhr was faithful to his wife. But, anyway, I just can't imagine what an attractive girl like Gabrielle would see in a guy like Niebuhr."

Duckworth glanced furtively over to Riordan, who let his head droop down and rubbed the back of his neck. "Look, Valmont," he said without looking up. "I know this is not your favorite topic, but Gabrielle—or whatever her name is—doesn't seem to be too discriminating. I don't know anything about Niebuhr, but I'm sure I wouldn't have to work hard to find someone even less desirable that she's slept with. For instance, if I'm right about Maitland—"

"Okay," said Ted Valmont hotly. "I get it. My time with Gabrielle was nothing special. Drop it, will you?" He lay back in the bed and closed his eyes.

Riordan and Duckworth made eye contact and Riordan gestured with his thumb at the door. They stood up.

"Sorry, chief," said Riordan, standing beside the bed. "We're going to leave and let you get some rest. You want me to keep going on the Niebuhr angle—trying to talk to the conference attendees and all that?"

Ted Valmont opened his eyes. "Yes, please do. I want Niebuhr found. Any way you cut it—he's right in the middle of all this."

Riordan started to reply, but just at that moment, the nurse returned to the room. She looked at Riordan and Duckworth. She looked at the disconnected tubes and wires, and then she looked at Ted Valmont lying tired and pale against the pillow. "What is going on here?" she demanded. "Who are you two? What happened to his IV? Get out. Get out this instant!"

Ted Valmont smiled thinly. "It's all right. They were just leaving, weren't you boys?"

Riordan nodded and tugged at Chris Duckworth's shirt. As the nurse hurried past them, he said, "See Chris. I told you not to play with the IV. It's very important for trauma patients to avoid dehydration."

Duckworth turned to slug Riordan ineffectually on the shoulder. "Bastard," he said, and strode out the door.

PUPPET FACTORY

"PortaPam is a whole new reason to play with your Palm!"
—Copy from the web site of defunct start-up Eruptor
Entertainment, describing their virtual Pamela Anderson for the
Palm computer

E ARLY IN THE AFTERNOON OF THE FOLLOWING day, Ted Valmont
got out of bed to go through the clothes in his closet. He held
up his shirt and trousers to examine the bloodstains, grimacing when
the sharp tang of tequila reached his nostrils. He picked up the single
Italian loafer and stared at it with a puzzled expression. He sighed
and chucked the shoe back in the closet, then closed the door deliberately as if to distance himself from the associated events.

He padded back to the side of the bed and pulled open the
nightstand drawer. Inside were his wallet, a ring of keys and his
Palm computer. Frowning, he swept a hand to the back of the
drawer, searching for something else. When nothing presented itself,
he grunted resignedly and reached for his wallet to flip it open.
"Figures," he said to the empty bill compartment. He returned the
wallet to its place and had the drawer partway closed when a muffled
beeping stopped him.

He slid the drawer open again and pressed the power button on the
Palm computer. The display flashed on and an envelope icon winked

in the upper corner of the screen. Ted Valmont stabbed at it with the nail of his index finger. The words "Receiving Message…" appeared like before, but this time a photograph of a small aluminum storage shed painted on the screen. The shed was built into the side of a grassy hill and the text, "Bring bolt cutters!" was written below it.

Ted Valmont snatched up the computer and held it less than six inches from his face. Wrinkles came into his nose and forehead as he scowled down at it, bunching up bandages in both places. He seemed not to breathe for a long moment, then he blew air through his lips and flopped onto the bed, flinging the computer to one side.

He lay huddled in this position for nearly half an hour, his eyes focused on a distant corner of the room. When at last he roused himself, he moved with the heavy reluctance of a deep-sea diver. He hauled himself upright, slid off the mattress and trudged back to the closet to get his clothes. He went into the bathroom to put them on, and was standing in his stocking feet with the single loafer under his arm when Nurse Flynn came through the door. She carried a vase of flowers and another gift basket.

"What a popular fell—" she began, then stopped abruptly when she caught sight of him. "Why, you're dressed!"

"Yes, I've got to go out."

"But you can't, Mr. Valmont. You're not well enough. And you don't have a signed release from Dr. Olson."

Ted Valmont took the loafer out from under his arm and nestled it in amongst the pears and hickory-smoked sausage of the gift basket. "Give this to Dr. Olson with my compliments. Tell him I'm sorry I missed him."

He went around her to the door.

Wearing new pants and a new shirt with the creases still in it, Ted Valmont sat in a rented Taurus outside the Maitland estate in almost exactly the same place as he had parked the Jaguar four days before. It was ten minutes after five in the afternoon.

On the seat beside him was the Palm computer with the picture of the storage shed showing on the display. Beside that was a plastic shopping bag containing a flashlight, a pair of gloves, binoculars and a hacksaw. He rummaged in the bag for the binoculars and trained them on the line of hills that guarded the eastern edge of the property. There were several structures in the vicinity, but only one was made of aluminum and only it appeared to butt directly into the hillside. He worked the zoom control of the binoculars, cropping the image to almost an exact copy of the picture on the computer. He kept his eyes pasted to the glasses for a long minute, then grunted to himself as he pulled them away. He started the car again, wheeled it around in a tight U-turn and drove back the way he came.

At the Silverado Trail, he turned right and followed it into Calistoga, the town at the northernmost end of the Valley. He parked on the main drag near the Mount View Hotel and started across the street to the hotel entrance. As he turned to look for on-coming traffic, his eyes ranged to a hardware store less than a block away. He veered off in the direction of the store, slipping inside just as a slouching, teenaged clerk with baggy pants was getting ready to lock up. For nearly two hundred dollars in cash, he purchased a monstrous set of bolt cutters and carried them back to the Taurus where he dumped them onto the floor of the front seat.

He made it across to the hotel without further distractions and cut through the lobby to the adjoining saloon of the Catahoula Restaurant. Cajun music played loudly and the TV hanging from the ceiling was tuned to a Giants and Braves game that was tied 1-1 in the bottom of the first. The game went into extra innings, but the Giants eventually won in the 11th off a bases-loaded double hit by

Barry Bonds into deep left field. During the course of the game, Ted Valmont sat at the rustic bar and consumed a plate of cornmeal-fried catfish and four non-alcoholic beers. He also engaged the beefy bartender in a running debate about Internet search engines—the bartender liked Yahoo, Ted Valmont liked Google—and was given cocktail napkins with phone numbers written on them by two women.

As the play-by-play men were reading off the final stats for the game, Ted Valmont reached across the bar to shake hands with the bartender and waved good-bye to the second of the two women, who watched him walk out of the bar with a wistful expression from the booth she shared with two of her girlfriends.

Ted Valmont returned to the Ford and pointed it back up the Silverado Trail and over to the now familiar road beside the Maitland property. Parking farther down than he had on the previous occasions, he got out of the car and went around to the passenger door to retrieve his gear. He found the plastic bag would not hold the weight of the bolt cutters, so he carried the bag in one hand with the cutters by his side in the other.

He pushed the car door closed with his butt and looked over once more to the Maitlands'. There were lights on in the main house and a few of the outlying buildings, but there was no sign of activity on the grounds. Ted Valmont took a deep breath, said, "fuck me" in a toneless voice and walked slowly over to the barbed wire fence. He heaved the equipment over the uppermost strand of wire and wriggled delicately through the middle pair. He winced as he leaned down to pick up the bag and the bolt cutters, then jogged in an oblique angle from the fence in the direction of the hills and a surrounding fringe of oaks.

By the time he reached the cover of the trees he was already sweating. He jogged right—towards the storage shed—and picked his way through the oak over uneven ground. Part way through the trees, he caught his foot in a rodent hole and went sprawling onto the dirt with a heavy thump. He made no cry, but his face was twisted in agony as he sat up to massage his ribs and brush the dead leaves and twigs off his shirt. He staggered upright again, and although he stumbled twice more, managed to keep his feet under him until he came to a break in the trees. There, less than fifty yards ahead, the aluminum shed glimmered dimly in the moonlight.

He covered the distance with relative ease, and after dumping his equipment on the ground in front of the small structure, examined the shed with a sober expression. It sat on a concrete slab and was built flush to the hillside with a sleeve of concrete blocks around the corrugated roof and sides. The sliding door was secured with a special, hardened metal padlock and no hint of light or sound escaped it. He turned from the shed and looked behind him. The main house was more than a half-mile away to the south and west. Another, larger storage building lit by floodlights loomed closer. He stood still and silent looking at the other building for a long time. Finally, with a faint twitch of his shoulders, he put his back to it and leaned down to take hold of the bolt cutters.

Bending at the waist, he clamped the jaws of the cutters around the shackle of the lock and squeezed. Neither he, the cutters, nor the lock seemed to move for a moment. Color crept into his face from the strain and his arms began to shake. A low, stuttering groan escaped his lips, and then—just as it seemed he must succeed or explode—the cutters bit through the metal of the shackle and the lock fell to the ground, clattering down the side of the shed as it went. Ted Valmont stood hunched over like an old man, using the handle of the cutters as a support while he massaged his ribs and sucked down air. When he had recovered enough to continue, he pulled on his gloves and yanked open the shed door.

It opened with a loud scraping noise, prompting him to duck and grit his teeth as if he were expecting a blow. The interior was pitch black. Ted Valmont retrieved his flashlight and shone it around the room. Dozens of smudge pots, three or four spools of bailing wire and a pallet stacked with bags of alfalfa seed filled the interior. A second door stood at the back of the shed—complete with another padlock—but the door was blocked by the pallet of seed. Ted Valmont spat the words, "*On est foutu!*" when it became clear that he would have to move the seed to get through the opening.

He put the flashlight down in front of the pallet and bent to the task of moving the alfalfa seed. The first few bags he picked up with dispatch and set down carefully well away from the door. As the count climbed, however, the manner in which he hefted the bags grew sloppy and the distance he carried them grew shorter. Soon his breath was coming in deep gulps, his face was covered in sweat and he could barely stagger between the pallet and the uneven, elongated mound he had established to one side. In the end, he was reduced to bulldozing the bags off the pallet on his hands and knees.

When all the bags had been dealt with, he crawled crabwise to the front of the pallet and pulled it forward, away from the rear door. Then he collected the bolt cutters and the shopping bag from the dirt in front of the shed and pulled the outer door closed. With only the eerie light thrown from the flashlight to illuminate the room, he looked dishearteningly from the padlock to the bolt cutters and then back again. He slumped against the concrete blocks of the back wall, his eyes closed and his head hanging down between his knees. He stayed that way for several minutes, moving only to draw in deep, ragged breaths. The tableau was broken abruptly when he snapped his head upright and yanked over the shopping bag to draw out the hacksaw.

He half-turned to face the door, and steadying the lock with one hand while working the saw with the other, managed to score the surface of the shackle. He drew the blade carefully across the cut several more times and then fell into a regular—albeit slow—rhythm of strokes. The thin cut ate across the shackle, silvery filings of metal floating down, powdering the floor, his shoe and pant leg beneath the lock. Several times the blade got stuck and he had to yank on the hacksaw with both hands to free it. It was stuck again near the very end, and once more using both hands to free the blade, he cut through the last millimeter of metal and flew ass over teakettle into the mound of seed bags.

He twisted off the padlock—and aiming the flashlight at the center of the heavy fire door—cleared the hasp and pushed the door open. The beam shone down a tunnel with rough plastered walls and a level concrete floor that ran deep into the hillside. No lights were on, but at a distance of fifty yards or more, it was barely possible to make out a "T" intersection. The air coming from the opening was cool and moist and it seemed to carry with it the faint hum of running machinery. Ted Valmont picked up the shopping bag and stepped across the threshold, flashlight held before him like a weapon.

He crept down the tunnel, trailing his fingers along the surface of the right wall. When he got to the "T," he shone the light in both directions of the new passageway and paused to listen. Nothing but tunnel could be seen in either direction, but the humming noise seemed to be coming from the left. He went that way. The new tunnel was wider than the old and the flow of air through it seemed stronger. There were also light fixtures dotting the ceiling, but no obvious switch to turn them on. Twenty yards down on the right, Ted Valmont came upon a metal door. He turned off the flashlight, walked cautiously up to the door and put his ear to it. There was no sign in his face that he heard anything inside. He reached for the knob and attempted to turn it. It was locked.

His fingers were shaking as he took them away from the knob. He stepped back from the door and drew in a deep breath. Then he whispered, "Come on, Valmont," to himself, snapped on the flashlight and pointed it ahead. He moved resolutely down the middle of the tunnel. The humming noise grew louder as he progressed, and seemed to resolve itself into three distinct sounds: a continuous metallic hum, an intermittent, high-pitched whine and an occasional thump. The halo of the flashlight beam drew across the outline of another door on the right. Ted Valmont flicked off the light and came quietly up to the door.

He placed his ear against it, and this time it was clear he perceived the noises came from within. Biting his lower lip, he squatted by the doorknob and reached over to grasp it. When the knob turned easily in his hand, he released his lip and let his lower jaw sag. He eased open the door. Little or no light came through the gap, but the noise grew very loud. He inched his head around the edge of the door and looked into the room. Nothing except the faint glow of colored lights could be seen, but from the resonance of the sound, it was clear that the room was quite large.

Two of the colored lights winked in and out of shadows as Ted Valmont watched. His breath caught sharply: someone was moving in the room, blocking the lights from view.

"Hello," he called out weakly.

There was no answer. There was only the sound of machinery and the strange movements in the dark. Ted Valmont picked up the flashlight and pointed it into the room. He flicked it on.

The beam fell on a factory floor with a conveyor belt that described a large, continuous oval around the room. The belt was moving slowly, transporting mechanical components in various states of completion along a manufacturing line. Manning the line at stations with pneumatic wrenches, screwdrivers, grinders and other equipment were men wearing identical orange coveralls. Their movements were precise and economic, and they did not turn or acknowledge the intruder in any way.

Ted Valmont shrank from the threshold, hiding behind the partially open door. When it became apparent that no one or no thing was paying the slightest attention to his presence, he slipped back through the opening to shine the light along the inside wall.

A set of four light switches came into view and he mashed them all up at once.

Overhead, banks of fluorescent lights flickered on and the room filled with a stark, cold light that had Ted Valmont and the other men squinting and blinking to adjust. But unlike Ted Valmont, the workers did not wait for their pupils to contract—they continued working as if nothing had changed. With his own eyes fully open, Ted Valmont could see there were close to twenty men on the line, all working in a scripted, robotic fashion. All were Hispanic, all appeared emaciated and all were very poorly groomed. Scraggly beards, unkempt hair and urine- and feces-stained uniforms were common. And, as the workers turned to pick up tools or components, Ted Valmont could see that they all had silvery metal boxes attached to the back of their necks.

As he watched assembled components move from the last work-station, around the oval to the beginning of the line—where they were dutifully disassembled by workers, only to be reassembled by others further down— he whispered, "Jesus, no."

Slowly and cautiously—as if he were afraid of disturbing something—he walked up to the nearest of the workers. He was a short man with badly pockmarked skin and large, flat nose. He was working with a pneumatic hammer, fitting a metal collar around a machined aluminum spindle on the components that went by him on the assembly line. His eyes tracked Ted Valmont as he approached, but he did not pause or hesitate in his repeated routine. When Ted Valmont was less than a foot away, he reached out and took hold of the man by the shoulders. He shook him—hard. The man staggered on his feet like the mast of a bobbing ship, but he did not stop his work with the hammer.

Ted Valmont stepped back and peered into worker's eyes. "Can you hear me?" he said loudly. "Give me a sign."

Nothing changed in the man's wooden expression, but the pupils of his eyes vibrated wildly. He blinked furiously.

Ted Valmont took a deep breath. "Okay," he said. "You can hear me." He stepped in back of the worker to get a closer look at the sliver box. It was about two inches long and a little over an inch wide and it was strapped to the man's neck by means of a nylon band that ran around the front of his throat like a choker. Ted Valmont pulled a penknife from his pocket and hesitantly slipped the thin blade under the nylon band. Seemingly oblivious to what Ted Valmont was doing, the worker continued moving to and fro while Ted Valmont attempted to saw through the band without stabbing the man in the neck. For all the difficulty the moving target presented, the little blade was sharp and it cut through the nylon material easily. As the knife twitched clear, the separated lengths of the nylon band fell away, but the box did not detach itself.

Ted Valmont cursed and moved directly behind the worker. He brought his hand up and slowly closed his gloved fingers around the sides of the box. He pulled at it gently, seemed to sense a slight resistance, then yanked it away.

The worker collapsed in a heap on the floor, the pneumatic hammer dropping from his grasp as he fell.

Ted Valmont stared at the pair of wicked-looking metal spikes sticking out from the back of the metal box. He looked down at the worker. Blood welled from the wound in his neck where the spikes had penetrated the skin. He dropped to the floor and rolled the man over. His eyes were closed and he appeared unconscious—or worse. Frantically, Ted Valmont pulled off a glove and shoved a finger against his neck to feel for a pulse. He did not seem to find one. He slapped at the man's face. He moved his head from side to side. He pulled open an eye to see the pupil rolled back in the socket.

"No, damn it, no," said Ted Valmont in a quivering voice.

Other sounds asserted themselves over the hum of the factory machinery: shouts and the sound of running feet. Ted Valmont jumped up in time to see a door open at the back of the room. Ramos's henchmen, Mario and Luis, boiled through the doorway carrying pistols. Mario spotted Ted Valmont immediately and pointed at him. Both men leveled their pistols and fired. The shots came so close in succession that it was impossible to distinguish between the explosions. Slugs zinged through the space Ted Valmont had been standing in and crashed into the wall behind. Ted Valmont, who was now crouched below the assembly line, grabbed the silver box and scuttled back toward the rear door.

Mario and Luis fired again. One bullet kissed off a roller on the assembly line and sent it spinning wildly. Another slammed into the midsection of a worker who was working a pneumatic wrench. The force of the impact knocked him off his feet, but even lying on his back with blood flowing from his gut, he continued the motions of picking up bolts and tightening them down with the wrench.

Ted Valmont did not even glance behind him to see where the shots went. Running in a crouched position, he reached the back wall and flung up a hand to the light switch. Darkness spread across the room, arrested only momentarily by muzzle flashes from two more shots aimed in his direction. He flinched at the sound of the guns, and then slipped through the door, slamming it closed behind him. He broke into a full sprint, racing down the right side of the passageway toward the smaller tunnel that led back to the storage shed.

By the time he had covered fifty yards, the sound of someone turning a doorknob came to him. This was followed shortly by the glow of light from behind. At seventy-five yards, the bank of lights above him began to flicker on, and when he was just a few feet from the opening to the storage shed tunnel, the sound of another shot rang out and a chip of concrete flew up from the wall and into his cheek. He dove into the opening for the smaller tunnel and rolled head over heels into the left side. He scrambled back to his feet, and now limping badly, covered the remaining distance to the storage shed door.

As he stepped into the shed, he spotted the bolt cutters lying on the floor where he had left them. He reached down to scoop them up and limped over to the outer door. Pulling it open with a loud scrape, he then dodged back to the rear wall of the shed, where he crouched behind the mound of seed bags. He had waited less than twenty seconds when an arm holding a 9mm automatic poked through the doorway. After the arm came the rest of Mario, who ran straight for the second door without bothering to look around. He was completely gone from view by the time a second 9mm automatic poked through.

Ted Valmont drew up and silently raised the bolt cutters over his head. When the back of Luis' head was in range, he brought the metal jaws of the cutters down with a vengeance. Luis made a sound like deflated football being kicked and went down in a jumble on top of the seed bags. His automatic fell from his hand and slid across the concrete slab to the edge of the outer door. Ted Valmont dropped the bolt cutters and bounded over to the door to take hold of the pistol. He pushed his head out of the opening and looked into the night.

Mario was about fifteen yards away, walking back to the shed from the direction of the oak trees. Ted Valmont did not hesitate. He thrust the automatic through the doorway and squeezed off three shots in quick succession. Mario appeared bewildered at first, but when he saw dirt kicking up in front of him, he yelled something in Spanish and sprinted toward the larger storage building. Ted Valmont fired at him once more and then took off in the direction of the trees. Although he still limped, he covered the ground quickly, and he was well into the oaks before Mario regained his wits enough to return fire. His shots thudded harmlessly into the trees. Ted

Valmont made a token response by blasting the final few rounds in the automatic over his head while he ran.

With dead branches snapping underfoot, he made it to the outer boundary of the oaks and sprinted directly for the barbed wire fence. As he came up to it, he flung the automatic off to one side, and incautiously thrust his torso between the middle strands of wire. The sleeve of his shirt caught on a barb, and cursing with a crazed vehemence, he savagely yanked it clear, leaving a three-inch long strip of fabric fluttering on the wire.

Now he moved down the road in an awkward, hopping gate that betrayed a heavy fatigue. When at last he came to the Taurus, he jammed the key home, flung the door open and threw the silver box he still carried across to the front passenger seat. He dove behind the wheel, ground the starter hard and was well into a wheeling, gravel-spraying U-turn before he managed to pull the car door closed.

Less than a half-minute behind, Mario came cautiously up to the fence and watched as the dust from the fleeing Taurus formed pale, billowing clouds in the moonlight.

THE FIFTH CHUKKER

"The site sells everything from cigars to gifts for women—even if the mind reels at the thought of buying an engagement ring online from TheMan.com."
—Timothy J. Mullaney, e-business writer, *Business Week*

T HE NEXT MORNING, TED VALMONT CAME OUT of an office supply store at the Stanford Shopping Center with a bubble-cushioned mailing envelope and a box of stationery. He walked to a bakery-cum-coffee shop, ordered a croissant and an espresso and went to sit at an outdoor table under a white canvas awning.

While the coffee grew cold and the croissant sat untouched, he filled five pages of the stationery with a succinct, unemotional account of the events of the prior evening. The narrative began simply with the statement, "On the night of June 18th, I, Ted Valmont, witnessed the following on the property of Douglas Maitland," and was addressed to no one in particular. When he had finished, he reread the pages—crossing out a word here, amending a sentence there—and sat back in his chair sipping his espresso. The coffee gone, he picked up the envelope and examined it thoroughly front and back. He had the air of a man who occupies himself with trivialities in order to avoid making a decision.

He sighed, dropped the envelope on the table and reached into the breast pocket of his jacket to extract August Riordan's business card. He copied Riordan's address onto the "To:" lines of envelope and then shoved the handwritten document inside. He slapped at the side pocket of his jacket and pulled out a small cardboard box, such as might be used for a gift of jewelry. Something in the box rattled as he took it out, and when he pulled off the lid to look inside, sunlight glinted off the silver metal of the device he had taken off the worker's neck the night before.

Dried blood still adhered to its prongs. Ted Valmont touched an index finger to the tip of one of them, and shuddering visibly, clapped the lid back on the box. He flexed open the mouth of the envelope and dropped the box in as if disposing of a dead rat. Suddenly in a hurry, he took a monstrous bite of the croissant and jumped up from the table, leaving the remainder of the pastry and the nearly full box of paper behind. His final business at the shopping center was a return visit to the office supply store, where he used their Federal Express services to overnight the envelope to Riordan.

The midnight blue Ferrari was parked in the back lot of the center, near the Sand Hill Road entrance. Settled into the driver's seat with the motor idling, he said, "Larry" into the hands-free microphone of the car's cell phone. The phone acknowledged the request, and a moment later, the voice of Larry Breen's secretary, Samantha, came over the car's speakers:

"Mr. Larry Breen's office. How may I help you?"

"Sam, it's Ted. Awfully formal, aren't we?"

"Oh, hey, Teddy boy," said Samantha in a looser, almost seductive tone. "That's the way I have to answer now. He even calls the office number to check up on me periodically."

"Larry obsessed about unimportant details? I'm shocked—shocked to find that anal retention is going on in here."

Samantha laughed. "You're better looking than the Claude Rains character. You could be Bogie—only taller."

Ted Valmont smiled and twisted the rear view mirror to look at himself. "I don't know, Sam," he said lazily. "You might not say that if you'd seen me lately. I'm definitely worse for wear."

"Sorry. We heard about the accident. Maybe you better come over to my place this evening so I can examine you—thoroughly."

"Don't get started with that again, Sam."

"I never stopped. You got that engagement ring for me yet?"

Grinning to himself in the mirror, Ted Valmont went through the motions of patting his jacket. "Must have left it in the other suit. I was thinking of swapping out the stone for a bigger rock anyway. I'll bring it next time I come in."

"Golly, we've got to be up to about twenty carats by now," Samantha said sarcastically.

He twisted the mirror back and cleared his throat. "So is his nibs available? I need to talk with him."

"Back to business, huh? No, he's not here. He went to a breakfast meeting in the East Bay and got stuck in the Caldecott Tunnel. Now—"

"Was he driving or walking?"

"Cute. What I was going to say is he's running late so he went straight to his polo match. It's Wednesday, remember?"

"Of course. How stupid of me. Canada Park in Woodside?"

"Yep. I think it starts at eleven. But you know he doesn't like to be bothered there."

"That's just too bad," said Ted Valmont harshly. "I'll pull him down off the damn horse if I have to."

Samantha's voice came through the speakers softer, more serious. "Go easy, Ted. He's just an overgrown adolescent. Don't let him get to you. God knows I couldn't have worked for him for four years if I took him seriously."

Ted Valmont stared down at his lap. "That's where you're wrong, Sam," he snapped. "We all need to start taking him seriously."

Samantha said nothing for a moment. "Take—take care of yourself then, Ted. I'll talk to you later."

"Right. Bye."

Ted Valmont shoved the Ferrari into low gear and launched out of the parking lot with a snarling whine. He drove up Sand Hill Road, past Basis Ventures and shot onto Highway 280 heading north. He stayed on the freeway for less than two miles before pulling off on the Woodside Road exit. The polo club was a short distance from the town center on a broad strip of green acreage that bordered Canada Road. Ted Valmont drove under an arch made of rough-hewn timber with the wrought iron silhouette of three polo players galloping along the top. He went up a straight road with polo fields on either side—two of which had games in progress—past several barns and an exercise track and up to a low building with a flagstone facade.

A portly, gray-haired man behind the desk with burst capillaries in his nose and a too-ready smile directed him to the nearest of the fields, so he trudged back down the road, walking on the well-groomed strip of grass between the asphalt and the shoulder-high fence. He went through a gate at the field and then along a path that paralleled the road to a set of stands with a dozen or so people sprinkled across four levels of seats. The majority were middle-aged women with wide-brimmed sun hats, casual but well-made clothing and a great many carats of precious gems. Several with picnic baskets were sipping wine and snacking on fruit and cheese. Most were deeply engaged in conversation with their neighbors, with only an occasional glance directed at the distant grouping of horses and men, now charging across the field in a ragged line, now worrying over the unseen ball like a cluster of wild animals about a fallen prey.

Ted Valmont sat down near a wiry young man with a goatee and a cast on his wrist who seemed an exception to the spectator demographics. Not only was he young and male, but he had a set of binoculars trained on the action and was following it closely. "Excuse me," said Ted Valmont. "Can you tell me what chukker this is?"

The young man looked up from the binoculars with trace of annoyance showing in his smooth, tan features. "It's the fourth—the last. This is just a club match. They're only playing four. You know someone who's playing?"

"Yes. Larry Breen."

The young man set the binoculars in his lap and looked at Ted Valmont more closely. "You a friend of his?"

Ted Valmont drew down the corners of his mouth and shrugged. "I work for him."

The young man looked through his glasses again. "If he manages people anything like the way he plays polo, you must be in for a lot of abuse. He's scored two of his team's goals—and committed all of their fouls. Two of the penalty shots resulted in goals for the other team, so I'd say it's a wash. They're tied 8-8 right now and there's only about a minute left."

Ted Valmont nodded and looked out on the field. The players were well away from the stands, but even at a distance of nearly a hundred yards, the eye was drawn to a player on the yellow team. One distinguishing characteristic was his girth. He and his horse were considerably heftier than the other players and animals. Another was his aggressiveness—he rode hard on the ball wherever it went, often bumping other players, sometimes riding them straight into the sideboards that bounded the field.

Now he and an opposing player from the red team broke free from the pack, chasing an errant pass. They collided at a point fifty yards from the red goal, just as they closed on the ball. There was a rough jostling, a blur of mallets swinging and then the red player tipped from his saddle and fell on his shoulder. His pony reared and checked up limping. The yellow player chased down the deflected ball and hit a swooping shot under his horse's neck. The ball zinged through the red goal.

"Bastard!" said the young man beside Ted Valmont. "He's done it again."

"I take it you're not referring to the goal."

The young man jerked his head around to look at Ted Valmont squarely, his eyes glittering with malice. "No, I don't mean the goal. I mean injuring another player." He held up his wrist defiantly. "How do you think I got this? Your boss sent me flying over the neck of my horse is how."

Ted Valmont looked at the young man soberly and nodded. "Sorry to hear that."

The young man made a dismissive gesture, jumped up and strode down the stairs, taking two steps at a time. Polite applause broke out among the other spectators in response to the end of the game. With the exception of the injured player—who walked along the margin of the field gripping his arm—the players on both teams formed a line and rode by the stands in a slow procession. When Larry Breen came by—mud-splattered, sweaty, flushed, but wearing a huge grin—Ted Valmont called out to him. Breen looked over and grinned all the wider. "Valmont," he shouted. "Meet me down here."

Breen dismounted with a ponderous grace and led his horse along the fence to the far end of the grandstands. With his tall boots, knee guards, too-tight breeches and well-stuffed yellow jersey spilling down over his waistband, he looked like a character from The Beatles' movie *Yellow Submarine*. He yanked on the chin strap of his helmet, tossed the helmet to the ground and leaned jauntily on his polo mallet as if it was a Malacca walking stick. When Ted Valmont came within earshot, he said, "Glad to see you up and around after your accident. Did you see that last goal? Wasn't it a beauty? You should take up the sport, Valmont. It's exhilarating. Better than sex, even."

Ted Valmont looked at Breen woodenly. He jerked his chin in the direction of the injured player, who was still making his way to the clubhouse. "Think he feels the same about it?"

Breen made a wry face. He shook his head. "Pshaw, Valmont. Pshaw. It's part of the game. Just like sex. After all, it's not uncommon for the deflowered virgin to bleed a little, is it?"

"You've an odd mind, Larry."

Breen ran a gloved hand through his matted hair and chuckled. "Who can say? I'm not prepared to pass judgment on anyone's psychology—my own included."

Ted Valmont closed on the fence and took hold of the railing with both hands. "I need to talk to you."

Breen nodded. "About starting back at the firm. Good—I'm glad to see that you've put that NeuroStimix business behind you."

"No, Larry. It's about NeuroStimix that I want to talk. I went to Maitland's winery last night. I know what he's done with Niebuhr's technology. I think you're right in the middle of it. You and Niebuhr had a considerable e-mail correspondence before he disappeared."

Ted Valmont watched as Breen's face closed and hardened. He plowed on:

"I think this whole business with Niebuhr's disappearance, cutting funding to the company and the sabotage was your way of getting a corner on the technology and ensuring that it never came to market the way NeuroStimix intended. You and Maitland apparently have some very sick ideas about how it should be used instead."

Breen's horse tossed its head and stamped its front hooves. Breen yanked cruelly on the reins to quiet the animal. When he looked back at Ted Valmont, his manner was very somber. "You're making some big assumptions here, Ted, and you have no proof. These are very deep waters and I'd advise you to go slowly."

Ted Valmont barked a laugh. "Slowly, hell. I'm going straight to the cops."

Breen looked down and tapped the head of the polo mallet absently on the heel of his boot. "There's a lot you don't understand, Ted. As it happens, I do know Douglas Maitland. He's a member of the Napa Polo Club and we often play together. Why don't you meet with us and talk before you do anything ill-advised." He looked up from his boot. "In fact, I feel sure that a meeting could be of positive personal benefit for you—and perhaps for your most unfortunate brother."

Ted Valmont sneered. "Is that a bribe or threat?"

"Neither, Ted," said Breen mildly. "It's merely a suggestion that you could benefit financially from a venture in which you've already played a very important role. To say nothing of your brother, who might gain access to a cure much sooner than either of you ever imagined. What could be more reasonable than that?"

Flushing at the mention of his brother, Ted Valmont looked into Breen's face as if trying to gauge his motives. He said nothing for a long moment. Then: "After all that's happened, I don't trust you, Larry, and I certainly don't trust Maitland. There's no way I'm going to meet with you two alone."

Breen smiled broadly, reassuming his usual jovial demeanor. "You're over-dramatizing, Ted. You really are. But if it makes you feel better, we'll meet in a public place. A restaurant, say. In fact, why don't we have dinner tonight? You pick the place—that way you'll feel more comfortable about it."

Ted Valmont looked past Breen to the field beyond. "All right," he said in a cautious voice. "We'll meet at Spago's in Palo Alto. I know the *maître d'* and can get a table on short notice."

Breen laughed. "There's a surprise. What *maître d'* in the Bay Area don't you know?"

Ted Valmont didn't acknowledge the jibe. "What time, then?"

"Shall we make it ten? That will give Douglas plenty of time to get down from Napa."

Ted Valmont nodded curtly. "Ten it is. But I'm warning you, I've given all the evidence I've collected to a reliable third party. If anything happens to me, it will be hand delivered to the police and the newspapers."

"Oh please, this is Silicon Valley in the 21st century, not some tawdry 1950s detective show." Breen continued with an exaggerated buoyancy, "You'll feel much better about all this after we've talked, I'm sure. Now I've got to get Sir Winston here back to the stables."

Breen leaned down to pick up his helmet and then remounted the horse with much creaking of leather and a heavy thump as he hit the saddle. He yanked the reins to one side, turning the horse's head. "See you tonight, then," he said and spurred the animal into a trot across the field.

Ted Valmont stood by the rail without moving until Breen rode out of view behind a barn and then turned and trudged slowly back to his car.

UNDERCARD

"What is the provenance of this stuff?"
—Dan Lynch, Silicon Valley venture capitalist, commenting on his decision to sit out the record-setting auction of 83,000 cases of wine from failed start-up Wine.com's inventory

TED VALMONT HELD A GLASS OF GOLD-COLORED wine up to the light and swirled the contents. He watched as the "legs" of the wine glissaded down, then set his teeth on edge as a tremor in his hand caused the wine to jiggle and splash. He slammed the glass down on the linen-covered table, snapping the stem from the base.

"Ted," said a voice that came from the aisle behind his booth. "I hope you're not developing a case of nerves. We wouldn't want that."

Ted Valmont twisted around to see Spago's austere, white-haired *maître d'* looking down at him with a concerned expression, but it was not he who had spoken. The voice belonged to Larry Breen, who stood a short ways back with Douglas and Gabrielle Maitland at his elbow. Ted Valmont rose awkwardly, still holding the broken wineglass.

"Let me take that for you, Mr. Valmont," said the *maître d'*, deftly relieving Ted Valmont of his encumbrance. "We'll be moving you to another table now that there's a fourth in your party."

Ted Valmont's gaze snapped to Gabrielle, who did not meet his eyes. "Oh," he mumbled, "I see."

Breen laughed heartily and came up to clap Ted Valmont on the back. "I believe you already know Gabrielle Maitland, don't you, Ted?" he said in an insinuating tone. "And of course you remember Douglas."

Ted Valmont sidled out of the booth and away from Breen's meaty paw. "What's she doing here?" he said in a more collected tone. "I thought we were going to talk business."

"Relax, Valmont," said Breen. "Of course we're going to talk business, but as you'll see, Gabrielle here has as much to do with it as anyone. Isn't that right, Gabby?"

Gabrielle pressed her lips together and looked down at the floor. She nodded almost imperceptibly.

The *maître d'* ahem'ed politely. "May I escort you to the larger table?"

"Yes, please," said Breen with enthusiasm. "This is quite a late dinner for me."

The *maître d'* led the party to a table in the center of the room. Ted Valmont and Breen sat on one side; Douglas and Gabrielle Maitland settled in on the other. Ted Valmont tried once more to make eye contact with Gabrielle, but she sat still and rigid with her head bowed.

There was an awkward silence. Breen nodded to Douglas Maitland, who—dressed in a business suit in place of bib overalls—looked like a different person entirely. "I appreciate your agreeing to meet with us, Ted," he said gruffly. "I'm enthused about the possibility of us working together." If he was aiming for genial tone, he missed by a considerable amount.

Ted Valmont laughed without amusement and shook his head. "You're not nearly as good as Larry at spreading the fertilizer, Maitland. You wouldn't be here at all if I hadn't got the goods on you."

Maitland worked his face slowly and methodically into a horrible smile, like an undertaker rearranging the expression of a corpse. "I'm not sure I understand."

"Then let's take Gabrielle as an example—if that's even her real name. I know she's not your niece."

There was no change in Maitland's expression. With the horrible smile stuck firmly in place, he dipped his head slightly in acknowledgment. "That's right, Valmont. You have done your homework, haven't you?" He held up a hoary, calloused palm. "Look, there's no point in flinging accusations back and forth across the table like this. Larry assures me that you are a reasonable man, and for my part, I want to apologize for the misunderstandings that we've had in the past. Once you hear the full background on all this, I think you'll see things differently."

Ted Valmont started to reply but a waitress came up with menus and the bottle of open wine that had been left at the other table. She sat the bottle in front of Breen and said, "Shall I bring glasses for everyone?"

Breen picked up the wine and examined the label. "Yes, please do," he said pleasantly. "Douglas, this is an excellent Val du Grue chardonnay. Have you had it before?"

Maitland took the bottle from Breen and looked it over carefully. "I've heard you make some great wines, Ted. I've never tried this vintage, but I'll be eager to taste it."

Ted Valmont rapped the table, causing the silverware to bounce and rattle. "Let's cut out the false pleasantries and get down to it," he said sharply. "You say you have things to tell me. Let's hear them."

Maitland's face dropped, assuming its usual forbidding mien. Breen made a clucking noise. "Patience, Ted, patience," he said gently. "We'll have plenty to tell you in moment, but please, let us order first. It's late, and I, for one, am quite hungry."

The waitress came back with glasses and poured out the wine. No one spoke or made eye contact while she did this, but Gabrielle put her hand over her glass to signal that she didn't want any of the chardonnay. Perhaps daunted by the grim mood, the waitress asked tentatively if they were ready to order. Breen gave an emphatic yes, and proceeded to order a meal that was a combination of two of the beef entrees on the menu, with elaborate instructions on the degree of doneness he required and a request that a sauce from yet another entree be used in place of the ones that were normally employed.

The waitress dutifully noted all this down and then inquired what Gabrielle would like. Before she could respond, Maitland ordered the salmon for her and himself. Ted Valmont said he would have the chicken, flipped his menu closed and thrust it out to the waitress, then stared pointedly at Breen. "Are you ready now?" he demanded.

Breen seemed not to notice the heat in Ted Valmont's tone. He sipped some of his wine and smiled. His eyes wondered to the ceiling. "I think," he said contemplatively, "it would be best to start with Gabrielle's story. Gabby, why don't you tell Ted a little more about the unfortunate incident in your adolescence."

Gabrielle nodded without looking up from her lap, twisting her napkin in her hands. She spoke in a soft monotone. "I told you before that I was in a riding accident when I was fourteen—that was true. What I didn't tell you is that I was completely paralyzed from the neck down. I spent six years in a wheelchair, unable to do anything for myself except press buttons on the chair console with a stick I gripped in my teeth. Sometimes I even had trouble breathing." She looked up at Ted Valmont with tears welling in her eyes and her voice quivered out of its monotone. "It was a horrible existence. I had very little to live for." She tried to continue, but a half sob choked off her words and her tears began to flow in earnest.

Maitland reached over and put his hand on her shoulder. She didn't quite flinch. He made a noise deep in his throat like a lawn mower starting. "Perhaps it's best if I pick up the story. I first heard about Gabrielle when I was visiting my sister-in-law in England. She happened to tell me the story of a girl in their village who had been horribly injured in a riding accident. The girl was a friend of my real niece. Like Larry, I play a bit of polo, and that sort of accident is the kind of thing you fear most. Well, the story made an impression on me—although at the time it never occurred to me that I might be in a position to help the girl.

"Sometime later, I was back in Napa playing polo with Larry and I myself was thrown from my horse. It was nothing serious, but while discussing the incident afterward, I mentioned the girl in England. Larry told me that Basis Ventures had invested in a company that was developing technology to help people in just that situation, but he said that progress had been frustratingly slow and he doubted the technology would ever be viable. However, he did say that the Chief Scientist of the company was brilliant. It was the way the company was being run that was hindering development."

Ted Valmont narrowed his eyes and looked over at Breen. "Thanks for the big endorsement, Larry."

Breen smiled while mashing a full pat of butter into a piece of bread three inches square. He gestured with the knife. "That's the way I've always felt about the situation, Ted. I've never hidden that from you."

Maitland paid them no heed. "Anyway," he continued dully, "I began to think more about this, and I asked Larry if a different approach to the problem might yield better results. We kicked it around in the course of several conversations and eventually came up with a plan to fund separate work by Warren Niebuhr, permitting him to focus solely on R&D without the distractions he faced at NeuroStimix."

Ted Valmont fell back in his chair, flabbergasted. "I can't believe I'm hearing this, Larry. Everyone with an engineering role at a start-up—at any high tech firm for that matter—signs an agreement stating that the work they do in the company's technology area is owned by the company. Niebuhr had no right to work on this elsewhere."

Breen chewed on his bread and smiled. He dabbed at his beard with his napkin. "You're being naive, Ted. Those sorts of agreements are gone around all the time. Hell, three-quarters of the spin-offs in the valley are in technical violation of agreements like that. They are simply not enforceable. In any case, the break-through Warren ultimately made in the technology occurred because he took quite a different approach than the one NeuroStimix was following in its research."

"That's right, Ted," said Maitland quickly. "And Gabrielle here is the result. You see, when Niebuhr got to the point that he was ready to do human trials, I thought of the girl I had heard about in England. We flew her out and Niebuhr worked with some excellent surgeons to implant a vastly improved version of the device in her neck, attaching the electrodes to the severed nerves below the break in her spinal cord. Although it took a number of iterations in the design and programming of the device—and a lot of hard work and training on Gabrielle's part—the results are amazing. As you've seen, complete mobility has been restored. And with diligent work, she's restored full tone and strength to her atrophied muscles—in fact, she's in better shape than most people simply because she does not experience the fatigue and pain associated with exercise. She can work her muscles to failure without feeling a thing."

Ted Valmont looked over at Gabrielle, his eyes bright with thought. "That explains what I saw in the cabana by the pool," he said slowly. An idea seemed to come to him and he paled beneath his olive skin. "But if you can't feel anything below your neck," he stammered, "why do you—I mean, why would you ..."

Gabrielle's face spasmed and she twisted away from Ted Valmont. Breen laughed rudely. "Out with it, Ted: you mean why would she be so interested in sex?"

No one said anything for a moment. Then, with her back still turned, Gabrielle's spoke in a halting voice. The quietness of it made Ted Valmont lean forward.

"It's true I don't feel anything. And although I'd never been with a man before the accident, I hunger for the closeness of it. Just to be able to make love with someone makes me feel more human, more normal."

Breen nodded and smiled, as if he was agreeing with an observation about the weather. He took another bite out his bread and poked Ted Valmont sharply in the ribs. "Besides," he said with butter clinging to his mustache, "sex doesn't end at the neckline, does it Ted?"

When the full significance of the remark dawned on Ted Valmont, his face darkened with anger and he bared his teeth in a snarl. He took hold of Breen's wrist and forced his arm back, almost toppling him from his chair. "Shut up you pig," he hissed.

Maitland stared at Breen with an expression that was one part astonishment and two parts aggravation. "That was uncalled for, Larry."

Breen chuckled and shrugged elaborately. "It was a perfectly benign observation, it seems to me. But if I've given offence, I apologize." He laid his arm across the table in a placating gesture. "You'll forgive me, won't you dear?"

Quiet sobbing noises came from Gabrielle, but her shoulders and back did not move in rhythm with them. When she turned to face the table, there were fissures of black, mascara-stained tears running down her cheeks. She twisted and wrung the napkin in her hands and then wiped at the tears, leaving her skin red and raw. "I'm—I'm

going to wait in the car," she said hoarsely, still managing somehow
to convey a sense of tattered dignity.

Maitland scrunched his face up as if he'd swallowed something
foul. He looked from Breen to Gabrielle and back again. There was
an unspoken accusation in his eyes. "Perhaps that would be best,"
he said heavily. "I'll walk out with you and come right back."

Maitland rose and stood behind Gabrielle's chair. She knocked
the table getting up and let Maitland lead her out of the restaurant
in a funereal march. She did not look at or speak to Ted Valmont
as she went by.

Breen took a healthy sip of wine. He sighed and let his eyes
wonder around the table. "Will you look at that," he said abruptly
and leaned over to spear the linen napkin Gabrielle had left on her
plate. He dangled the rumpled cloth in front of Ted Valmont, a
six-inch tear running through the middle of it. "Talk about hand
strength."

Ted Valmont's face became heavily thoughtful. He stared into
his lap saying nothing.

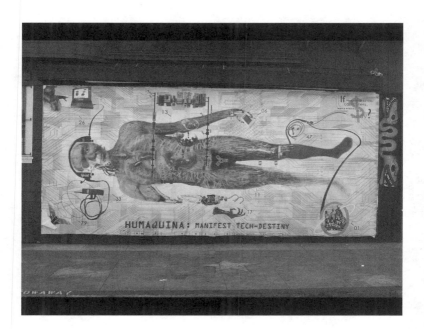

THE MAIN EVENT

"[T]he third or fourth time they went off, I was pretty sure we weren't going to be raising money from these guys."
—Brian Sroub, CEO, Chipshot.com, describing a funding pitch to a group of investors whose pagers were set to go off with sharp market drops

BY THE TIME DOUGLAS MAITLAND RETURNED, THE waitress had brought the food. Maitland looked first at Breen, who was already bent over his plate—sawing at his beef with a steak knife—and then at Ted Valmont, who was staring off to a corner of the room with his dinner pushed to one side. "She's fine," said Maitland with a trace of self-consciousness. "She's just going to lie down in the back of the limo. It's been a long day."

"Yes," said Breen with his mouth full of half-chewed filet mignon. "That's certainly understandable."

Ted Valmont roused himself and stared coldly at Maitland as he returned to his place at the table. "You've prettied up that story about Gabrielle. You've spun it so altruism is the motivating factor and you haven't even attempted to justify why you told everyone she is your niece. But pass that. What I want to know is how you explain the wine cave. Those men weren't moving of their own accord like Gabrielle. They were being forced to perform against their will. You've warped the technology somehow to override motor impulses from the brain and take control of movement. Electronic slavery—that's what it is."

Maitland's eyes glittered darkly. For an instant it seemed as if he were going to launch himself across the table and grab at Ted Valmont's throat. Instead, with an obvious exercise in self-control, he relaxed back into his chair and took a sip of water. "That's not right, Ted," he said with false calm. "You've misinterpreted what you saw. It is true that the factory in the wine cave represents a different application of the technology. In the system Niebuhr developed for Gabrielle, a transponder embedded under her neck relays motor signals from her brain to a remote computer. The computer interprets and translates them, and then sends the appropriate nerve impulses back to the electrodes attached to her spinal cord.

"As I'm sure you can appreciate, the heavy processing require-ments rule out the possibility of placing a computer directly under the skin: its size and power consumption would simply be too great. As a matter of fact, the need for a remote computer is one reason why Gabrielle's episode at the restaurant was so severe. When she's away from the estate, she normally carries the computer in her purse—it's about the size of a deck of cards. However, when you rushed her off to the hospital, you left her purse under the table, effectively paralyzing her. That's why she was so disconcerted when she regained consciousness. It is a distinctly unnerving experience for her to lose mobility again."

Ted Valmont looked down at the table and needlessly straight-ened his silverware. "You still haven't told me what was going on with the factory workers."

Maitland nodded and leaned forward, as if Ted Valmont's cul-pability had given him the high ground. "In the system used in the factory, the role of the computer is different. Rather than interpreting nerve impulses from the brain, it sends prerecorded signals to guide the movements of the workers. You see, Niebuhr has figured out a way to record and later replay the nerve impulses associated with movements in people who are not paralyzed. With the right filtering, he can even make records from one person and play them on another. For instance, if you wanted to teach a beginning golfer to swing as well as a pro, you could record the pro's swing and then replay it on the student. The student would then learn how it feels to make a good swing, and eventually be able to do it unassisted."

"But we're not talking about golf swings here," Ted Valmont said hotly. "What I saw looked like forced labor."

Maitland picked up his fork and mashed it into the table, bending one of the tines. He pressed his lips together until they were white and bloodless. "Will you please let me finish," he sputtered. "What you saw last night was a set of volunteers engaged in an experiment. We've been thinking about applications for the technology, and one of them clearly would be manufacturing. Regular workers get fatigued over time, lose focus, become less productive and make mistakes. On the other hand, if we could record the movements required for factory assembly when a worker is fresh and replay them with absolute fidelity when required, we would have a much more efficient worker, and by extension, a much more efficient assembly line. Traditional factory automation will never take us as far, because no matter how much robots advance, they will never achieve the dexterity and range of motion of the human worker."

Breen looked up from his plate and nodded. "This beef is excellent," he said with a contented belch. "But getting back to your concern, Ted, in this scenario the worker would only be under the control of the replay device during his shift. Even with reduced working hours to compensate for the extra fatigue, our experiments show a factory staffed by workers so equipped can be up to thirty percent more efficient. And our volunteers tell us they actually find the work to be more pleasant. They don't have to concentrate on the job at hand, so they are free to let their minds wander."

"That's right," said Maitland, warming to the argument. "And the work environment can be altered as a result. In some cases, there's no need to even light the factory floor. Workers don't need to see to perform their job and some actually find it more pleasant to be in a darkened setting. That was what we were trying last night."

Ted Valmont looked from one man to the other and then laughed in disbelief. "What do you take me for? If there was an experiment going on last night, it was to see how bad a working environment you could have and still run the factory. I've seen the dope on your operations, Maitland. My guess is you're planning to set up in Third World countries in the least expensive facilities possible and work the people to death. Either that, or use your zombie workers in manufacturing processes that involve hazardous materials without bothering with the expense of safeguards.

"One thing is for certain—the men on that manufacturing line were in a pitiable state. Not to mention that your goons shot at me and hit one of them instead."

Maitland stabbed at Ted Valmont with the fork. "You were trespassing. You actually did much more harm when you pulled the device from the neck of the other worker. He went into cardiac arrest and we barely resuscitated him in time."

Ted Valmont flinched and ran his hand down the length of his tie to smooth it flat. "I'm sorry that happened," he said carefully. "But I'm not sorry I kept the device. And don't think I won't give it to the authorities to prove what I saw."

Larry Breen made a clucking noise. He shook his head. "Look here, Ted. Douglas is right. You had no business being on his property. We are both curious to know what possessed you to break into that storeroom, but that can come later. The important point in all this is we have succeeded in perfecting the technology. It's clear there are many applications for it, including the very important one that Gabrielle helped pioneer. Perhaps manufacturing is not the best one to next exploit. I think even Douglas might concede that. But there are many others. Helping people develop motor skills, as Douglas suggested earlier. Physical therapy to recover from injuries or surgery. Strength or endurance training for athletes—the list goes on and on."

Breen paused long enough to snatch a honeyed carrot from Ted Valmont's plate and gobbled it down. "Now, I will acknowledge that we've achieved this success in a somewhat unorthodox manner. And frankly, I have used my influence at Basis Ventures to speed the demise of NeuroStimix so that there are no questions about technology ownership as we go forward. However, I have no doubt the company would have failed eventually, even without my intervention." He held out both hands in the gesture of a reasonable man. "That being said, I understand you—even without knowing it—have contributed significantly to the venture. You first recognized the potential of the investment. You started Niebuhr down the path that ultimately led to success. In recognition of that, Douglas, Warren and I are willing to bring you in as a partner." He laughed in a breezy way. "And parenthetically, I should mention that Tillman Cardinal is also involved."

"You mean you bought him off to get help in torpedoing NeuroStimix."

"Please, Ted, try not to be so hostile. We are here in good faith with an offer that we are by no means obliged to make. Come along with us. The profits will be off the charts, and there will be no limited partners to pay back as there would be with a venture investment. Once we bring the technology to market, I'm sure you'll make more money in six months than you've earned in your entire career. And let's not forget about family obligations. Can you imagine Tim Valmont out of his wheelchair moving under his own power like Gabrielle? Good lord, he could even return to platform diving and be as good or better than he ever was."

There was a long silence. When Ted Valmont finally spoke his voice was thin and empty of expression. "And you're saying Niebuhr is in with you?"

"Of course he is," said Breen heartily. "We couldn't have done any of this without his help. He is the technology."

"Then why did he go off like that? Have you got him locked up somewhere?"

"No, not at all." Breen gave a narrow smile that was somehow sly and coy at the same time. "We all thought that the maneuver with NeuroStimix would be helped by his departing from the scene for a few month's time. He is just laying low until we get the company assets sold off." Breen pushed back from the table and reached a hand over to Ted Valmont's chair. "Now, what do you say Ted? Are you with us?"

Ted Valmont looked soberly at Breen and then over to Maitland. Breen smiled at him in a friendly way, but Maitland could manage no more than a strained glare. "What if I decline?" he asked in a suddenly too-loud voice.

Breen removed his hand from the chair and shrugged casually. "Frankly, we simply earn more money without your participation."

"And if I try to stop you?"

Maitland brought his hand up from his lap and laid it on the table. He balled it into a fist so tight that his knuckles cracked. "We won't let you," he said coldly.

Breen snorted. "It's less a matter of not letting you stop us than simply continuing with our original plans. If you think about it, Ted, I'm sure you'll realize that you have no lever to use on us. You have no evidence of wrongdoing—primarily because there hasn't been any. But, for instance, if you were to show the device you took from Douglas' cellar to the police and claim it was evidence, what would it prove? A simple radio receiver with some odd protuberances.

Nothing illegal about that. And then there's the little matter of your credibility. I think that after your automobile accident, the Napa County Sheriff's Department—at least—has some reason to doubt the things you say."

Ted Valmont reddened and his breathing became irregular, but he said nothing.

"Take some time to consider the offer," said Breen, pushing his chair back still further. "In fact, we could hardly go wrong if we allowed you a little solitude now to think things through. Douglas has a long drive back, and we don't want to leave Gabrielle alone in the car any longer than necessary." Breen smiled abruptly. "You don't mind picking up the tab, do you my boy?"

Ted Valmont jerked his head no.

"Excellent. Then we'll be on our way." Breen and Maitland got up from the table. When Breen had maneuvered his girth behind Ted Valmont's chair, he paused and leaned down to ear level. "One more thing," he said low, insinuating tone. "If you elect not to come in with us, I'm sure you understand that your brother will never get access to the technology. And given his wife's departure, his drinking problems and his depression, just how do you think he will feel when he hears that a cure was available and you prevented him from receiving it?"

PAINFULLY, WHEN I'M UNDER STRESS

"We sell a substantial portion of our products at very low prices. As a result, we have extremely low and sometimes negative gross margins on our product sales."
—Buy.com prospectus

A MUFFLED POUNDING ON TED VALMONT'S FRONT DOOR woke him up the next morning at twelve minutes before noon. There was a brown crust on his lips and his face was pale and puffy-looking. He pried his head off the pillow, then collapsed back onto it and pulled another pillow over his face. "Go away," he said, barely audible through the linen and goose feathers. "Let the dead rest in peace."

A heavier, more insistent object pummeled the front door. The sound of wood tearing and a tremendous slam caused Ted Valmont to fling the pillow from his face and bolt upright. He slithered out from under the covers, banged his knee on the bed frame and limped down the hallway in his boxer shorts and black silk socks. At the entrance to the living room, he poked his head around the corner. August Riordan stood in the middle of the room drawing a steady and apparently quite deadly bead on his tousled head with a Glock semi-automatic pistol.

Ted Valmont jerked back, but lost his footing on the slick hardwood and fell face down, sprawled on the living room like a hooked marlin. "God damn it, Riordan," he said into the floor. "What in the hell do you think you're doing?"

Riordan straightened up from his stiff crouch and lowered the automatic slightly. "You okay?" he blurted. "You here by yourself?"

Ted Valmont pushed himself off the floor and sat upright to massage his elbow where he had banged it on the hardwood. "Riordan," he began, then paused to clear his throat savagely. "You know what you're like? You're like herpes: you always make your appearance painfully, when I'm under stress."

"Never mind the gags. Are you alone?"

"Yes, damn it. Thank God I didn't have anyone over. I repeat: what in the hell are you doing here?"

Riordan took a deep breath and let his arms fall to his side. He eyes flicked around the room, then returned to Ted Valmont. "I got your FedEx package with that electronic gizmo. I called your office and they didn't know where you were. I called here and didn't reach you. I was afraid something had happened."

Ted Valmont rolled over on his haunches and stood up. He glanced down at his torso self-consciously. "Not yet," he said, and folded his arms across his chest.

"Not yet, huh?" said Riordan, nodding to himself. "That's swell." He flipped his jacket up and shoved the gun under his waistband at the small of his back. "Say, those are some great looking socks you got there."

Ted Valmont spat the words, "Eat shit," and tromped out of the room. When he returned, he was wearing a silk kimono and a pair of slippers with no socks. Riordan had moved to the far corner of the room and was examining a cast metal sculpture on a marble pedestal. A paunchy, nondescript figure with both arms raised beseechingly to the sky, the statue omitted the particulars necessary to distinguish sex or age.

"Like it?" asked Ted Valmont. "It's *Sunrise Salutation* by Wild Horse."

"I thought it was *Touchdown* by Flabby Zebra."

Ted Valmont clapped his palm to his forehead. "I deserved that. I'm making coffee. You want any?"

"Sure. I kicked down the door of a Starbucks earlier this morning, but I could use another cup."

Ted Valmont made no comment to that but walked straight into the kitchen where he gestured for Riordan to take a place on a stool in front of the island. He got a pot of coffee brewing with some grinds he took from a vacuum-sealed jar in the freezer and sat down across from Riordan.

"Any more wisecracks you need to get out of your system?" he asked.

"Not just this minute, but you'll be the first to know if anything changes. Now what's going on?"

Ted Valmont recapped events from the time he left the hospital to the previous night's dinner. He concluded with, "And I don't have a fucking clue about what to do next."

"Call the cops. What's so hard about that?"

"Sure—I threatened them with that, but Breen's right when he says there's nothing to indicate wrong-doing." He paused. "And he's got me over a barrel with Tim. The main reason for investing in NeuroStimix was to help my brother. Breen knows that—and he also knows how desperate Tim is to find a cure. If the technology has been perfected to the point that Gabrielle can do the things she does, I don't want to risk losing a chance at that for him."

Riordan plunked both elbows on the marble countertop and picked at the heavy calluses in his hands. "The whole thing is pretty fantastic, Valmont. I still don't understand how this Gabrielle can move around of her own accord, while the factory workers are forced to follow a scripted routine. You said something about record and replay. We're not talking about video taping TV shows here, we're talking about people."

Ted Valmont nodded. "I know it's pretty far out, but the idea is simple: record the motor signals your brain sends to your muscles and then replay them to recreate the original movements. What scares me is the other applications they may have cooked up for the technology. A warped bastard like Maitland could have a field day."

"What do you mean?"

"They basically have the ability to create electronic slaves. Think of all the uses slaves have been put to throughout history. Forced laborers—they've got that covered. Next comes prostitutes, after that soldiers—or worse—terrorists and assassins. Speaking of which, I'm almost certain now that the suicide bomber at Buck's was an electronic slave sent by Maitland. The miserable wretch wanted no part of what he was doing and he even warned me off." Ted Valmont snapped his fingers. "Hey, that's something. There might be remnants at the scene of another of those devices."

Riordan did not quite frown. He leaned away from the counter and crossed his arms under his chest. "Please. You couldn't fill a baby's sock with what was left of that guy. Besides, you said yourself that the device doesn't prove anything."

Ted Valmont stood up to get two coffee mugs from a cabinet. "Yeah, I did. But we've got to find something solid we can go to the cops with." He filled the mugs and set them down on the island before returning to his stool. "How about the dope you found on Maitland and Gabrielle? That proves he's a liar at least."

"They don't prosecute rich old men who lie about their relationships with young, attractive women. The courts are overburdened enough as it is."

"You're right. I told you I didn't know what to do."

"What about going back to Niebuhr's wife? If you could convince her that her husband is really in trouble, maybe you could get the cops back on the case. Have them question Maitland or Breen for instance. That would stir the pot." Riordan took a sip of coffee. He blinked as a faint expression of surprise registered on his features.

"No," said Ted Valmont wearily. "I don't think that will fly either. I'm pretty sure she's in on it. She may not have known where Niebuhr was in the beginning, but I'm betting they clued her in as part of the business with the letter. If I approach her now, she'll just report it to Breen and Maitland."

Riordan nodded with his nose deep in the mug of coffee. "All right. How about contacting Gabrielle? She's living proof this thing you're talking about exists and we know she's got some pretty good ideas about what they've been up to."

Ted Valmont scowled and tugged the belt of his kimono tighter. "I don't want to risk it. Breen and Maitland aren't stupid. They must suspect that Gabrielle tipped me off to the zombie factory. Can you imagine the hold they have on her? If she doesn't do what they say, they could remove or disable the device. She would be a quadriplegic again."

Riordan seemed not to have heard what Ted Valmont said. He looked down into his mug: it was empty. "This is pretty good—you got any more?"

Ted Valmont got off his stool and poured Riordan another mug. "Glad you like the Blue Mountain coffee. Did you hear me?" he inquired tartly. "Gabrielle's out."

Riordan growled between his teeth. "If Gabrielle's out, then all we can do is stall for time."

Ted Valmont put down the pot and returned to his place. "Stall for time? I tell Breen I can't make up my mind about their evil plot and could I please have a week or so to think about it?"

"No, you moron. You tell him you're in—and you damn well better make it convincing."

Ted Valmont studied Riordan's face awhile before responding. "Okay. I can do that. But what does it buy us? What do we do in the meantime?"

"Stake out Maitland's property and hope for a break."

"A break? I'd like to think I'd be risking my neck for something a little more solid than a break."

"Break and neck may not be the best words to use together." Riordan smiled tepidly. "But what it boils down to is this: I'll watch the comings and goings off the estate and hopefully I'll see something incriminating or I'll have the opportunity to get one of the key players alone."

"Not Gabrielle," said Ted Valmont quickly.

Riordan shrugged. "Niebuhr would be best. From your description, it sounds like he would milk pretty easy. I might even be able to do something with one of Maitland's farm hands, if the circumstances were right. But as for Gabrielle, if I manage to tail her off the estate to neutral ground, you better damn well believe I'm approaching her. This is serious, Valmont. If you're right about the suicide bomber, these guys are stone killers. With even the slightest suspicion that Gabrielle sent you the message about the factory, why wouldn't they eliminate her? She's already served her purpose. The best way for you to protect her is to stop them as soon as possible. You got it?"

Ted Valmont tilted his coffee mug forward and stared fixedly at the circle of brown liquid at the bottom. "Yeah, I got it," he agreed softly. Nothing more was said for several moments.

A police siren wailed in the distance. It filled the silence between the two men, growing louder as it came closer to the house.

Riordan pushed off his coffee mug and stood up. He gave a lopsided grin. "Well, here's my ride."

The siren diminished as the police car went by on an adjacent street. Ted Valmont looked up at Riordan and shook his head. "You do belong in the back of a police cruiser. Now get out of here. I'll call you after I speak to Breen."

Riordan nodded and ambled out of the room. At the front door, he jiggled the wobbly knob and peeled back a six-inch splinter from the door casing. "Deduct it from my retainer," he called out.

Larry Breen stood in the middle of his office with his back to the door making a throwing motion with his right arm. Gripped in his hand was a paddle-shaped device with an LED screen centered in the middle, a row of plastic buttons below and a hand crank protruding from the side. A high pitched sound like that made by line unwinding from a reel emanated from the device. Breen moved the paddle-shaped thing to his left hand and wound the crank with his right. Suddenly, it seemed to twitch and shake and the sound of splashing water could be heard. Breen yanked the device towards him and struggled to turn the hand crank against what appeared to be stiff resistance. He glanced over his shoulder during his machinations and saw Ted Valmont standing in the doorway with a blank look of surprise on his face.

"Hooked a big one," said Breen in a strained voice. "Top water lure did the trick."

With the stiff demeanor of someone who does not want to betray what he is thinking, Ted Valmont inclined his head slightly to acknowledge the remark, pulled the office door closed and sat down in the guest chair. Breen continued his struggle with the device until a mechanical voice said, "Bass landed. Twelve pounds."

Breen relaxed and dabbed at his forehead with his shirtsleeve. He turned to smile broadly at Ted Valmont and held up the device. "My latest toy."

Ted Valmont returned the broad smile, but on him it seemed to have an unnatural manic quality. "So I gathered," he said. "But I didn't figure you for a bass fisherman, Larry."

"A virtual bass fisherman, Ted. There is a difference. No need to actually handle the slimy, stinky fish for one. And no need to worry about stray casts becoming tangled in the trees for another. But as for that, I've actually become quite good at casting. The motion is remarkably similar to the overhead thrust in saber. Did I mention that I was a champion saber fencer in school?"

"Yes, I believe that has come up once or twice."

Breen set the virtual fishing reel down and dropped into his high backed chair. He dabbed at his forehead once more and then folded his hands placidly over his bulging gut. "Well, Ted," he said in casual way. "I enjoyed our dinner last night. Excellent food—and wine. I may just have to order some of that vintage from your winery."

"It is good wine," said Ted Valmont slowly, seeming to reflect. "I'll tell you what. I'll have Bruce pull a case aside for you and ship it to your house. My treat."

"That's very generous of you, Ted. I appreciate it." There was nothing in Breen's face or actions to suggest that he was the least bit curious or anxious about Ted Valmont's visit. He looked across the desk with a relaxed, almost self-satisfied expression.

Ted Valmont nervously fingered the clasp of one of his cuff links. "I've been thinking about the offer you made last night, and I've come by to tell you that I'd like to accept. It is gratifying to see the technology pan out as I hoped, even if the—the vehicle for delivering it to market is not what I anticipated. And when you factor in the advantages of a more direct participation in the returns on the investment and an opportunity to help my brother—well...I'd be stupid to pass it up."

Breen smiled grandly, beneficently, like the pope on parade. "There really wasn't any other decision possible, was there Ted?"

Ted Valmont looked up from the cuff link and met Breen's eyes. "No, there really wasn't—once I had a chance to think it all through. But there's just one thing."

"Yes," said Breen, and leaned forward. A cunning look crept onto his face. "You wouldn't be worried about the split, would you?"

Ted Valmont bowed his head slightly and held out his hands in a gesture of acknowledgment. "You read my mind. I don't expect as big a stake as you or Maitland, or even Warren, but I certainly expect more than Cardinal. As you said last night, I did find the opportunity originally—and now that I'm back in—I think I can close down the NeuroStimix operation a great deal more smoothly than you would have otherwise been able."

Breen laughed. "Yes, it will be easier if we don't have to go around you all the time, won't it Ted? In any case, you seem to have hit upon the right answer. Our thinking is that you get a ten percent equity position, with an opportunity to earn another five percent based on how you manage things like the NeuroStimix shut down. Tillman is only in for five percent himself, so I think you'll have to agree that's more than fair."

Ted Valmont tugged on his earlobe and didn't say anything for a moment. "I can live with that," he said at last. "But I lied. There is one more thing: I don't want to deal with Maitland. I don't like him and I don't trust him."

Breen laughed harder, crinkling the skin around his eyes. "You're right, Ted. He's really not one of us, is he? I understand your position and will do my best to accommodate it. And, truth to tell, my strong suspicion is that Douglas, for his part, would like to limit contact as well. It should not be so very hard to arrange."

Breen pushed himself back from his desk and reached over to pick up the virtual fishing reel. "Well, I'm sure you have a backlog of work to catch up on since you've been away from the office, so I won't hold you up any longer. We'll get down to the contracts and such in a few months' time after we incorporate the new company. At that point, we can also look into making the technology available for your brother. In the interim, you know what you can do to most help the partnership along."

"Shoot NeuroStimix in the head," said Ted Valmont grimly.

Breen chortled and stood to resume his virtual fishing. "Exactly right," he said over the sound of unreeling line. He turned to catch Ted Valmont's eye as he got up to leave the room. "Oh, and Ted, thank you again for the wine. You won't forget to have Mr. Crane send it my way, will you?"

DINING WITH THE DOGGIE

"He is a mixed breed, very mixed. Rumors about his formative years include escaping from a washing machine, traveling with the professional arm wrestling circuit, and being dismissed from a doggy manners school."

—Pets.com sock puppet official biography

AUGUST RIORDAN SAT AT A WOODEN TABLE outside the Doggie Diner on Sloat Avenue in San Francisco. On the table next to him were a pitcher of beer and a bag of unshelled, salted peanuts. He had his knife out, and in between sips of beer, was carving something into the table.

A tired, haggard-looking Ted Valmont came up the sidewalk from the direction of the San Francisco Zoo, paused a moment to gawk at the seven foot sculpture of a dog's head on a pole above them, and then walked around the other side of the table to sit down. "Excellent choice, Riordan," he said snidely.

Riordan looked up from the table, shoved a glass in Ted Valmont's direction and poured him some of the dark beer. "Have a drink and give your pedigree a rest, Valmont. Did you bring it?"

Ted Valmont nodded, paying no attention to the beer. "Yes, I brought it." He pulled his Palm computer from the breast pocket of his sport coat and passed it over to Riordan. "Press the green button," he urged, when Riordan seemed not to know what to do.

Riordan mashed down the power button and watched as the screen flickered to life with a picture of a ramshackle bar. "Meet me at 8 on Saturday," was written below the photograph. Riordan grunted. "What's the name of the place again?"

"It's called the Smudge Pot. It's some kind of locals' dive bar, I gather."

Riordan passed the computer back to Ted Valmont. "You're getting a tour of the best places today, aren't you?" He gunned the remaining beer in his glass and poured another. "I still don't like it," he said after another swallow.

Ted Valmont had been watching the older man intently, as if looking for a sign of approval or agreement. Now he sighed and reached into the bag for a peanut. He cracked it distractedly against the table. "I don't like it either, but what choice do we have? You've been watching the estate for a week. The waiting is killing me—I don't know how long I can keep up the front with Breen."

Riordan picked up his knife again and returned to his work on the table. "You said you can't even tell if the message came from Gabrielle. It feels too much like a set up."

"I couldn't tell if any of the messages came from her. But they must have."

"Did you ask her?"

In an annoyed gesture, Ted Valmont swept the cracked peanut off the table. He rummaged in the bag for another. "No," he said sharply. "I never asked her directly. She more or less admitted sending the first one and I never got a chance to talk to her about the second."

"Let's hope you get a chance to ask about the third." Riordan used both hands to push the knife blade deeper into the wood of the table. "Where did you park?"

"At the zoo lot, like you told me."

Riordan nodded over his work. "Good. The decoy's driving your Ferrari down to Carmel. I've got the rental on a side street. You drive. I'm going to hide in the back."

Ted Valmont frowned. "Whatever for?"

Riordan leaned forward over the table, thrusting his chin out a little. "If it is a set up, it's better if they think there's one of us instead of two."

Ted Valmont looked at Riordan soberly for a moment and then reached into his coat pocket for a roll of antacids. He popped three of them in his mouth and quickly washed them down with a swig of beer. "Jesus," he said, "this never ends..."

Riordan finished what he was carving and threw the knife into the table. The quivering, stainless steel blade stuck in the wood near his handiwork—an old Burma-Shave jingle:

Road

Was slippery

Curve was sharp

White robe, halo

Wings and harp

Burma-Shave

"Everything ends, Valmont," he said. "It's just a matter of how."

Ted Valmont took a white tablet from his breast pocket. Bracing the steering wheel of the rented Ford Taurus with his forearms, he snapped the tablet in half. One half went out the window onto the asphalt of the Golden Gate Bridge, the other he swallowed dry.

"That didn't look like another of your antacids," said August Riordan from a cramped position on the floor of the back seat.

"It wasn't," said Ted Valmont shortly without turning his head. "Try speed instead."

Riordan gave a low chuckle. "Why'd you throw half away? Don't you know there are children sleeping in India?"

Ted Valmont twisted the wheel sharply to cut out from behind a lumbering delivery truck that came into his lane. He mashed down the horn. "Half a tablet should do me fine. I just need a little boost to get through this."

Thrown to the side by the sudden maneuver, Riordan struggled to right himself. He spat a carpet fiber from his mouth. "Good thinking, Valmont. Tired, edgy and hopped up on speed. That's the perfect condition for the meet."

"I guess you think drunk is better. You chugged most of the beer—and don't think I haven't noticed that hip flask. I just better not see any guns."

"Then you just better not look too hard."

Ted Valmont snapped a quick glance over his shoulder. "Damn it, Riordan. I'm serious. Gabrielle is very much at risk. We've got to be careful."

"At least we can agree on that." Riordan relaxed back onto the floor. "All right. No more out of you. If someone is following us, they're sure as hell going to think it's odd if you spend the whole drive talking to yourself. Why don't you get down to picking your nose or whatever it is you venture capitalists do by yourselves."

Ted Valmont lowered his hand below window level and flipped off Riordan. Thereafter, he replied to Riordan's sporadic questions with only a grunt or a quick shake of his head.

At a poorly marked farm road just inside the town limits of Rutherford, they turned west off Highway 29 and headed towards the foothills. A few minutes later, Ted Valmont wheeled the Taurus into the rutted, dirt parking lot of a dilapidated roadhouse. Three pickups, a motorcycle and an olive tree that had been maimed more than once by drunks on their way home were the only things in the lot. Ted Valmont parked well away from the other vehicles and cut his lights and motor. He looked across to the stucco building and stared at the flecked, two-foot high red letters along its side that proclaimed the name of the establishment in a crude block print.

"Welcome to the Smudge Pot," he said softly.

Riordan lifted his head and half rolled onto his hip. He extracted a silver flask from his back pocket and unscrewed the cap. "Everything you hoped for?" he asked.

"Everything and more. If Gabrielle was looking for a quiet, out-of-the-way spot, it would be hard to do better—or creepier."

Riordan took a long swig from the flask and wiped his mouth on his sleeve. "Still think I'm being paranoid?"

Ted Valmont went through the motions of unbuckling his seat belt. "I'm not sure," he said, his lips moving only slightly. "But if you're drinking to cover it, let me say that I prefer sober paranoia to drunken courage."

Riordan smiled and took another swig. "Relax. There isn't enough in two flasks to get me drunk. Do you see her car?"

"We're about ten minutes early." Ted Valmont brought his hand up to his mouth as if to cover a cough. "I don't know what she drives, but I'm guessing it's not a pick-up or a Harley—and those are the only choices."

"Okay, go in and wait for her. I'll hang back until I see her arrive. If she doesn't show in a little while I may come in on my own. But whatever I do, don't wait more than twenty minutes for her. Got it?"

"Roger Wilco," said Ted Valmont softly and popped open the door. He stepped into the lot, paused to wipe his hands nervously on the back of his jeans and then slammed the door shut and quick-footed it over to the roadhouse. The interior of the bar was a lot of knotty pine scarred with bar patrons' initials, a cement floor covered by sawdust and peanut shells, greasy stuffed animals with dusty glass eyes and the overpowering bouquet of stale beer, cigarettes and the kind of cigars with plastic mouthpieces that come five to a box at the local Wal-Mart. A jukebox with two busted legs stood balanced on pair of overturned ashtrays playing the Sons of the Pioneers' "Tumbling Tumbleweed." A couple of Latino farmworkers were bent over a coin-operated pool table at one end of the room, and at the other, three Anglos with baseball caps, farmer's tans and cowboy boots sat in a rickety wooden booth with quart bottles of beer and a plate of hardboiled eggs. There was no sign of Gabrielle.

Ted Valmont's eyes flitted around the space. He mashed his palms into the back of his jeans once more and walked stiffly up to the bar. Behind it was a hefty, middle-aged blonde with a penchant for aquamarine eye shadow—and plenty of it. Behind her were a chipped, oval mirror and a shimmering electric waterfall sign for Olympia beer of early 1960's vintage. The bartender slapped a napkin on the warped metal surface of the bar causing her charm bracelets to jangle dully. "What ya drinkin' tonight, sugar?" she asked.

Ted Valmont seemed surprised by the question. He gestured at the Olympia sign. "How about an Oly, then?"

The bartender broke into a wide grin that revealed a spate of yellow teeth encrusted with a mass of silver and gold fillings. "Drink a lot of Oly, do you?"

Ted Valmont smiled like it hurt. "Yes, yes I do. Why do you ask?"

The bartender cackled. "Because the good folks in Tumwater, Washington sold the brewery to Miller. We kept the sign, but we haven't had the beer in years."

Ted Valmont jerked his chin in annoyance. "Give me whatever you have on draft."

"We don't have anything on draft."

"Then just give me whatever can or bottle you come up with when you reach your hand into the ice box, will you?"

The bartender cackled again and bent down to open a cooler. She pulled out a bottle of Bud and expertly pried the cap off on an opener screwed into the bar. "That'll be two bucks, sugar."

Ted Valmont slapped three dollar bills down on the bar and took his beer to an empty booth near the door. He took a negligent sip from the bottle, made a face and set the bottle aside. A moment later he pulled it back and picked at the band of paper around the neck. The jukebox played Patsy Cline's "Crazy" and then shifted into a scratched rendition of The Band's "The Weight." The needle got stuck on the opening lyric, "I pulled into Nazareth/Was feelin' about half past dead," repeating it a number of times until the bartender came out from behind the bar and gave the machine a healthy whack.

A loud exultation in Spanish marked the end of the pool game. The loser—a thickset man in a tank top with barbed wire tattooed around his arm—dug into his pocket for some more quarters, while the winner—a tubby, dark skinned man with a pierced eyebrow— chugged the rest of his beer and slammed the bottle down with a victory flourish.

Ted Valmont twitched his leg up and down and glanced at the gold Cartier on his wrist that had replaced the stolen tank watch. He watched as a man from the far booth got up, mumbled something about draining his lizard and went through a swinging door marked "Gents" across from the pool table. When he came out, Ted Valmont waited until he had rejoined his companions, then got up from the table on the same mission.

He was standing in front of a corroded, trough-like urinal in the rest room when the farmworkers from the pool table came into the cramped space. He turned to look at them, nodded, sidled further down the urinal and gave his full attention to the business at hand. Without warning or hesitation, the Latino with the tattoo pulled a wicked-looking leather blackjack from his hip pocket and swung hard for Ted Valmont's left ear.

Ted Valmont made a sound like an old man spitting out his dentures and crumpled to the floor, banging his forehead on the edge of the urinal as he fell. Urine soaked his trousers, then dribbled out of his exposed penis as he lay on the grimy linoleum in a curled position.

The Latino with the pierced eyebrow watched the proceedings without comment and then reached back to lock the door to the bar. The other man returned the blackjack to his pocket and fished out a key that he used on a door at the back of the rest room. It opened onto the night behind the roadhouse, where a pickup truck sat idling.

The tattooed man looked down at Ted Valmont and laughed. "Okay, Miguel," he said to his cohort. "I hit him with the blackjack. You stuff his dick back in his pants."

CELLAR TASTING

"We have a motto that you should get to know your coffin before you're buried in it."
—Brad Miller, co-founder, YourCoffin.com

WHEN TED VALMONT REGAINED CONSCIOUSNESS HE WAS lying on a narrow cot in a darkened room. The walls of the room were covered by rough plaster, and looming around him in the semi-light, were racks of oak barrels that reached nearly to the rounded ceiling. A lump the size of a robin's egg bulged from Ted Valmont's forehead. His skin was covered with a thin, glittering sweat and his eyes looked like sunken upholstery buttons. He groaned and reached for the back of his head, then bit his lip and winced as he probed the place where the blackjack had struck him.

"Ted," whined a male voice. "Are you okay? I was worried that you would never wake up."

Like an I-beam hoisted from the ground by a crane, Ted Valmont laboriously raised himself off the bed to rest on one elbow. He shaded his eyes against the dull light and squinted in the direction of the voice. Standing coyly beside the wine barrels was a pasty-faced man with wispy brown hair, and a tiny, puckered baby-like mouth. He wore oversized clear plastic glasses, a polo shirt and stiff blue jeans with a crease ironed down the middle of each leg. Steam drifted off a mug with a red plastic stirrer that he clutched to his chest with both hands, and in the face of Ted Valmont's intense scrutiny, he seemed ready to bolt from the room at any moment.

Ted Valmont slumped back onto the cot. "Warren," he said heavily, with equal parts resignation and annoyance. "Where are we?"

"We're in the Maitland wine caves."

Ted Valmont took a deep breath and exhaled slowly. He covered his eyes with his forearm. "I guess that's not a big surprise. Do you know how I got here?"

Warren Niebuhr crept closer to the cot. "Some of the winery workers brought you in. They didn't tell me where they found you—or how you got to be the way you are."

"You mean how I got beat up?" Ted Valmont put in harshly. He waved his hand. "Pass that. Rhetorical question. What are you doing here?"

Niebuhr gave a girlish shrug. "Well, I've been staying with Maitland since I left the conference."

Ted Valmont sighed. "I know that, Warren. I meant what are you doing here with me? What are they planning?"

Niebuhr stirred his drink and considered. "I'm not sure, Ted. When you came in, the workers came and got me to look after you. I didn't know exactly what to do, to tell you the truth. I mean I certainly know a fair amount of brain physiology and all that, but I really don't know the first thing about treating head injuries. I'm just glad you've regained consciousness. I know that's a good sign."

Ted Valmont struggled upright and glared at Niebuhr incredulously. Niebuhr colored, and trying to cover his embarrassment, hunched over to take a sip of his drink using the plastic stirrer as a straw.

This seemed to provoke Ted Valmont further. "Cut that out," he growled. "Grown men who've created technology to enslave others do not drink their fucking tea through a fucking plastic stirrer."

Niebuhr drew back. "You're not being fair, Ted. Maitland and Larry Breen are the ones who've applied the NeuroStimix technology in ways that I did not intend. They've kept me here. I had no choice in the matter."

"The hell you say. Somewhere along the way you made the choice to quit NeuroStimix and throw in with them. Everything else is a consequence of that decision."

Niebuhr's voice became lower, more conspiratorial. "I tried to help you stop them. But you botched it."

"What?"

"Who do you think sent those messages to your Palm Pilot?"

Ted Valmont raised his eyebrows and then grimaced from the pain it brought. "I thought Gabrielle did," he said softly.

"No, it was me. Except for—except for the last one. They made me send that." Niebuhr stirred his tea, considering. "I even changed the bomber's programming so he could speak to warn you. I took some incredible risks."

"You're a true hero, Warren."

Niebuhr got a foxy look on his face and leaned forward. "Maybe you never intended to stop them. Maybe you were just angry that they had cut you out of the action. They tell me you're with us now. You're part of the new company we're going to form."

Ted Valmont laughed rudely. "Sounds like you're having trouble deciding whether you're with them yourself. I had to make them believe I was in to buy time. Now shut up and let me think."

Ted Valmont collapsed onto the cot once more. Niebuhr made a face at him and took another sip of tea—still drinking through the stirrer.

"Warren," said Ted Valmont in a calmer voice. "Did they bring anyone else with me? I mean, was there anyone you didn't recognize as a Maitland employee with the men who brought me?"

The sound of a bolt being thrown back cut off Niebuhr's reply. A door at the rear of the room swung open and through it stepped Maitland and his foreman Ramos. Maitland had jettisoned his business suit for a return to overalls and he had his thumbs hooked under the bib in a cocksure way. "Yes, Valmont," he said, not bothering to hide the jubilation in his voice. "We bagged Mr. Riordan well before we got to you. A man is pretty vulnerable lying on his back in a car with a 9mm automatic shoved in his nose."

Ted Valmont's eyes squinted a keen hatred into Maitland's. "Where is he?"

Smiling, Maitland unhooked a thumb to scratch his ribs. "Believe me, Valmont, it's a great relief to know that I'll never have to answer another of your prying, impertinent questions again. But thank you for answering one of mine."

"I'm not following."

"I never believed you'd come over to our side, but knowing for sure makes it so much easier to convince Larry about what needs to be done." Maitland turned to Ramos and jerked his head in the direction of Ted Valmont. "Grab him. I'll take the other one."

Ramos lumbered over to the cot and took hold of Ted Valmont by his lapels. He yanked him off the bed and pulled the taller man to eye level on bent, trembling legs. "*Hola, novia*," he hissed, then cuffed him—hard—with an open hand. Ted Valmont's head lolled to one side, and Ramos dragged his limp body across the room and out the door.

Niebuhr had retreated against the rear wall. Maitland wheeled on him and slapped the mug of tea from his hands. Niebuhr yelped as hot liquid splashed down the front of his shirt and the mug exploded into shards on the concrete floor. "Chamomile-swilling freak," snapped Maitland, shoving Niebuhr roughly in the shoulder.

They followed Ramos and Ted Valmont down the corridor to another door. Ramos held Ted Valmont up on his knees with one hand while he pounded on the closed door with the other. Silver flashed at his wrist.

Ted Valmont caught the flash through half-closed eyes, and rousing himself, took hold of Ramos's thick arm. "That's my watch, you bastard."

The door jerked open suddenly and Ramos grabbed two handfuls of Ted Valmont's shirt and flung him across the threshold. Ted Valmont lost his grip and landed in a sprawl about two yards into the room. A woman's voice screamed his name. Ramos strode over to where he lay and reached down to unfasten the expensive Cartier. "No," exulted Ramos, "that's my other watch you're wearing."

Mario stepped out from behind the door. Maitland launched the now blubbering Niebuhr towards him and pulled the door closed. "Stand him up over there with Gabrielle," he ordered.

Mario bent Niebuhr's arm behind his back and frog-marched him to a metal table piled high with electronics. Beside the table was a wheelchair, and seated naked in the wheelchair with a broad plastic brace to hold her chest and head upright was Gabrielle. Her pale arms and legs lay dormant and purposeless against the cruel, bright chrome of the chair. She wore no makeup and her hair was a flattened tangle, as if she had just woken from a long sleep. Her eyes darted around the room in a panic and her breathing was rapid. Tears squeezed out from the corners of her eyes.

"Tears, bitter tears," said Larry Breen in a fulsome tone. He stood at the back of the table, twirling a Phi Beta Kappa key on a chain. "I think there's a sonnet there somewhere."

At the sound of Breen's voice, Ted Valmont stirred on the floor and turned his head to look his direction with a single dull eye. His glance slid from Breen to Gabrielle, who whimpered inarticulately when she met his gaze.

"Well, hello, Ted," said Breen with warmth. "It looks as though you've wet yourself."

"Asshole," croaked Ted Valmont. "What have you done to Gabrielle?"

Breen smiled and walked behind the wheel chair, where he took hold of the handles and rocked the chair gently back and forth. "What do they call it when musicians do without electric amplification? Playing unplugged? This is Gabrielle unplugged."

A horrible strangling noise rose up in Gabrielle's throat. Her eyes were marbles of anguish.

Ted Valmont gulped an involuntary breath. "Turn her back on," he shouted. "This has nothing to do with her."

Breen wagged his finger. "I'm afraid it does, Ted. Gabrielle is altogether too infatuated with you. Eventually, she would have betrayed us."

Ted Valmont pushed himself off the floor. He stared at Breen woodenly. Then, looking down, he mumbled, "Where's Riordan?"

"Why, he's right there beside you. And what is that sticking out of the back of his neck?"

Ted Valmont managed a painful turn to his left. August Riordan was sitting bolt upright on a cot with his hands pressed flat against his thighs. His shirt had been stripped off and a silver box very much like the one Ted Valmont had taken off the factory worker protruded from his neck. He made no movement, and except for a wild, terrorized look in his eyes, seemed unaware of his surroundings.

Douglas Maitland clapped his hands impatiently. "Enough of this, Larry. We need to get going."

Breen nodded. "I apologize for grandstanding, Douglas. This is your show. Do as you think best."

Maitland gestured at Ted Valmont. "Up against the wall with him, Ramos."

Ramos came up with a 9mm automatic and yanked Ted Valmont to his feet. He spun him around and backpedaled him to the rough brick wall at the rear of the room. With Ramos training the 9mm on a spot between Ted Valmont's eyes, Maitland came up to hover malevolently like an enormous praying mantis.

"You and Riordan are going to have another accident," he said cozily. He took a fistful of Ted Valmont's hair and pulled his head over to speak into his ear. "A fatal and self-inflicted accident."

Ted Valmont's eyes took on a stricken look and his whole face became suddenly haggard. Maitland laughed and shoved Ted Valmont's head to the side. Then he cursed, muttering, "little faggot," as he wiped mousse that had come from Ted Valmont's hair onto his overalls. "Bring the other stimulator," he shouted at Mario.

Mario came hurrying up with a second box, which he passed to Maitland, then took hold of Ted Valmont's collar and yanked it open. The first two buttons flew off and Mario spun Ted Valmont around once more to shove his face roughly into the wall. He grasped the back of his collar and hauled the material of his shirt well past his neckline.

Maitland held the silver box close to Ted Valmont's face, steel prongs jutting out from it like the fangs of a snake. Ted Valmont ran a thick tongue across crusted lips. His breath came ragged and shallow. "Don't move, Valmont," said Maitland with the intimacy of a lover. "This part's a little tricky. I'd hate to do any...damage."

Just as he mouthed the word damage, Maitland jammed the prongs home. Ted Valmont cried out, twitched his hand up to his neck. Ramos hammered it down and augured the barrel of the gun into his temple. "Keep your hands at your sides, *chilito*," he hissed.

When Maitland stepped away, the silver box clung limpet-like to Ted Valmont's neck. Trails of blood trickled down from the puncture wounds. Mario peeled Ted Valmont from the wall, and Maitland came around to fasten nylon straps under his throat, cinching the device firmly in place. "There," he said. "Now you're a good little zombie like your friend Riordan."

Ramos hustled Ted Valmont over to the cot and pushed him down on it. Maitland made a detour to the table where Breen, Niebuhr and Gabrielle still waited. He picked up a Palm computer with a wireless modem attached and handed it to Mario, then walked over to stand in front of Ted Valmont and Riordan.

He chuckled without mirth. "I doubt the computer manufacturer ever anticipated it, but thanks to some programming by Dr. Niebuhr, Mario can read his e-mail, keep track of his appointments and control both of you—all with the same Palm computer."

"I don't think Mario has any e-mail or appointments, boss," Ramos interjected.

"No, I suppose not." Maitland's gaze went back and forth between Riordan and Ted Valmont. "We'll start with Riordan, I think. That way, Valmont, you can see what's coming and have an opportunity to think about it long and hard."

Ted Valmont sank his head into his hands. "You were born at the wrong time in history, Maitland. You belong in a dungeon with a black hood over your head."

"Ted, I really would not antagonize the man if I were you," chided Breen. "You don't know what you're—"

Maitland cut him off. "That's enough, Larry. Valmont knows everything. It's his defining characteristic. These dot-com punks are no different than the smug, know-it-all, old money bastards I've fought my whole life. It all comes down to entitlement: whether the money comes from the Internet or daddy's trust fund."

Ted Valmont looked up from his hands to stare at the tall, white-haired man. "Feel better now?"

Maitland laughed. "Better than you will. Since we've had the ability to record and replay sequences of motion on the device, Ramos has come up with some very creative ideas for—how did Larry phrase it—self actualization."

Ramos made a scissors gesture with his fingers and Maitland laughed again. "Yes, my favorite is the pruning shears. We give the subject a pair of shears and, well, you can imagine the rest." He sighed. "Unfortunately, we really can't do anything that creative with you two. Your injuries need to be consistent with a car accident. Bruises, broken bones and so on." He patted his bald pate and then hooked his thumbs back under the bib of his overalls. "Get Riordan lined up," he said to Mario. "And freeze Valmont so we don't have any more sass out of him."

Mario used the stylus of the Palm computer to touch a button on the display. Ted Valmont snapped into a rigid position exactly like Riordan. Sitting together on the cot, they looked like a pair of stone lions guarding the entrance to a library. Mario flicked the stylus over a menu on the display and selected an entry marked "standing." Riordan jumped to attention, and then Ramos came up to guide him by the shoulders to a line on the floor marked with masking tape about ten feet in front of the brick wall.

Riordan's face was drawn: thin and rigid with lines of strain around the mouth. His unblinking eyes were prized open unnaturally and they had a dreadful, glassy appearance. The scar on his chin shone pale and waxy.

Ramos stepped to one side and grinned at Mario. "On your mark…"

Mario worked the stylus once more and Riordan bounded forward in a full sprint. He covered the distance to the wall in less than two seconds and strode directly into it without hesitation. He hit with a sickening thump and rebounded onto the ground, where his head whiplashed against the concrete. Blood flowed immediately from his mouth and battered nose, but he lay exactly as he fell and made no cry or sound of any sort.

Niebuhr shrank into himself and dissolved onto floor, a blubbering heap. Gabrielle choked off a sob, tried to wrench her head around to look at Breen. "Stop them, Larry, please."

Breen lost some of his own florid color. With an obvious effort to master himself, he took a deep breath and passed his hand over his beard. "No," he said with a hoarse and gritty voice that did not achieve the admonishing tone for which he aimed. "You should understand that we are showing you this for a reason. Both of you. If you ever get out of line again, this will be your fate. And Warren, please don't labor under the misapprehension that you are indispensable. We have several men on the staff now that know as much or more than you. And they are ever so much easier to work with."

Maitland walked over to where Niebuhr lay and prodded his butt with a work boot. Niebuhr flinched and scuttled out of range. "What Larry says is very true, Warren. Very true. And don't let's forget Dr. Frankenstein was destroyed by his own creation." Maitland laughed sourly "Let's go," he said to Mario. "Set him up again."

Mario again selected the menu entry marked "standing" and Riordan bounded to attention. Ramos came up to him and slapped him on the back. "I guess you thought you were Superman, didn't you buddy?" Nothing changed in Riordan's appearance or demeanor to indicate he heard the remark, and Ramos guided him—stiff-legged and bleeding—back to the mark on the floor.

Riordan was made to run into the wall again. When he came to attention, his right eye was swollen shut, the ear on that side was cut and badly abraded and it appeared that many or all of his front teeth were broken or dislodged. He walked back to the line with an odd gait that prompted Maitland to comment, "Must have broken a kneecap."

The third time Riordan did not get up. He lay prostrate on his back like a store mannequin that fell from its display window. The bare skin of his chest was bruised and marked by the rough mortar of the brick wall, and blood from his nose and now gaping mouth formed a shiny crimson pool at his ear. Mario worked the stylus of the Palm computer furiously, then announced, "He's dead or too far gone to keep going. I'm not showing any feedback from him now."

Maitland cracked a hoary knuckle on his index finger and grunted in a satisfied way. "Okay," he said. "Let's get Valmont going. Give me the phone book." Ramos pulled a thick book of yellow pages off the table and handed it to Maitland. "All right. Hands out," said Maitland.

Mario selected a new setting from the menu. In response, Ted Valmont thrust his hands out in front of him with his fingertips touching in a circle. Maitland rolled up the telephone book tight and slipped it into the circle. "Have him grip it," he commanded. Mario touched the display once more and Ted Valmont's hands closed tight about the book near the bottom.

Maitland squatted down to look Ted Valmont in the eye. He smiled in a confidential way. "You know, Valmont, prisoners are often beaten with phone books because they leave no marks. Yet the beatings can be remarkably painful." Maitland pushed the rolled phone book further into Ted Valmont's grip. "I think we'll make an exception to the usual gag policy and allow you to give us your impressions."

Maitland glanced back at Mario. "Stretch him out," he said. Mario's command caused Ted Valmont to straighten his legs out in a V and freed him of the electronic gag.

"You twisted, pathetic pile of flea dirt," he yelled. "I'm going to—"

Mario flicked his stylus once more and Ted Valmont leaned over and swatted fiercely at his right shin with the phone book. He bit off his words and his eyes bulged out. His arms brought the phone book down on the same place three times in quick succession. A tremendous howl escaped his lips.

Maitland and Ramos turned to grin at one another. "What a talker," said Maitland. Ramos gave a belly laugh and wiped moisture from the corner of his eye.

Like a kind of demonic machine, Ted Valmont continued to pummel himself methodically with the phone book. The blows alternated between legs and inched slowly toward his groin, Mario's commands insuring that every square inch of flesh was subjected to a torrent of impacts before the phone book moved higher. By the time Ted Valmont reached his kneecaps, sweat flew from his face and arms and he could no longer even form distinct cries in response to the blows. He was reduced to continual stream of whimpers and mournful groaning sounds.

"Please stop this. Stop this now!" yelled a shrill female voice.

Everyone in the room—everyone but Ted Valmont—turned to look at Gabrielle. Her lower lip trembled and her bloodshot eyes begged for mercy. The plastic brace that cupped her chin was dripping wet with the tears and mucus that had run down her face. "Please, please," she repeated.

Maitland smiled viciously. "What a big tough guy your boyfriend turned out to be. But there's nothing to be done for it now."

As if to punctuate Maitland's assertion, a horrible wail lacerated the room: Ted Valmont swung the phone book directly into his groin. His face clenched in a spasm of unmitigated pain.

Larry Breen went completely pale. He stroked his beard with a trembling hand. "Douglas," he said, straining to be heard over Ted Valmont's cries. "These two have seen enough. Perhaps it would be best if I took them back to the main house."

Maitland eyed Breen critically. Breen seemed to wilt under the duress of his scrutiny. "All right, Larry," Maitland said at last. "Take them to the house. But I'm sure you'll want to come right back."

Breen nodded and reached down to pull Niebuhr from the floor. "Come on, Warren," he urged. "You push Gabrielle and we'll get out of this din." Shielding his eyes from Ted Valmont with one hand, Niebuhr took a handle of Gabrielle's wheelchair with the other and maneuvered it back and then away from the table. Gabrielle, Niebuhr and Breen then made a slow procession out of the room, pulling the door closed behind them.

Once they had gone, Maitland shouted to Ramos, "Weak-willed gas bag." Then gesturing at Ted Valmont, "We'll switch him to a backhand soon so he can beat his head."

Ramos grunted his agreement, but as Maitland watched, the tip of a stainless steel blade suddenly blossomed from his throat. With a look of stunned surprise, Ramos toppled to the floor, dropping his 9mm automatic.

Down on one knee—near the place he had fallen—was August Riordan. Chest heaving, his pant leg pulled up to reveal the rig for the knife and his right arm extended from the follow through of the throw, he looked like a catcher in a grisly game of baseball. As the 9mm clattered to the floor, he dove for it, grabbing it up with both hands.

Maitland whipped his head around to stare at Riordan. "Stop him," he shouted.

Mario jerked the stylus over the display of the Palm computer in a frenzy. Riordan struggled upright and grinned, and with his broken teeth, mutilated nose and one eye swollen completely shut, it was a hideous thing to behold. He yanked at the strap at his throat, pulled the damaged device free and flung it at the wall. "Turn off Valmont," he commanded through puffed, cracked lips.

Mario hesitated, looking to Maitland for direction. Riordan caressed the trigger of his revolver. A shot went zinging between Mario and Douglas Maitland. Mario quickly complied with Riordan's order. Ted Valmont dropped the phone book mid-swing and slumped onto the cot.

Riordan rose unsteadily to his feet, favoring one leg, but kept the automatic trained squarely on Maitland. Maitland pasted him with a supercilious stare, but said nothing. "Tell me I won't get out of here," croaked Riordan.

"You won't get out of here," said Maitland, calmly and slowly, as if talking to a child.

Riordan twitched the automatic over to Mario, fired. A bullet slammed into his neck, spilling a stream of blood over the tattoo of flames. Mario was blown from his feet, landing in a dislocated heap behind Maitland. The Palm computer flew from his hands, skittering across the floor. "I don't want to get out of here," said Riordan. "I just want to be sure that you don't either."

Maitland and Riordan locked stares for a long moment: the bull and the matador. The bull blinked first. Maitland turned abruptly and dove for the door. Something cold and horrible gleamed in Riordan's one open eye as he lowered the automatic and squeezed off a shot. Maitland screamed. The slug caught him in the back, and he writhed on the ground under Mario's empty gaze, less than a foot away from the Latino's dead body.

Riordan threw the automatic to one side and limped over to the cot, where Ted Valmont had managed to pull himself upright. Ted Valmont looked up at Riordan, mumbled, "thanks." There was nothing to show that Riordan saw or heard him. He reached down to pick up the phone book, turned slowly and hobbled back over to Maitland with a ghastly leer on his face.

Stopping near Maitland's head, he dropped awkwardly to his knees as if he was going to pray. He rolled Maitland over and then swung the flat of phone book against Maitland face with tremendous force. Maitland howled and his head was driven to the side. Riordan wound up again and smacked Maitland's head the other direction. And again.

By the time Ted Valmont had lurched from the cot to wrap Riordan in a bear hug, Maitland face was a mass of bruises and he had long since lost consciousness. "Stop it," yelled Ted Valmont. "You'll kill him."

Riordan shrugged off Ted Valmont's embrace and fought his way to his feet. He probed his lower lip with his tongue, then bent over to spit a tooth and a mouthful of blood to the floor.

"And your point is?" he demanded, wiping his mouth on the back of his hand.

Ted Valmont started to reply when the sound of running footsteps came from the corridor outside. Riordan retrieved the gun, while Ted Valmont scurried to the side of the entrance with the phone book raised over his head. The door flew open and Gabrielle ran naked into the room. She checked up at the sight of Riordan taking aim at her belly button.

Ted Valmont came up from behind and touched her neck. She spun round, squealing to wrap him in a hug. "Oh my God," she said breathlessly. "I was sure you were dead."

"What's—what's happening?" said Ted Valmont, stupefied. "Where are Niebuhr and Breen?"

Gabrielle turned her head away. "Warren switched me on again as we were going down the corridor. Breen tried to stop me from coming back here, and I...I broke his neck."

TED, MEET WINIFRED

"We were both shocked at how well it worked."
—Paul Kunz, creator of the first web site, commenting on the reaction he and Tim Berners-Lee (the father of the World Wide Web) had on the first transatlantic demonstration of the technology

TED VALMONT EDGED STIFFLY DOWN A HOSPITAL corridor, leaning on an aluminum cane. The back of his head was swathed in a large bandage and a smaller one was pasted over his right eye, but his color was good and he smiled and nodded blithely at a curvy blonde nurse who greeted him with:

"The beautiful Mr. Valmont returns for a visit."

He came up to a closed door and pulled it open a few inches. Chris Duckworth could be seen standing next to a hospital bed with a Victoria's Secret shopping bag in his hand. Grinning, Ted Valmont paused with the door partially open to spy through the gap.

"What are you doing here?" said the occupant of the bed in a slurred but familiar voice.

"You said to come at eleven," replied Duckworth.

"That's a half hour from now."

Duckworth glanced down at his wrist. "Really?" he said. "This crappy watch you gave me must be fast."

"Probably to keep you company."

Duckworth stamped his foot. "That's libel!"

"I think you mean slander. But come off it, Chris. If you were brought up for lewd and lascivious, there's not a jury in California that would acquit."

Duckworth reached into the Victoria's Secret bag to pull out a bra with an enormous cup size. He held it up to his flat chest. "If the cup don't fit, you must acquit!"

"Ha," retorted the slurred voice. "I see you got yourself a new model."

Duckworth wreathed his upper body sinuously. "Yes, you likee big sailor man?"

"Well, it's not your grandfather's push-up bra, that's for sure."

Ted Valmont pulled the door fully open and stepped through. "Talk about your Norman Rockwell moments," he said.

Duckworth grinned hugely and dropped the bra from his chest. "Ted! It's great to see you! You're looking ever so much better."

Ted Valmont returned the grin, but the expression seemed to have more to do with inner amusement than a shared pleasure in the meeting. "It's nice to see you too, Chris." Pointing at the hospital bed and its occupant with his cane, he said, "How's our boy?"

August Riordan lay propped up in bed on two pillows. His nose was a mass of gauze and packed cotton, both eyes were black and it was clear that the tooth fairy owed him a lot of money. A topographical survey of all the scratches, cuts and bruises on his face would have run to pages, and his left leg—covered in a fiberglass cast from hip to ankle—hung from a traction bar at a thirty degree angle.

"Hail the conquering hero," said Riordan, his words slurred by swollen lips and missing teeth.

Ted Valmont advanced into the room under Duckworth's solicitous gaze. He shook his head. "If you can stand the sight of it, you should say that to a mirror. You're the one who stopped them."

Riordan snorted. "I've two things to say to that. One—" He held up blunt index finger. "I screwed up big time at that shit-hole of a bar. They should never have gotten either of us. Two—" A second finger joined the first. "My guess is in another minute, Gabrielle would have come into the room and done the job as good or better."

Ted Valmont eased himself into a chair. "I don't think I had another minute."

"Yeah, sorry I hung back so long," said Riordan. "Everything okay...down there?"

"No permanent damage. I'll be wearing a foam rubber codpiece for a few weeks is all. What I want to know is how you broke free."

"Yes," said Duckworth. "I've heard the story three times now, and you still haven't explained how you were able to pull that knife off your ankle."

Riordan gave a gap-toothed grin. "I'm here to tell you—drinking saved my life. I'd be a dead man if I hadn't had the beer and drained that hip flask in the parking lot waiting for Gabrielle to show."

Ted Valmont reached down to straighten his leg and grimaced. "You're going to have to explain that."

"I'm not sure I can entirely. Niebuhr gave me about twenty minutes of geek-speak on the topic this morning, but I didn't really follow. All I know is this: after my first run into the wall, I noticed that the control the device was exerting on my movements was breaking down. Not in my legs—I couldn't stop them from running—but I felt some latitude in the movements of my arms and torso. So, on the second and third runs, I twisted my shoulders and neck into the wall as I hit."

Duckworth slammed his fist into his palm. "To smash the device," he said eagerly.

Riordan looked at Duckworth and suppressed a smile. "Now don't go getting butch on me here, Chris. It hurts to laugh."

"Fuck you, August. Just finish the story."

Riordan lifted his head from the pillow and laced his hands behind it. "All right," he said, looking up to the ceiling. "Yes, the idea was to smash the device, or at least dislodge it. And on the final run, I did manage to smash it pretty good and I felt it shut down. After I bounced, I hit the ground and played dead, waiting for a good opening."

Ted Valmont brought his cane up and laid it across the arms of the chair, running his hand across the smooth metal. "I think I know what was going on with your drinking. Maitland told me the seizure Gabrielle had in the restaurant was caused by her drinking too much wine. Said it triggered an epileptic fit. What it really did was affect her ability to control her movements through the device."

"Bingo," said Riordan. "Niebuhr said that alcohol not only affects the brain, but the central nervous system as a whole. That means that signals from the device to your body get scrambled, and in my case, allowed my brain to call some of the shots again. In Gabrielle's case, it must have short-circuited everything since she has no other means to move."

Duckworth screwed up his face. "That's pretty obtuse. I expected your drinking had saved you in a much more pragmatic way. Like your enlarged and cirrhotic liver shielded your other internal organs from injury."

"Leave my liver out it," snapped Riordan.

Ted Valmont rapped sharply on the cane. "Let's talk about the knife, then. Why didn't they take it away from you?"

Riordan pulled a hand down and gently traced the slope of his nose. A distracted look came over his features, but then his expression sharpened and he stared at Ted Valmont. "Maitland's goons were so happy to nab my Glock and the silver flask when they frisked me that they didn't bother to check any further." Riordan showed off his gummy smile and looked over to Duckworth. "Yet another way in which drinking saved me."

Duckworth chortled, and in a gesture in which he and Riordan seemed to have engaged before, held up his palm to be slapped. "Hey Pancho!" he said in a bad Mexican accent.

Riordan reached across the bed to slap Duckworth's palm and responded, "Hey Cisco!" with an accent that was—if not even less authentic—certainly more slurred.

Ted Valmont sighed and looked at them with bored indulgence. Then his features hardened. "Hey," he said sharply. "That's my Cartier, Riordan." And snapping his glance over to Duckworth's wrist, "And that's my tank watch. You bastards have got both the watches Ramos took from me."

Riordan laughed and reached down to unfasten the Cartier. "Christ, Valmont, it took you long enough to notice. I never got my flask back, but I thought I might as well liberate the watches from Ramos before they ended up in Deputy Whozit's evidence locker. I pulled them off Ramos while you were running around playing Sir Galahad to Gabrielle."

Duckworth passed the watches over to Ted Valmont, who strapped the tank watch on and dropped the other into a coat pocket. "Well, speaking of Deputy Olken, I've got to get going." He rose slowly to his feet, Duckworth nearly tripping over himself for the privilege of holding his elbow. "I'm due at the Sheriff's office to sign my statement. I just wanted to swing by and see how you were doing before I went."

Riordan tugged on the covers of his bed and nodded. "Thanks. I'm fine. Three or four more days and then I can go home." He passed a thin tongue over puffed lips. "Of course, it will be a while before I lose the cast—and then a couple months of physical therapy before I can walk normally. Then there's the dental work. And they say I need more work on my nose." Riordan shook his head slowly. "Actually, I'm not doing so good at that."

"Better than Maitland or Breen," said Ted Valmont. "Breen's alive, but he's a quadriplegic. And your bullet caught Maitland in the spine: he's paralyzed from the waist down."

Duckworth made a tsk-tsk noise. "There are two sales NeuroStimix won't be making."

The woman Ted Valmont knew only as Gabrielle Maitland bobbed and surged through the water of his swimming pool in a powerful breaststroke. When she reached the far end of the pool, she grasped the wall, swung her legs round and pushed off smoothly for the return lap. She kicked with increased force and blitzed through the remaining water to the near end of the pool, where she ceremoniously tagged the tile. Hanging by one arm from the diving board, she peeled off her bathing cap and goggles and loosed her hair. It flew out in a luxuriant strawberry sweep, the tips of it settling on the water where it curled and darkened as it danced on the turbulence of her wake. Gabrielle swung both legs onto the pool decking and hauled herself out of the water in a quirky, gymnastic show of upper body strength.

"Bring me a towel, will you?" she said.

Two feet swung over a patio chair to land on the cool deck beside it. The tip of an aluminum cane joined them. There was a grunt. "This is hard. I can barely stand."

Gabrielle looked up and smiled. "Trust me," she said. "It'll get easier." She reached to accept the towel.

The back door of the house opened and out walked Ted Valmont. He frowned in the direction of the pool. "Careful you two," he said. "I leave for one minute and you head straight for the diving board."

Tim Valmont—tanned, muscled and wearing a brightly colored Hawaiian shirt with baggy shorts—turned awkwardly to sit on the edge of the board next to Gabrielle. He put the aluminum cane across his legs. "Don't worry," he said with a huge smile. "Sitting is the only thing I'm doing on one of these things from now on."

Ted Valmont came up to them and gestured at Gabrielle. "What would you think of her as NeuroStimix's Director of Physical Therapy?"

Tim nodded. "Excellent choice. I only worry that the board will object to the new CEO's decision to hire his girlfriend."

"Bastard." Gabrielle swung the towel playfully in Ted Valmont's direction. "You didn't say anything about going to NeuroStimix."

"It was the only way I could convince Niebuhr to stay on as CTO. Besides, I've had a belly full of venture capital."

"I think it's a wonderful idea," said Gabrielle. "And if you're serious about my joining you, I'd be honored."

Ted Valmont reached down to take a corner of the towel. He dabbed at water on Gabrielle's face. "Under one condition," he said in a mock-serious tone.

"Which is?"

"You tell me what name goes on your business cards."

"My real name? It's awful. It's worse than awful. Winifred. Winifred Smythe."

"Ted and Winifred," groaned Tim. "God bless us, every one."

The faint tapping of a door knocker carried out to the backyard from the front of the house.

"Your public calls," said Winifred.

"Yes—with sickening punctuality." Ted Valmont leaned down to kiss her check. "Be good, you two. I'll be back shortly."

He jogged to the rear door, through the house and up to the front door. Pulling it open, he found Amelia Crenshaw standing on his porch with her slope-shouldered producer Hal directly behind. They were both smiling ferociously. "Oh, Mr. Valmont," she said brightly. "I'm so pleased that you agreed to gave us the exclusive on your story."

Ted Valmont crossed his arms and gave a shrug like Jack Benny. "Something told me I owed it to you."